Mai Tai Butterfly

JOANN BASSETT

Mai Tai Butterfly

Second Edition
Published by Lokelani Publishing
Green Valley, AZ 85614

www.joannbassett.com

First edition published in 2008, by Dog Ear Publishing, Indianapolis, IN

***

This book is a work of fiction. Places, events, and situations in this book are purely fictional and any resemblance to actual persons, living or dead, is coincidental.

***

Also by JoAnn Bassett:

"THE ISLANDS OF ALOHA MYSTERY SERIES"
Maui Widow Waltz
Livin' Lahaina Loca
Lana'i of the Tiger
Kaua'i Me a River

Discover the latest titles by JoAnn Bassett at
http://www.joannbassett.com

ISBN: 978-1492340140

For Kaye Haberer, a solid 24K sister

CHAPTER 1

My life ended with a letter bomb. It made for a quick exit—like a magician's trick: now you see her, now you don't. The limb-from-limb pain came later.

At 3:17 on a Thursday afternoon, Mike, our graying hippie mail carrier, plopped a damp rubber-banded stack of mail on my reception desk at All Seattle Realty.

I'm sure of the time because although Mike scoffed at most postal service regulations—picture Ozzy Osbourne doing court-ordered community service—he seemed to pride himself on strict adherence to the mail carrier creed of reliability. He'd clocked his route like a NASA shuttle launch, and the ETA for our office was 3:17p.m., rain or shine.

"Hi, Mike. Got anything good for me in there today?"

"Well, I didn't see anything from the lottery commission, but you never know." He didn't break stride, smiling and clicking me an index-finger salute as he pressed his shoulder against the glass door on his way out. A chill blast of late October wind carried a smattering of soggy alder leaves onto the entry mat.

"See ya mañana, Nola." And he was gone.

The cream-colored number ten envelope hid near the bottom of the stack. It was addressed to my husband, Frank, but as office manager of his real estate company it was my job to open the incoming mail. The letter opener zipped through the back flap with the ease of a scalpel.

I pulled out a single sheet of "Bayside Floral" letterhead. As I unfolded it, a little white card fluttered to the floor. Two handwritten lines in black ink scrawled across the page: *We failed to include the message card with your most recent order. Please accept our apology.*

Pushing back from the desk, I bent over and groped under my chair for the dropped card. As I sat back up, black splotches slid into view, obscuring my eyesight and threatening a fainting spell.

I took a deep breath, squeezed my eyes shut and visualized my carotid arteries expanding to allow blood flow to my brain. I hadn't exercised in months—okay, years—and whenever I felt stressed, or got up too fast, I risked ending up in a heap on the floor.

The dozen or so extra pounds I'd gained since turning forty didn't help either. From the neck up I still looked pretty good—hazel eyes, a straight nose, and a thick mane of curly medium-brown hair. I'd let my stylist talk me into highlights in an attempt to see if blonds had more fun. But the constant pinch at my waistband reminded me I wasn't fooling any salesclerk worth her salt as I flipped through the size sixes on the Nordstrom sale rack.

Opening my eyes, I was relieved to find I could see again. I'd assumed the dropped card was a business card, but it turned out to be a floral enclosure. Printed at the top was a trio of blood-red roses, and below, in my husband's unmistakable spiky left-slanting handwriting, it read: *Thanks for the nooner. You're the best. Love, Frank.*

Nooner? I didn't know normal middle-aged people used that word. Besides, for the past ten years the naughtiest lunch we'd shared involved splitting a slice of banana cream pie. I dropped the card into my purse and zipped it tight. Then I stuffed the high-priced handbag into my bottom drawer and slammed it shut. Didn't help. Even hidden away, that Dooney and Bourke hummed like a high voltage wire.

Frank was sitting in his private office no more than thirty feet from me. The right thing to do was to march in there and demand an explanation. But, on second thought, maybe I should give myself a few minutes to think. I rose from my chair, but the black blotches returned and I plopped back down. Leaning my elbows on the desk, I dropped my face into my open hands. My fingers felt cool against my fevered cheeks. *Deep breath, deep breath,* I silently prayed.

The phone started ringing. The insistent *chirr-chirr-chirr* jangled me into decision mode. Fight or flight? Neither seemed especially appealing.

"Nola? You out there?" Frank yelled. "For God's sake, pick up the phone."

Frank hated answering his own phone. He alleged it made him look small-time if the caller didn't have to wait at least fifteen seconds before he took a call. When I first came to work with him, I didn't believe he'd actually sit there counting, "one-thousand one, two-thousand two" up to fifteen before picking up a waiting call. But that's exactly what he did.

A second line started up, joining the first in a double-time effect. I had to get out of there. Needed some space. I was supposed to ask for phone backup if I left my desk, but I couldn't imagine what I'd say.

It seems Frank's sent flowers to his bimbo and I'm feeling a little woozy. Or maybe, *Frank's been sleeping around during noon hours so I need a minute to go throw up.*

To tell the truth, my brain wasn't as shocked as my heart seemed to be. For months Frank made long outgoing calls after silently shutting his office door. He'd disappear for hours on end "checking on his listings." For a hotshot real estate broker he certainly didn't seem to care much about being available. He offered all kinds of excuses when I asked why he didn't pick up calls forwarded to his cell phone. Even our son, Frank Jr., in his third year at the University of Washington, commented he'd given up trying to reach his father.

I made my way to the back door and slipped outside. An invisible vice squeezed my chest as I staggered across the rain-slick parking lot. I approached my beige, or more precisely "desert sand, "Ford Taurus and dropped the keys before I could manage to unlock the door. Bending to retrieve them, I came nose-to-nose with the white magnetic sign on the driver door. It featured a photo of a grinning Frank, alongside his contact numbers and the company tagline: "East-side, West-side, We Do 'Em All!"

I pressed the remote on my car keys. Heard the *peep peep* of the doors unlocking. Fumbling the door handle, I broke a nail but didn't stop to check the damage. I just had to get inside. Shut the door.

In the hush of the snug car I heard my heartbeat drubbing in my neck. I stared through the windshield, reviewing the past few months like a foreign movie I'd been unable to translate.

I'd always figured our marriage to be about average. After twenty-two years it'd taken on a mellow tone—no stunning highs, but no yawning lows either. Frank started the real estate brokerage fifteen years ago, and I'd worked for him for the past ten. I didn't take a salary because what was the point? We shared everything. I figured we made a good team.

Frank wasn't that into sex. Oh, every now and then on a weekend morning we'd sleep in and he'd roll on and off me in about a seven-minute act. Then we'd go out to brunch. I must admit, my favorite part was the brunch.

But last month while using Frank's computer to locate a market analysis he'd done, I clicked on his Internet "history" section. In the drop-down list, it showed URL's like "hotlove.com" and "sockittome.com" We had a bunch of practical jokers in our office so I'd figured someone had sent the links to him as a gag. I'd even chided him about it.

"Yeah," he'd said. "You know Brad, the new guy from California? Well, he attached a couple of porn sites to an email he sent me. I clicked on them without thinking. Wow, there's some pretty graphic stuff floating around cyberspace."

His face darkened. "You know me, Nola. I'm a solid family man and I expect the same of my agents. I probably need to have a chat with him about office protocol. No more goofy stuff on the company computers. Besides, those sites carry viruses." He'd scowled as he gravely thanked me for bringing it to his attention.

The cell phone in my purse began chiming. I fished it out and stuffed it in the center console to smother the sound. Then I turned the key in the ignition, backed out of the parking stall and aimed my car for home. Good thing the car knew the way. I was in no frame of mind to be navigating.

I pulled into the driveway and pressed the opener button on the visor. The garage door lurched up in a creaky 'welcome home.' Once safely parked inside, I hit the button again and the door slid back down. I turned the key to "off" and listened to the *tick, tick, tick* of the cooling engine. It was spooky in the dusky gloom of the three-car garage, but I felt cozy inside the warm car. Like being the smallest doll in a set of *matryoshka*—those Russian nested dolls that get smaller and smaller one inside the other—I had layers of protection buffering me from what lurked outside. My breathing slowed, warmth returned to my fingers, and I tilted my seat back to rest my eyes for a moment before going inside.

After a minute or so, I felt ashamed. I'd leapt to a pretty damning conclusion based on rather flimsy circumstantial evidence. Besides, I wasn't some ingénue catching her boyfriend out behind the bleachers with the school skank. Middle-aged men stray. It doesn't mean they don't love their wives. I wanted the facts, but first I needed to calm down so I wouldn't come off sounding like a shrew.

I rehearsed the call I'd make as soon as I'd gotten a grip. First, the office phone would ring about twelve times before someone finally picked up.

"Is Frank there?" I'd say.

"Sure, Nola. He's been really worried about you." Whoever answered would want to chat, but would realize Frank was anxious to know I was all right.

I'd wait on the line the required fifteen seconds.

"Darling, where are you?" he'd say. *"I've been going nuts here. Are you okay?"*

"Yeah, I'm fine. But I need to ask you about something."

"What's wrong, honey?"

I'd tell him about the flower card. He'd launch into a perfectly plausible explanation about Brad being up to his tricks again. He'd be furious about the forgery, and would want to fire him for unprofessional behavior—not to mention causing me major mental distress.

I'd admit that at first I'd been upset, but after thinking it over I realized it was just a bad joke. Then I'd say I didn't think he should let Brad go over a juvenile stunt, but he should be put on notice because he'd seriously breached the rules of acceptable office conduct.

Frank would commend me for my sensible attitude and offer to take me out to dinner—anywhere I'd like to go.

Feeling much better after coming up with a credible scenario to explain the smarmy little card in my purse, I took a deep cleansing breath, hunched my shoulders into the back of the car seat, and drifted off.

When I awoke, I panicked for a couple of seconds before remembering why I was dozing in my car in the shadowy garage. Sitting up, I opened the car door. The overhead light came on and the alarm dinged to remind me my keys were still in the ignition. I turned the key. The lights on the dash sparked to life.

The digital clock glowed 5:32. Anxiety shot through me as I did the math. I'd been gone for two hours and hadn't called in. Frank would be worried sick.

I dug out my cell phone and dialed the main office number. Sunny, a mortgage broker Frank brought in to do in-house loans, picked up after two rings.

"Hey, Nola," she said. "What happened? You didn't tell anyone you were leaving."

"I know. I felt really sick all of a sudden. Sorry."

"Well, Frank said to put you right through if you called. Hold on. I'll see if he's still here."

I started counting. Frank came on the line after only four seconds.

"Where the hell are you? We had clients out front and no one to greet them. You know you're not supposed to leave without getting someone to cover for you."

Not exactly the greeting I'd imagined. Probably best to hold off mentioning the florist card until he got home.

"I didn't feel well so I came back to the house."

"That's no excuse. What's the problem?"

"Uh. I'm not sure. I just felt sick and needed to come home."

"Since when do you just waltz off the job and leave me in the lurch? Maybe you haven't noticed, but I'm trying to make a living here."

"Make a living? So, tell me, does that 'living' include buying flowers for your nooner girlfriend?" I honestly have no idea why that popped out of my mouth. I felt my cheeks heating as I waited for his reply.

"What the hell are you talking about?"

"In today's mail you got a note from Bayside Floral. They were returning a message card that said, 'Thanks for the nooner.' It was signed 'Love, Frank,' and it sure looked like your handwriting." I prayed he'd launch into an outburst of indignant fury.

Instead, he granted me the decency of a long pause before saying, "We need to talk."

That remark ranks right up there with *There's been an accident* or, *We've found a lump*. Just four little words and yet when I heard them I knew my life, as I'd known it, was over.

CHAPTER 2

I couldn't make myself go into the house. No way was I ready to hear Frank's confession, or worse yet, his lies. I pressed the garage door opener and the door drew up to reveal dusky darkness outside. Where to go? Driving around aimlessly wasn't an option I'd entertain with gas prices what they were, so I called Malia Spurling, a girlfriend I hadn't seen in at least two months.

"You okay, Nola? You sound a little shaky."

"I need to get away from the house for a little while. Can I bring over some dinner for you and Jim?"

"Thanks, but Jim had two surgeries this afternoon. He called and said one of them didn't go well." She paused and I took in the gravity of her remark. Jim was a pediatric thoracic surgeon—a children's heart surgeon—and when a surgery didn't go well, it usually meant someone's child died.

"Sorry." I cringed at how pathetic I'd become, fretting over a philandering husband when a mother had lost her child today.

"So, what's going on with you?"

"Oh nothing, really. Frank and I had a little tiff and I'm not ready to deal with it. That's all."

"Come on over. I have no idea what we're doing about dinner, but you're more than welcome."

"Thanks. I'd really like to pick something up, though. What do you guys like?"

"Anything's fine. Pizza, Chinese, Taco Bell, whatever. I'm pretty sure Jim won't be very hungry, but you never know. It'll be good to see you. We haven't had a chance to catch up in a while."

On the way across town I stopped at Peace-A-Pie on University Avenue and picked up a gourmet veggie pizza. I like to go out to the U District because Frank Jr. lives out there and I always hope I'll run into him. He usually emails or calls me once a week, but I don't get to see him face to face very often. Frank sees him because they work out together at the Seattle Athletic Club on Wednesdays and Fridays.

I parked at the curb in front of the Spurling's house just as Jim pulled into the driveway.

"Hey Nola, long time no see." He didn't ask why Frank wasn't with me. Malia must have called and clued him in to the situation.

Malia sat at the kitchen table. She'd set it for three using her best china and heavy Lenox water glasses. She'd created a centerpiece of five ivory pillar candles. A silver ice bucket sat at the empty place at one end of the table next to a pair of ice tongs poised to hygienically plop ice cubes into the waiting glasses.

"Anyone want a soda, or sparkling water or something?" She jumped up and pulled a six-pack of

Diet Pepsi and a large bottle of Pellegrino water out of the refrigerator.

A nervous energy infused the room. Frank and I had socialized with the Spurlings since early in our marriage, so it felt strange with only three of us at the table.

"Great pizza," Jim said, breaking the silence. He nodded, pointing to his third piece in less than fifteen minutes.

"Yeah, it's really hearty for vegetarian. You don't even miss the meat."

Jim didn't mention his failed surgery; and no one asked for details on why I was there by myself. At one low point in the conversation I heard myself asking Jim who he thought might win the Super Bowl this year. Like I cared. I didn't have a clue who'd won the Super Bowl last year, or any year, for that matter.

When Malia picked up my plate a half hour later I'd only nibbled the point off my pizza slice, but I'd downed two cans of Diet Pepsi.

"Didn't you like the pizza?"

"No, it was fine. I'm just more tired than hungry, I guess."

Malia and Jim insisted I relax while they cleaned up the kitchen. I sat at the table feeling like a disaster victim at a Red Cross shelter. I glanced at the ice bucket, remembering my unfinished business waiting at home. Anxiety gripped my chest so tightly I found myself gulping oxygen like a guppy out of water. Then I flashed on Jim in his scrubs talking to the dead child's parents and shame at my petty self-indulgence washed over me like a chill wind.

"Would you like to stay over, Nola? You can sleep in Leila's room. She won't be home until Thanksgiving." Malia must have sensed my reluctance to hit the road.

"Thanks, but I probably need to get home."

"You want to talk first?"

Jim's eyes darted toward Malia as if she'd just pulled a hand grenade out of the cupboard. "If you ladies will excuse me, I've got some consult emails to get out before I get ready for bed."

"Oh no, you don't," Malia said. "I think we may need a man's perspective here. Your emails can wait another half hour or so." She gave his cheek a quick peck, and he leaned against the counter with a sigh.

I told them about the florist returning the nooner card and I'd just begun a play-by-play of both my imagined and real phone calls with Frank when Jim interrupted me.

"What did Frank say when you told him?" Jim apparently wasn't one to suffer the details.

"He said we need to talk."

I caught a swift glance pass between Jim and Malia.

"What? You guys know something, don't you?"

"No, I mean...I've heard some gossip, but…" Jim bobbed and weaved like a prizefighter.

"C'mon, please tell me what you heard."

"It's not pretty."

"As if finding a 'thanks for the nooner' card from my husband was?"

"Well, for starters, I think that florist doesn't want any more of Frank's business. I can't imagine them being so stupid they'd return a card like that to a customer's workplace," said Jim.

"Yeah. That was amazingly dumb," Malia added. "I'd think they'd be more sensitive to privacy issues."

"So," I said, completely indifferent to the florist's lack of customer service skills. "Do you think he's having an affair?"

"It looks that way, kiddo." Jim said.

I'd come this far, no sense turning back.

"Do you know who it is?" I consciously took in a deep breath and held it, preparing for a body blow. I squirmed at the possibility it was Dixie, a buxom bottle-blond real estate agent who worked for Frank. Although she played up to the men in the office, she treated other women like dirt. She acted especially dismissive of me even though—or maybe because—I answered her phone, made her coffee, and brought in a cake every year for her birthday.

"I've got a pretty good idea." Jim took the gentlemanly lead, allowing Malia to sidestep the bloodletting.

"Blond?"

"Not exactly," he said. "I think the correct term would be 'chemically' blond."

"Young?" I figured Dixie for early thirties, even though she'd claimed to be turning twenty-seven for the past couple of birthdays.

He nodded glumly. He fixed his eyes on his Nikes as if willing the shoelaces to burst into flame and create a diversion.

"I knew it. I'm such an idiot. There I sat taking messages for Frank while he was supposedly out showing houses. Instead, he was out *playing house* with Seattle's answer to Pamela Anderson."

"That's not exactly the visual I got," he said.

"What do you mean?"

Malia sighed and put a hand over her eyes as if to avoid witnessing the final thrust of the knife.

"Let me get us all a tall shot of Johnnie Walker and I'll tell you the locker room buzz I've overheard at the club," Jim said, glancing at a cabinet above the refrigerator. He worked out at the S.A.C. as often as his schedule allowed and he often ran into Frank and Frank Jr. there.

"Honey, you know Nola doesn't drink." Malia leaned across the table and laid a hand on my forearm.

"Correction, Malia," I said. "Frank's the one who can't drink. I just went along with the on-the-wagon thing to be a supportive AA wife. Personally, I don't know Bill W and I don't want to."

"Great. So, whaddaya say?" Jim opened the cabinet door and brought down a half-filled gallon jug of Johnnie Walker Black. He wagged it back and forth in front of me like a hypnotist with a pocket watch.

"I say line 'em up. I have a feeling after what you're going to tell me, I'm going to need all the courage I can get."

"Right. Well, for starters," he said, pulling out three highball glasses and pouring a heavy shot of scotch into each one. "I'd guess Frank's lover's name is probably more likely "Paul" or "Peter" than "Pamela." He paused, allowing time for the significance of that to sink in.

"That doesn't make sense," I said. "Frank may be a lot of things, but *gay* certainly isn't one of them." I pressed my fingers into my temples in an effort to thwart the throbbing.

"This isn't first-hand information," Jim said, his voice a rough whisper. "Only rumor."

I nodded and tipped my glass to my lips, draining nearly half of the amber liquid. I held it in my mouth for a few seconds, and then forced myself to swallow. Tears rose in my eyes as I fought back an urge to cough.

Jim held my gaze. Malia got up and walked behind me and lightly placed her hands on my shoulders.

"I'm so sorry, Nola. If there's anything we can do…" she said.

Jim topped off everyone's glass.

I sat there wondering what I possibly could have done to make Frank turn gay. Or, had he fooled me and been gay all along? No, he'd fathered a son. We'd celebrated over twenty wedding anniversaries together.

"It doesn't make sense. Frank's way too fond of women to be gay. He's always noticing this woman's hair, or that woman's figure or whatever. I just don't believe it."

"Time will tell, I suppose. But that's the scuttlebutt I've heard."

"Poor choice of words, Jim," said Malia.

By this point we'd all drunk enough straight liquor to bark a laugh at her gallows humor.

"Nola, I don't think you should be driving tonight." Jim's words reverberated in my ears as if his voice was hooked up to a *waa-waa* pedal.

"I agree," said Malia, sounding a half-mile away. "You've had a rotten day and God knows how the hooch will affect you after twenty years of abstinence. The last thing you need is a DUI."

She offered me their daughter's room once again, but I opted for the sofa bed in the family room.

"Well, at least these will make it a little more comfortable," she said. She handed me a feather pillow and a puffy down comforter. I snuggled into them, numb with scotch and shock.

Light and shadows played across the walls as cars glided by on the road outside. I laid awake listening to the unfamiliar night noises of a strange house. In the dark still hours right before daybreak my head pounded with a painful backbeat but my thinking had cleared. I needed to hear what Frank had to say. I felt guilty I hadn't allowed him a chance to explain himself before I blabbed to Malia and Jim. Maybe there'd been a misunderstanding. Or maybe it was simply malicious gossip. Frank was an exceptionally successful real estate broker and more than likely he'd ticked off a few folks in the process of getting there.

Silvery shafts of light streaked the ceiling. I must have finally fallen asleep because when I glanced at my cell phone the time showed 6:05 a.m. My stomach roiled from the unholy trinity of no food, lots of alcohol, and the memory of yesterday's events.

I needed to call Frank. I knew he'd be up; he usually left for the office at 6:30.

After three rings, an unfamiliar male voice answered. "Hello?"

"Uh, hello. Is this 555-2341?"

"I'm not sure what the number is here. Do you want to talk to Frank? Hang on a second, he's in the shower."

"No. Just tell him his *wife* called, will you?" I disconnected before the stranger could reply. I pressed my hand against my mouth as I my made my way to the guest bathroom.

Gripping the toilet rim I threw up every last remnant of scotch churning in the pit of my stomach. I had no urge to cry, only to vomit until I'd scoured my insides clean.

After three days of hiding out at Malia and Jim's house watching CNN, Dr. Phil, and Oprah—those were the daytime TV shows I'd *admit* to watching—I found my niche in the Spurling household. I took over the job of cook.

Jim and Malia loved all kinds of food. Unlike Frank, who refused to eat anything round, red, or spicy (which knocked out most foreign cuisine except maybe Norwegian) the Spurlings were adventurous foodies like me.

For the past few days we'd avoided talking about my situation with Frank. I knew they were dying to know what I was thinking, or if I'd talked with him, or even how long I planned to maintain squatter's rights on their sofa. But they never asked.

My life was a train wreck about to happen. They knew it, I knew it. We were all just waiting for the sound of screeching brakes and shattering glass.

By Wednesday night we were ankle deep in broken glass.

"Frank Junior stormed out of the weight room at the club today." Jim said pouring us each a glass of cabernet before dinner. "I feel like a heel not giving him a heads-up earlier, but for the life of me, I couldn't figure out how to approach the subject."

I knew exactly what he meant.

For days I'd been meaning to call Frank Jr. and tell him what happened, but I just couldn't face it. I mean, how does a mother tell her twenty-two-year-old son that his dad's batting left-handed after passing himself off as a solid right-hander for almost fifty years? Just thinking about it made me want to spoon rat poison down my throat.

About eight o'clock the next morning my cell phone rang. I was still wrapped in the comforter on Malia's sofa, but I'd been awake since six. I picked up the phone and saw Frank Jr.'s number on the caller ID. I let it ring two more times, mentally rehearsing my lines, but when I finally screwed up the courage to answer, the line went dead. The city of Seattle is a jumble of hills and tunnels so it wasn't unusual to lose a cell call. I waited five minutes. When he didn't call back, I called him.

"Hi sweetie, did you try to reach me earlier?"

"Hey, Mom." His response came out clipped, with a raspy tone that reminded me of driving him home after an especially tough soccer game.

I waited. He said nothing. "Frankie, are you still there?"

"Yeah."

"Did you call me earlier?" I honestly don't know why I was so bent on getting him to admit he'd called me first.

"Mom, is it true?"

Under normal circumstances I'd have asked what he was referring to, but I'd been prepping for this question like a well-rehearsed *Jeopardy!* contestant. I wasn't going to play coy and make him choke out '*Is Dad gay?*' It'd be cruel, even though I longed to welcome another guest to my self-righteous pity party.

"I'm afraid so, honey. I'm staying at Malia and Jim's until I figure out what I'm going to do."

"What do you mean, 'what *you're* going to do?' Haven't you done enough already?"

Huh? Maybe I wasn't answering the right question after all.

"Frankie, are we talking about the same thing here?"

"Mom, I'm so pissed at you right now. I can't believe you'd do this to me. Why couldn't you two have held it together for just one more year? One lousy year, that's all I needed." He hung up.

I felt like I was in one of those low-budget crime movies where the clueless wife comes home and finds her husband shot dead on the floor. She picks up the gun lying next to the body just as the cops rush in. The only crime I was guilty of was blind naïveté. That seemed like pretty small potatoes compared to Frank's egregious breach of fidelity.

But tell that to my son.

When Jim got home that night he said Frank Junior called during his lunch hour. "He wanted me to tell you he's quit school. He said he's probably leaving Seattle."

"I need to talk to him."

"I wouldn't do that right now, Nola. This is so embarrassing for him. I think he needs to get away for a while."

"I can't blame him. Hell, I'd like to run away too. But why's he mad at *me*?"

"You're part of it. That's all he knows. And kids don't like to be forced to take sides in these situations."

All day Friday I called Frank Junior's cell number. Every time, a recording came on saying "the cellular customer you are trying to reach has either turned off their phone or is out of range. Please try again later." On Saturday, it changed to "the number you have reached is no longer in service."

My hands shook as a surge of grief erupted from my core, and once again, I dashed to the bathroom.

My husband maintained his innocence right up until my attorney slapped a packet of private detective's photos down on the conference room table. Luckily for everyone present those photos never emerged from the sealed nine-by-twelve envelope. I'm pretty sure I'd have thrown myself through the plate glass window to avoid viewing full-color glossies of my husband's betrayal. Since we were thirty floors up I'm pretty sure that would've resulted in even more equally ghastly photos.

"Since there's no prenuptial agreement, no minor children as a result of the marriage, and Washington's a community property state, we're asking that the parties' assets be sold at fair market value and then divided fifty-fifty." Frank's attorney said this as though he were talking about cutting a doughnut in half to quiet a couple of squabbling kids.

"But I didn't do anything wrong. You're talking about selling my home, my furniture, my memories. I didn't break my marriage vows. I didn't humiliate my family." My voice pitched up an octave with each line of protest. The word, "family," echoed in the hushed room like a struck gong.

My attorney tapped my forearm. I looked at him and watched his mouth morph from a frown into a tight smirk.

"That seems fair enough," he said, turning to face Frank's attorney. "We're including the sale of the real estate brokerage as part of the community assets, correct?"

"No way," Frank leaped out of his chair sending it skidding against the back wall. It seemed I wouldn't need to be pitching myself through the conference room window after all—Frank would be happy to do it for me.

I walked out of the lawyer's office with the promise of a cash settlement once everything was liquidated. Frank agreed to sell our sprawling home in West Seattle through his real estate company for no commission and we'd split the proceeds. He was also required to get a valuation on the brokerage business and pay me half its worth. This was all to be completed within the six-month waiting period before the divorce was final.

It seemed so cut and dried. So tidy and bloodless. Twenty-three years of marriage wafted to the wind like a child blowing on a dandelion puff. The loss of my title as Mrs. Frank Stevens hit me hard. Not because Frank had been the love of my life, or an irreplaceable soul mate I couldn't live without. But more because I'd never been anything else. Daughter, wife, mother—that pretty much summed up my life. My dad was dead. My mother was down in Portland absorbed in her latest religion of the moment—was it Kabbala or Taoism this month? And now with Frank and Frankie gone I feared I'd look in the mirror one morning and there'd be no one looking back.

"I don't know where to go," I told Malia. "There's no way I can go back to my house after hearing that guy's voice on our phone."

"Don't worry about it. You're welcome to stay here as long as you want." She gave me a hug that felt like I'd just told her I had a terminal disease.

Frank moved to Capitol Hill to be closer to his lover, his new lifestyle and God knows what else. He left it to me to explain to our friends and neighbors that my soon-to-be-ex-husband had taken up with a twenty-four-year-old with an uncanny resemblance to Ashton Kutcher.

Punk'd? For sure.

CHAPTER 3

In mid-November, Malia's sister called from Maui to announce they were planning a big birthday party for their dad's seventy-fifth birthday on December third. The family hadn't been all together since her mother's funeral two years earlier so Malia quickly agreed to come. That left me less than two weeks to find somewhere else to stay.

"You've been so generous in letting me hide out here these past few weeks," I said to Malia after Jim went to watch TV after dinner. "But I've got to find an apartment. Or maybe even move back into the house. I hate the thought, but without a job, I may have to consider it."

"It's been our pleasure. I never thought I'd have the luxury of Rachel Ray's clone as a live-in cook. I only hope Jim can adjust back to my less-than-stellar culinary skills once you're gone. But don't feel you need to leave just because I'll be gone for a couple of weeks. Leila will only be here a couple of days for Thanksgiving, and then she won't come home again until Christmas. It's really no problem."

"Thanks, Malia, but I've got to get out of your hair sooner or later. Besides I wouldn't feel right staying here while you're away."

"Well, there's always Plan B, of course." Malia's eager eyes let me know she had something up her sleeve. "Come with me. Jim can't go; he's got surgeries scheduled wall-to-wall until the end of the year. It would give you some time to think about what you should do."

"I don't know. It's a family visit. I wouldn't want to get in the way."

"Are you kidding? There's no such thing as getting in the way at a Hawaiian birthday party. I promise it'll be fun and my family will love you. You could use a little *aloha* after what you've been through this year."

"Well, it would be nice to slip away before I seriously start looking for a job. But I shouldn't spend the money. Who knows how long it will take to sell the house?" My thinking out loud sounded like I was wrangling for the pity vote, which I'd caught myself doing a lot lately.

"Don't worry. We'll stay at my dad's house. My auntie and the neighbors will cook up so much party food we'll eat like royalty the whole time. All you have to do is buy a plane ticket."

Airports are like hospitals. Heavy drama, both comedy and tragedy, happens there. When Frank and I were in high school, his idea of a hot date was to go out to the airport and watch the planes take off and land. I dreamed of being a stewardess—that's what flight attendants were called back in those days. I saw myself in a sleek beehive hair-do and crisp navy blue uniform taking off to exotic places, serving cocktails to celebrities in the first class section. The ultimate glamorous lifestyle.

"Forget it, Nola," Frank said when he'd picked me up for a date and I'd mentioned I'd been filling out airline applications. "With your luck, you'd get the turnaround flight to Bakersfield twice a week. And you know they weigh you every single day. My cousin says if you're even a pound over they pull you from the flight and put you on a really strict diet. Not only that, they plaster your name on a bulletin board in the stewardess lounge so everyone can see who the fatties are."

I tossed out the employment forms I'd painstakingly filled out for United, Delta, and Western Airlines. I'd hunt and peck typed them using the portable Underwood typewriter my parents bought me as an incentive to apply for college.

The next time I saw Frank I thanked him for saving me from the humiliation of life under a microscope. He returned the favor by surprising me with an engagement ring on Christmas of my senior year in high school. The ring held a barely visible chip of diamond, but he promised he'd "upgrade" it later. For more than twenty years, I'd held my breath every birthday, anniversary, and Christmas, anticipating a velvet ring box. But the upgrade never happened.

Funny, but I never considered saying, "No" to Frank's proposal. At eighteen, I loved the idea of being a grown-up married woman. I didn't exactly pull honor roll grades in high school, so who knew if I could handle college? And, more importantly, what were the chances

I'd ever get another proposal from a handsome, confident guy like Frank? I seized the opportunity and considered myself lucky that my life had fallen so easily into place.

Malia rummaged through her carry-on bag, pulled out a romance novel and started reading. I'd forgotten to pack a book but I didn't want to risk missing the boarding announcement while looking for a newsstand so I busied myself eavesdropping on nearby cell phone conversations.

"I love you too, Muffin," a woman with tiny palm tree decals on her lethal-length nails cooed into a sequin-studded phone. "Now give the phone to grandma, okay?"

"...the merger isn't open for discussion until after the meeting on January fifth," bellowed a guy with his jaw set in a grimace that brought to mind Martha Stewart as she was being hauled off to prison. "Focus on getting the Bailey account. That's what's important now. I'll be back in a week. Just one week." His flared nostrils and hand raking through impeccably-coiffed hair signaled a guy who was long overdue for a vacation.

The intercom at the podium hissed and an almost-familiar male voice announced Flight 32, nonstop service to Kahului, Maui. I knew that voice. Who was it? I squinted my eyes shut, trying to recall the name.

"First class passengers may board at any time. Then we'll board the main cabin by row number, starting from the back of the cabin." Johnny Depp! That's it. The guy sounded just like Captain Jack Sparrow in "Pirates of the Caribbean." I turned to share the news with Malia but she was already standing, gathering up her carry-ons.

"That's us. We'll be next since we're in row forty-nine," she said. We moved into line, readying our boarding passes for a gate agent in a vivid purple blouse.

As we stepped from the jetway onto the plane, a flight attendant stationed at the door tapped Malia on the arm.

"Malia? Is that you? It's me, Ana Malukea, from Kamehameha High. My sister is going to freak out when I tell her you're coming home. How long will you be staying?"

A man, wearing a size XXL aloha shirt that strained against the buttons, stepped onto the plane directly behind me. I gritted a "what can I do?" smile at his sweat-shiny face as we were both stopped short by the chatting women. He cleared his throat with a loud gargle that more than got my attention, but didn't cause Ana or Malia to even flick an eye his way.

"Oh, Ana Banana," Malia cooed, hugging her friend's sister. She seemed oblivious to the fact that by then the guy had managed to tightly wedge himself between me and the bulkhead wall. He'd lowered a shoulder like a linebacker throwing a block and was trying to squeeze through.

"Ladies, some of us would like to get to Hawaii today," he snarled.

Ana flared her nostrils as if smelling a foul odor and put out an arm to halt his progress. "What's your seat number, sir?"

"49 J"

"Cross the galley to the other side, please."

As if.

I scrunched up, spoon-style, behind Malia giving him as much room as possible. He returned the favor by invading my personal space requirements way beyond acceptable standards. He either had a pair of rolled up athletic socks in his pants pocket or he had a low arousal threshold. I mentally batted away an image of a bull, ready for some action, moving in on a worried heifer in a cattle chute.

Ana winked at Malia and nodded in the direction of the first class cabin.

"What?" Malia said. "Are you saying you can get us an upgrade?"

"No problem. We're a few people light up front. Just don't sit down until everyone is buckled up in case anyone wants to switch seats."

As Malia and Ana shoved our carry-on bags into closets and overhead bins, I watched men in ninety-dollar golf shirts urgently chattering on cell phones as if they were about to be shot into space. Newlywed brides whispered into the ears of husbands smug with relief after surviving "the perfect wedding," and poised for some consummation payback.

Ana went to the front galley and examined the manifest. She directed us to seats 3 A and B, then rummaged through the overhead bin across the aisle, pulling out pillows and blankets.

The guy in 3 C lifted an upper lip in disgust as Ana handed Malia two plastic-wrapped blankets. He clearly resented our intrusion, shooting me a fierce look.

"Sweetheart," he said, tapping Ana's thigh. "Be a good girl and bring me a Chivas on the rocks before we take off. That is, if you can tear yourself away from your little buddies over there."

Ana nodded, a stiff smile putting her well-defined cheekbones on full display. So much for the glamorous life of a flight attendant, I thought. But once she went into to the galley, I overheard her passing off Mr. Chivas' request to a male flight attendant who somberly served the drink a few minutes later.

Leather reclining seats with footrests, soft Hawaiian music on the sound system, and a steady stream of jaw slackening mai tais made the almost six-hour flight feel more like a day at the spa than a post-9/11 airplane ride. I dozed off in the middle of the movie and awoke to the urgent *ping!* of the intercom followed by the captain's voice announcing our arrival.

"Crew prepare for our final descent into Kahului. Take your seats please."

The plane swooped low over the ocean before banking sharply to the right. Below us I saw a ruffled fabric of aquamarine water giving way to a dense carpet of green sugar cane fields. The plane's thrusters kicked on and I watched out the window as the iron-rich red earth of Maui rose up to meet the landing gear. The tires chirped once and then we bumped along the tarmac as the engines whined in reverse.

I felt free of Frank's constant scrutiny for the first time in more than twenty-five years. I sat up a little straighter as we taxied to the gate.

"We're here. You ready for this?" said Malia.

"I can't believe Frank and I never came to Hawaii in all the time we were married. He'd never consider it. Said it was touristy and too expensive."

"Well, it's gonna be great. My family is hardcore Hawaiian, but you're gonna have fun like you never dreamed. Crazy, *kama'aina* fun. No doubt, girl." Her voice had changed on the trip over. She'd adopted the clipped sing-song style the Hawaiian flight attendants used when making the on-board announcements. Every sentence ended on a high note, almost like a question.

We made our way toward baggage claim along an open-air elevated walkway. A moist warm breeze swirled away most of my rum-induced stupor, and I gaped at the dazzling beauty around me. A towering cloud-capped mountain rose to the right, and on the left, a row of palm trees stood sentry against a bank of stark-white clouds floating in a brilliant azure sky. It reminded me of a painted backdrop for a high school production of "South Pacific."

As we exited the security area, Malia's family crowded the bottom of the escalator, lei poised, everyone talking, pushing forward to engulf us. Cameras flashed as we wended our way through a forest of brown arms raised to place strings of fragrant white pikake blossoms and purple orchids over our heads. I felt like Oprah Winfrey striding in on a red carpet, fans and paparazzi swarming on all sides. Even though the raucous welcome was all for Malia, I basked in the reflected glow. Okay, so maybe I wasn't Oprah, maybe I was Gayle King. Still good.

"Dad," Malia cried as a sinewy-built man with toffee-brown skin and wearing a battered baseball cap stepped to the front of the pack. He reached out and clasped both sides of her face, pushing her lips into a fish-face pout. He gazed at her as if committing the moment to memory. Then he dropped his hands and tenderly kissed her on both cheeks.

"Your mother should be here. She'd be so happy you've come home." He blinked back tears from dark eyes that disappeared into a fan of deep creases at the outer corners.

"Mom's here. I can feel her." Malia gripped her dad in a tight hug. Releasing him, she turned to introduce me.

"Dad, this is my friend, Nola Stevens, from Seattle," She bobbed her head and shoulders in a quick bow. "And, Nola, this is my dad, Kailealoha—or 'Al' for short."

"Ah, Nola." He reached out for my hand. I felt hard calluses on his palms. Looking into his face I was unnerved by his intense gaze. It felt as though he could see right through my skull and into my brain. Not a guy I'd want to try to lie to.

"Here on Maui your name would be Noelani." He turned to the rest of the family and with an open-palmed gesture made his pronouncement, "This is Malia's friend, Noelani Stevens. She's *ohana*."

Ohana seemed to mean something good, because everyone smiled and nodded. The guys lifted their hands in a shaka sign—thumb and little finger extended, three middle fingers folded down. But for all I knew, *ohana* could be shorthand for 'middle-aged woman whose cheatin' gay husband dumped her after more than twenty years of marriage." If so, that would have saved me a lot of explaining.

The boy cousins clamored to carry our bags as we bustled into the baggage claim area. I pointed to my small black rolling suitcase as it slid onto the revolving belt.

"That's just a little one, I'll get the next big one," the eldest-looking boy said, flexing his bicep as if welcoming an excuse to show off in front of a gaggle of teenaged girls waiting for their luggage. His display brought on a wave of giggles, whispers, and hiding behind hands as a group of teenaged girls from a Japan Airlines flight lightly elbowed each other in mock embarrassment.

"That's all I have," I said.

A dozen heads swiveled in my direction.

"No, you have more," Al said, as if he wasn't falling for my ruse.

"Nope, that's it."

"Remember when Malia went to Honolulu for her senior year party?" In a booming voice Al posed the question as if it were the first line of a long shaggy dog story, but right away everyone laughed. I didn't get the joke. Malia clued me in that every family member knew all about her showing up with about eighty pounds of luggage for a two-day trip to the neighbor island.

"Well, Dad, nothing's changed."

We waited as she said, "There's one," at least six or seven times as hefty pieces of tapestry luggage dumped onto the carousel. One of her overstuffed suitcases sported a neon green tag from the airline. It simply said, HEAVY.

"Now that's more like it," said the buffed-up eldest cousin. He jealously guarded the spot where the baggage first slid down from the belt. He reached over and heaved one whale of a bag after another onto an already overflowing airport luggage cart. The effect of the growing mountain of bags precariously piled atop the spindly cart brought to mind ten clowns stuffing themselves into a minuscule vehicle and zooming around a circus ring.

We trundled out to the parking lot where Al pointed to an ancient brown Chevy minivan. By the looks of the paintjob it hadn't been waxed since the day it left the dealership. Decades of sun and salt air had bleached it to the color of a Hershey chocolate bar left in the refrigerator for about a month.

"Oh Dad, you're still driving that thing?"

"What's that? You embarrassed to ride in the *ohana*-mobile?" There was that word again.

"No, I just thought that by now it would be smushed flat and stacked on a barge headed for the Honolulu wrecking yard."

"Don't talk like that in front of her. She's still going strong."

The aunties, uncles and cousins piled into a couple of equally dilapidated vans while Malia and I climbed into Al's. Malia insisted I ride up front.

"How long does it take to get to your house?" I said, not really caring about the answer but trying to make conversation with Al.

"It's on the Westside, so about forty-five minutes. But we can see the ocean the whole way so it seems less."

On one side of the van a shimmering expanse of water stretched to the horizon; the glittering flatness broken only by two islands off in the distance. Out the other side, steep verdant mountains with deep folds of valleys rose to such heights the peaks were hidden by a band of pink-tinged clouds. The ridged landscape reminded me of those spiky-backed dinosaurs—what were they called? When Frank Jr. was seven, I knew all the scientific names for the major dinosaur species. I'd learned them because I'd planned to teach them to my grandchildren one day. I sucked in a quick breath. Thinking about what I'd left back in Seattle caused a pinch in my chest. I pushed aside those thoughts and refocused on the view.

As we approached Lahaina Town traffic slowed to a crawl. The scenery deteriorated into a moonscape of bulldozed red dirt, clumps of shabby palm trees, and water-stained stucco buildings. A handful of brown-legged boys in baggy yellow soccer jerseys ran laps on a dusty sports field. At one point traffic completely stopped. We idled beside a pocket-sized cemetery.

"Whoa," I said. "That's a pretty sad looking place."

Bare red dirt blanketed the tiny scrap of hallowed ground. About four or five untrimmed palms loomed over the graves like ancient beasts of burden, their sun-bleached fronds bent toward the ground. Each of the graves was outlined with a ring of softball-sized stones. A few sported bouquets of what appeared to be plastic or fabric flowers; the colors bleached pale by the harsh sun.

"That's Ki'i ho'omana'o Cemetery," Malia said. "It's a traditional burial place. You know, most of what you see in Hawaii nowadays is fake. My ancestors would've laughed at stuff like high-rise condos with chlorine swimming pools. But that's what happened when the *haoles* took over."

I held my breath. With my curly hair and hazel eyes, there was no dodging my heritage. Every schoolchild knows the grim chronicle of the American westward expansion—explorers and missionaries, land grabs and Indian reservations.

"My mother's in a cemetery just like that one," she went on. "She's buried the way native Hawaiians have been laid to rest for hundreds of years. Not like some land-grabbing mainlander who puts their loved ones in a place that looks like a golf course."

The edge in her voice let me know she'd defended her family's customs before. I'd been put on notice that while on Maui, I'd best be thinking twice before offering up an opinion of what was "sad" or "weird."

"Malia," Al's voice carried a warning tone. "Noelani is *ohana* while she's our guest. We don't insult family members with talk about local politics."

Ah, so *ohana* meant 'family'. I liked the word. It slipped through the lips like a softly exhaled breath.

We pulled into the short driveway at Al's house. People milling in the yard rushed the van, making it necessary to get them to move back before we could open the doors. Once again, I felt like a celebrity. In the short hour I'd been on Maui I'd attracted more interest than I had in the past ten years—not that I was complaining.

Malia's aunt, Al's younger sister Momi, came out of the house wearing an honest to God *mu'u-mu'u* dress and a flower above her left ear. Her serene nut-brown face was a mirror of Al's, but fuller. She was probably five feet tall, but she weighed at least two-fifty, maybe more. Hard to tell under the puckered tent of brightly printed fabric. She could have passed for fifty-five, but I knew she was seventy, because Malia told me her dad was five years older than his last remaining sister.

"Malia," she stopped short, arms open wide. The loose skin above her elbows flapped like wet laundry on a clothesline.

"Auntie Momi," Malia bounded out of the van and fell into her arms. I pictured a seven-year-old returning from summer camp after a couple of weeks of hard-core homesickness.

Malia introduced me to Aunt Momi and about two dozen other relatives with names like Kono, Tomo, Kimo, and Timo. I had no idea how I'd possibly remember them all.

"We made *kalua* pig, just for you and Noelani," Aunt Momi winked and pointed toward the path to the back yard. Al shot her a disgruntled look, and she added, "Oh, and for your dad's birthday, of course."

Walking around the side of the house, I imagined a big hog with an apple in its mouth turning on a spit. I was surprised to find the minuscule back yard pretty much empty. No barbeque pit, just a smattering of ancient aluminum lawn chairs. A small shed with fogged-over windows huddled against the back fence. A massive splintery picnic table groaned under the weight of a dozen wooden bowls full of various types of salad and fruit. Two plastic dishpans were piled high with lavender-colored dinner rolls.

On the far side of the yard, three burly men with crossed arms stood watch over a dirt patch about the size of a ping pong table. They wore only rubber sandals and baggy board shorts. Their mahogany brown brows glistened as if they'd been working, but I couldn't see any evidence of labor. As I considered whether to go in the back door or circle around to the front, I saw a single puff of smoke come from a crack in the dirt.

"Ah, the pig's under there," I said aloud, pleased to have solved the mystery of the missing swine.

"Yep, dead and buried, as they say." The deep voice came from someone standing close behind me. I was so startled I jerked my head as if I'd been tapped with a cattle prod. I turned to look into the sage green eyes of the most compelling face I'd ever seen. Not native Hawaiian, but trying hard to be. He was deeply tanned, with salt and pepper hair and a light scruff of days-old beard. His well-defined biceps, triceps, and other types of ceps I couldn't even name, contrasted nicely against a faded blue tank top. My eyes lingered on his upper arms, and for a moment I shared solidarity with men who stare at big-breasted women, unable to tear my eyes away. I longed to reach out and stroke those muscles, if only to verify my hunch that the tactile would, no doubt, trump the visual.

"Hello, I'm Aidan," he said. "You must be Noelani, Malia's friend from the mainland."

I felt my pulse thudding in my temples as I struggled to form a clever response. Nothing popped into my jet-lagged brain so I settled for what I hoped passed for an engaging smile.

"I hear you caught your husband doing the 'down low' thing with some young stud." His eyes glinted with mock pity, like a pool shark who'd cleared the table before his opponent had even taken his first shot. "That's gotta feel like fifty shades of ugly."

CHAPTER 4

Malia appeared in the nick of time. I'd fallen into an awake version of that nightmare where I'm buck naked in a crowded room and can't find the door. Aidan's remarks, along with being tired, hung over, and feeling two hours ahead of the current time zone, had turned me to stone.

"I see you've met Aidan, our resident *artiste*," said Malia, threading her arm through his and giving his brawny bicep a squeeze. Envy prickled through me as I realized I still harbored a desire to stroke those muscles.

"Yes, he introduced himself," I finally managed.

"We were discussing Noelani's depressing state of affairs back home," he said. "But she hasn't had a chance to fill me in on the details."

"Oh, Aidan, you old gossip. You know better than to stalk my friend to dig up dirt. Besides, we're beat from the trip over. Today we're not going to think about any of that. We're just gonna chill, right Nola?"

Okay. I'll admit I'd been blindsided by Frank's 'don't ask, don't tell' lifestyle, but I'd wised up a lot in the previous six weeks. I didn't need to burn many brain cells figuring out this buffed-up, gossipy *artiste* probably had Elton John's private number on his speed dial. Once it dawned on me this guy was just Frank with a deep tan, I relaxed. No need to come off as cute or witty and certainly no need to defend myself to the likes of him.

"Yeah, Aidan, my life's a freakin' soap opera. But Malia's right. I'm too fagged out—pardon the pun—to go into it right now."

His eyes narrowed and he flashed a hesitant smile. His cover blown, he seemed to step back a notch and rethink the wisdom of taking me on.

"Sorry," he said. "I didn't mean to pry. Is it acceptable to ask how long you'll be staying here on Maui?"

"Ten days," said Malia, leaning her head coquettishly against his bulging pectorals. "We need to get back before Christmas."

"Pity. I've got an opening at the Waterfront Gallery the first of the year. I was hoping you two might come. We'll be serving champagne. The good stuff." He smiled, and I imagined those gentle eyes and dazzling grin working magic on art aficionados from both sides of the sexual divide.

"Aidan's work is incredible," Malia said. "Maybe I could bring Nola by the studio for a private showing before we have to go?"

"You're always welcome. But give a call first. It gets so hot in there I've been known to work in the nude."

Gay or not, that image was hard to dismiss.

"Malia, Noelani, come on in girls." Aunt Momi's lilting voice wafted from the back step. "Your dad's getting ready to open his presents."

"I hope your dad likes my gift," I said as we made our way to the house. "I had no idea what to get him."

"You didn't need to bring anything, Nola. But that's so sweet of you. And don't worry, my family loves everything. I've gotten some pretty weird things—"

"Remember the time your *tutu* gave you the BB gun?" I heard Aidan's resonant voice behind me as I climbed the three steps to the back door. Malia laughed, recalling a memory of her since-deceased grandmother.

"Oh yeah. That was pretty funny." She stopped and turned to me, "I came home from college one spring break and told my *tutu* about hiking in the mountains around Seattle. I said I usually set up a tripod to shoot birds and animals that came into the campsite. I was talking about photography, but she thought I was catching dinner. So Christmas rolls around and she's all excited 'cause she's sure she got me the perfect gift—a new pellet gun and a box of ammo."

Aidan held the door open, giving Malia's cheek a light kiss as she passed through. She seemed so relaxed around him. It was as if they'd known each other for years. Maybe he'd even been attracted to her at some point, before he'd fully embraced his nontraditional lifestyle choice.

We made our way through a tangle of bodies jammed into the kitchen. Al was holding court in the living room so we zigzagged through the crowd until we saw him. He was sitting on an ottoman with the youngest granddaughters and grandnieces clustered at his feet.

He'd already opened a half-dozen presents, including a case of beer and a new baseball cap with "Old Guys Rule" emblazoned on the front. He'd laid the cap aside, however, and instead wore a mass of brightly colored bows that the little girls had tied on his head. It said a lot about Al's love for his family that he was willing to sport bridal shower plumage with such good humor.

"Ah, Malia, I was waiting to open your present. And yours too, Noelani." He pointed to two wrapped boxes tucked near his bare feet.

Picking up the gift from Malia, he shook it as if trying to guess the contents. Whatever was inside thunked back and forth as he shifted the box. I guessed it was a hardbound book.

Malia had secured the shiny red package with only a thin strand of white ribbon tied in a simple bow. Al tugged at one tail of the bow and the ribbon fell away like an errant hair. He lifted the box top. Inside, a three-inch thick book with a fawn-colored leather cover was nestled between a few sheets of wadded-up tissue paper.

He lifted the book and gazed at the cover. I stood on tiptoe and saw it was a hand-made photo album, with "The Kanekoa Family" burned into the leather. The center of the cover was cut out to form a frame and a photograph had been placed in it. Al gazed longingly at the picture of himself and Lokelani, his wife of 48 years, on their wedding day. All chatter and fidgeting ceased as he held up the album and slowly panned the room so all could see.

"I will enjoy looking through this at a later time," he said. He blinked a couple of times and cleared his throat. "*Mahalo*, Malia. This is more precious than pearls."

The flat, rectangular box with the stark black and white domino-print paper seemed out of place next to the others swathed in vibrant yellows, blues and reds. When I'd wrapped it in Seattle I thought it looked sophisticated and stylish. Now, a small fist of doubt gripped my windpipe. Not only was the wrapping paper out of place, I had reservations about the gift itself.

"And this one's from Noelani?" Al winked at me as he plucked up the domino-patterned box and gave it a squeeze.

Rip one side, rip the other side, and then peel the center. Al's efficient gift opening method would have smoked any six-year-old on Christmas morning. He stared at the cover of the large-format pictorial book in his hands, his face transforming to a Buddha-like serenity.

"Ah. Connie's first book. A classic." He held it up. The cover of *Easy Orchids* by Constance Bergstrom sported vivid photos of a half-dozen exotic blooms.

Malia's eyes darted to mine. I could almost hear the splash as a wash of angst dumped into her brain.

"Dad, how nice. I told Noelani you liked orchids. You'll have to show her your greenhouse."

"Al has his own registered hybrid orchid," Aidan said in a languid *gotcha* tone. The put-down had a regrettably familiar ring to it.

"In fact, if I'm not mistaken," he went on, "You were president of the Hawaii chapter of the American Orchid Society a few years back, isn't that right Al?"

There was nothing I could do but live through the moment, praying Al would quickly move on to the next present. I'd never known a man who grew flowers. I'd taken Malia's offhand remark about her father's interest in orchids as a mild curiosity that might be satisfied with a pretty coffee table book. Now I squirmed from the awkwardness of my 'coals to Newcastle' gift.

"This is perfect," Al said, directing his monk-like expression to the small cluster of girls huddled around his legs. "I can share this with my *keiki mo'opuna*, so they'll know what their *kupuna kane* is talking about when he tells them about his orchids."

"Yes, yes. Good idea!" Auntie Momi clasped her hands together like a pleased schoolmarm. She beamed at me. "How sweet of you to think of giving something he can pass down to the little ones."

I nodded, trying to avoid looking as embarrassed as I felt. I imagined myself stumbling, and then a hand tenderly reaching out to offer support. *Living aloha* was beginning to take on real meaning beyond the trite slogans dished up by the Hawaii Tourist Board.

Al laid the book aside and proceeded to carve the huge pile of presents into twin mountains of wrapping paper and opened gifts. Among the offerings were many variations of his trademark baseball cap. He sat among a rainbow of colors and styles. They ranged from a black cap with the D.A.R.E. drug prevention logo from a niece who worked as a Maui County Sheriff's deputy to a bright teal cap that read "Show 'Em Your Woody!", the logo of a local surf shop. The woody cap was a gift from a shaggy-haired great-nephew with red-rimmed eyes who scooted a bit closer to the door when the female deputy locked eyes on him.

Al threw aside the wrapping paper from the final gift, signaling it was time to eat. I marveled as the group noiselessly stood and made their way out. Like a school of fish swimming in formation, everyone headed to the back yard.

Without discussion, the eldest helped the youngest fill their plates while the middle-agers—and I assumed I fit into that category—hung back and quietly chatted.

Next, the elders went through the line. This feeding technique, invented by ancestors long since dead, honored each generation with a specific position in the family hierarchy. The little guys got the food they needed; it honored the old people who'd paved the way; and it required the robust ones to patiently watch and wait.

When it was our turn to step up to the table there was barely a dent in the amount of food available. Bowls overflowed with fresh pineapple, papaya, and strange-looking fruits I couldn't name. Beyond the fruit were steaming bowls of rice, followed by green salad and a ghostly-white version of macaroni salad. Heaping plates of teriyaki chicken and fragrant pulled pork from the *imu* pit came next. At the end of the table, a medium-size bowl held a strange concoction consisting of pale pink translucent chunks mixed into some sort of flaccid stringy greens. The mixture looked like an emerald-green hairball hawked up by an enormous cat. I leaned over to sniff it just as Aidan stepped up behind me. I straightened back up. I didn't want to appear to be an unsophisticated hick, or worse yet, a finicky guest. I took a spoonful.

"Are you a *poke* fan?" he said.

Polka? Did I hear him right? Maui didn't seem like the kind of place where polka or much of anything

German would fit in. I figured most likely he was joking, so I played it cool.

"I'm not much of a dancer. But I like all kinds of music."

His eyes squinted in confusion. Then he opened his mouth in a silent *ah*. His straight white teeth suggested an affluent childhood complete with years of monthly trips to the orthodontist.

"Not polka. *Poke*."

With a hint of New England still evident in his vowels, the two words sounded exactly the same to me.

"You just put some *poke* on your plate," he went on. "Most mainlanders won't eat it."

"Oh. This here? I thought it looked interesting."

"It is. It's a traditional Hawaiian party food. Chilled raw fish and seaweed. Sometimes they use octopus, but generally it's *ahi* tuna. They mix it with onion, seaweed and kukui nut paste. It's kind of an acquired taste."

"Oh. Then I'll have to try it. I consider myself something of an intrepid eater."

"Well, *bon appetit*. Let me know what you think." He bobbed his head signaling his good-bye and moved to other side of the table.

Malia was chatting with a cluster of cousins on the back porch. I made my way over to her feeling a bit disappointed Aidan hadn't asked me to join him. There must be some truth to the maxim about seeking the familiar over the prudent, because why I'd want to spend time with a gorgeous gay man who tweaked my self-confidence at every turn was a mystery even to me.

"Hey, there you are," Malia said. "You and Aidan seem to be hitting it off."

"Oh, yeah. He's really enjoying playing 'gotcha' with the dorky tourist from the mainland."

"You're taking it wrong. Aidan's a joker but he's sweet. And he's shy. Mostly keeps to himself."

"Makes it hard to score in the bar scene, I'll bet."

"Bar scene? Aidan?" Malia chuckled as if I'd said the guy had twelve toes.

"Well, maybe gay culture is different over here. Frank's new lifestyle seems to involve a lot of hanging around bars ogling strangers. Or so I've heard."

"You think Aidan's *gay*?" Malia eyebrows disappeared under her bangs, and her jaw dropped open like a mailbox flap.

"If he is," she managed, choking back laughter, "Then he ought to get the Rock Hudson Lifetime Achievement Award for best performance by a leading man. He's pretty quiet, but believe me, Maui's littered with women who can attest to his gender preference."

"He's an artist, right?"

"Yeah."

"And you called him 'gossipy', right?"

"That was just to take him down a peg. All the guys over here are snoopy. It's part of the charm of island life. No one can keep a secret."

"And what about his gym-perfect physique?"

"Aidan's a hard worker. That body didn't come from pumping iron in front of a mirror."

We both slid our eyes his way. He was lifting a little girl of about two who'd been whining and yanking on her mother's *mu'u mu'u* to pick her up. She laid her head on his shoulder and began sucking her thumb.

"I'm sorry, I just thought..." I stopped there. It'd take more time than I had to figure out the ins and outs of Maui culture. My ten days would be best spent seeing the sights and working on my tan.

"Don't worry about it. I won't say a word." She grinned and draped an arm across my shoulders. "C'mon the *keiki* hula show is about to begin out front. It's my dad's favorite part of his birthday."

We went through the house and out the front door. They'd cleared people, pets and sports equipment off the small swatch of lawn to make way for the children's hula show. The elders were seated in white plastic chairs along the driveway. Everyone else stood.

One-by-one eight little girls and three boys slipped out of the carport and onto the open lawn, all eyes on their *kumu* or teacher. Standing together they looked like a funhouse mirror where the same image is repeated over and over, getting a bit smaller with each reflection.

The girls wore what we used to call "granny dresses" instead of the grass skirts I'd expected. A lei of small flowers—white and bright orange—encircled their slight shoulders. Matching flower rings crowned their heads.

The boys were in white cotton drawstring pants and loose fitting long-sleeved shirts. Their lei were made of what appeared to be round shiny black stones. On their heads, they wore a wreath of dark green leaves.

With a quick clap from the *kumu hula*, the girls formed two lines. They bowed to Al, their palms upturned to show respect. Someone punched a button on a boom box and a haunting song, sung in Hawaiian and featuring slack-key guitar, filled the yard with sound. The girls moved flawlessly in sync with the music and each other—feet, arms, and bodies shifting in a languid wave of body language portraying the story being sung.

"How cute is that?" I whispered to Malia, but she put a finger to her lips.

When the girls' took their bow, the crowd cheered and whistled as if we'd witnessed a home team touchdown. The boys took the stage and although the music and dance moves suggested more of a warrior dance, they exhibited the same choreographed precision as the girls.

As I watched, an ache pinched my sternum as I recalled my son Frankie's self-discipline when he was first learning to play soccer. He'd kicked the ball against the garage door for hours learning to control it with the side of his foot.

Al had tears in his eyes when the kids took their final bow. One by one they approached him, bowed and kissed his cheek. Each shyly wished him happy birthday—*hau'oli la hanau.* Then they took off their lei and slipped them over his head. When the last boy added his, Al's neck and chin disappeared behind a yoke of flowers.

"An orchid for your thoughts." Aidan said, creeping up behind me once again, startling me from my reverie.

He held out a mai tai in a plastic cup garnished with a single delicate purple and white orchid. As my hand closed around the cup, he plucked the orchid from the drink.

"Would you like me to put it over your left or your right?" he said, pantomiming placing it above each of his ears.

"I don't know. Does it matter?"

"Left side if you're spoken for; right side if you're available."

I gotta say that sure beat the heck out of *Come here often?* as an effective pick-up line.

CHAPTER 5

I woke up at six-thirty the morning after Al's party. I expected a nasty hangover from that final mai tai, but sunshine poured through the guest room window melting away any twinge of a headache. What a joy to see the sun. Unlike Seattle, where December brings fifteen hours of darkness and nine hours of gloomy drizzle, Malia explained that Hawaii typically sees the sun rise and set at about the same time, winter or summer.

I slipped into a yellow knee-length tee-shirt dress and dragged a brush through my tangled hair before making my way to the kitchen in search of coffee. Surprisingly, the kitchen was already bustling. Auntie Momi and Malia's sister Lani, along with her husband and their two teenage daughters were all huddled over the Kanekoa family photo album. Malia was in a corner chatting quietly on her cell phone.

"Morning, Noelani. You sleep okay on that guest bed?" Lani poured herself a refill from the coffee maker and then pulled a clean cup out of the cupboard and raised it in an offer of coffee. I nodded gratefully.

"No offense to Malia," I said. "But her sofa bed could learn a few tricks from that guest bed. I slept like the dead in there."

Everyone stopped talking, and the activity in the room ground to a halt. Clearly, I'd said something wrong. I was pretty sure it involved my apparent lack of appreciation for Malia's kind offer to put me up on her sofa bed for the past few weeks.

I guessed Malia was talking to Jim, and my hunch was confirmed when she whispered, "Love you too, babe," before hanging up. My throat tightened as I flashed back on what it felt like to have someone to say "I love you" to when you ended a call. Those days were over for me, and like my stress-induced fainting spells, it was one more reminder I wasn't twenty-five anymore.

"Good. I see you're up and about." Malia tossed her phone in her purse. She had a look in her eye that signaled her agenda for the day included me.

"Yeah. But I need at least one hit of caffeine before you get me out on a surfboard or taking hula lessons, or whatever other crazy scheme you've got in mind."

"I'm not going to make you do anything—promise. But it's a gorgeous day, and I thought I'd walk down to the farmer's market and pick up some fresh papaya. Want to come?"

I sighed. Knowing Malia, the farmer's market was at least three miles away, perched on a steep hill. But after dissing her hospitality to the rest of the group I felt I needed to make amends.

"Sure. I'd love to go. I'll need to change into some walking clothes, though."

"You're fine the way you are. It's just down the block. Put on some slippers and we'll head out."

Slippers? People went to the market in slippers?

"I don't have slippers. Just my sandals."

"That's what I mean. Over here, sandals are called slippers—or more accurately, *slippas*." She drew out the "ah" sound to make her point.

As if on cue, Al burst into the kitchen from outside, shucking off rubber flip flops and adding one more pair to the pile by the door.

"Hello, my treasures." Al kissed each of his two daughters on the cheek. He turned to me and, with the slightest of bows, asked if I'd slept well. The room once again grew still, as if everyone expected me to blunder a second time.

"I slept very well, thank you. Of course I've also slept remarkably well at Malia's house these past few weeks. She and Jim were extremely kind to let me stay with them."

I waited for some response to my sucking up but everyone seemed engrossed in sipping their coffee, buttering their toast and watching *The Today Show* on Al's big flat screen TV.

"Were you out watering the lawn?" Malia asked her dad.

"Doing my tai chi. I am now fully prepared to start the first day of my seventy-sixth year."

Everyone murmured and nodded as if he'd uttered a snippet of dazzling wisdom. Once again, I marveled at the respect bestowed on Hawaiian elders.

While we walked the five blocks to the farmer's market I mentioned I was pretty sure I'd come off as ungrateful and offended her family.

"I hope you aren't mad I whined about your sofa bed. I can't imagine what I would have done without you guys."

"No problem. And just so you know, that wasn't it."

"Okay, then I'm confused. All I said was I'd slept way better last night than I had on your sofa bed."

"No, I overheard you saying something about sleeping like the dead. Over here that's considered *kapu* or taboo—to reference the dead in a joking matter. The spirit world is very sacred in Hawaiian culture and any mention of the dead should be done with respect."

"Geez, I feel like the Ugly American in the fiftieth state. I'm so sorry."

"Don't worry about it. My family acted that way because it made them uncomfortable. But now it's ancient history. Let it go."

"I need a crash course in all things Hawaiian."

"Ask Aidan. He's a mainlander turned *kama'aina*—that's the word for a native or local person. He had to learn everything from scratch, just like you."

"Like he'd get a real kick out of tutoring a short-timer while he's trying to get ready for his big art show. By the way, what kind of art does he do? Oil painting, watercolors, maybe photography?"

"Mostly he's a bronze sculptor."

Well, that explained the beefy biceps.

"His work is all over the island," she said. "He has pieces in all the best hotels, and some in the county buildings, and even on the local campus of the University of Hawaii. He's got a big following on the mainland, too. We should go see his studio. You'd be amazed. And I'm sure he'd love to see you again."

Before I could comment on her doomed matchmaking efforts we'd arrived at the farmer's market. It wasn't a large market, like the Pike Place Market in Seattle. It looked more like a garage sale or a small swap meet made up of folding tables loaded with ancient cardboard boxes stacked high with produce. Above us, flimsy white tarps tented the tables against a sudden shower. The market was set up in the narrow parking lot of cluster of shops including a tiny Mexican grocery store, a real estate office, and a storefront espresso stand. Unshaven hippie-types, both men and women, worked the crowd passing out small samples of fresh fruit and baked goods. One guy looked so much like Mike, our mailman back in Seattle, I considered asking him if he had a twin brother in Washington State.

Wherever I went there were reminders of Seattle. A fresh-faced teenager wearing bold print board shorts and a brilliant white tee-shirt enthusiastically wolfed down every sample offered. I thought of Frank Jr. and wondered if he was hungry, or maybe even homeless. Not knowing where he was or how he was doing cut like a rusty razor across my belly.

"You okay?" Malia held up a clear plastic bag heavy with papayas. They ranged in color from goldenrod to bottle green. "You look kind of pale."

I laughed in response. In that crowd the Coppertone kid would look pale.

"I'm just missing Frankie and wondering how he's doing."

"Oh, Nola. That whole thing makes me sick. I'm sure when we get back he'll get back in touch. He just needs some time."

I noticed grapefruit-sized onions piled high in a tattered cardboard box and went over to investigate. They cost three times as much as onions back in Seattle. The hand-lettered sign said simply, "Maui Onions."

"Maui must think pretty highly of their onions. I've never seen such a ridiculous price."

"They're special," Malia said. "Very sweet. People have bags of them shipped back to the mainland."

"Really? Well, I've got a recipe for a sweet onion tart I'm dying to try. Do you think your family would be game?"

"To eat? Hey, I come by my ravenous appetite honestly. Trust me, they'll love anything you're willing to make."

I selected a half-dozen firm shiny globes and slipped them into a thin plastic produce bag. The bag was so full I could barely get a firm grip on the top.

While we waited in line to check out, my mind drifted back to Seattle and Frank Jr.

"Jim didn't mention he'd heard from Frank Jr. did he?"

"Nola! Give me some credit. I promise if I hear anything at all I'll tell you right away. Good or bad, I won't keep it from you."

The five-block trudge back to Al's house seemed longer now that I was carrying a knot of worry over Frankie as well as five pounds of Maui onions.

We kept to the far right of the sidewalk, making way for the constant stream of joggers, walkers, and buns-of-steel moms pushing strollers. I'd never seen so many fitness freaks in one place. Even in my few forays to the gym—which usually resulted in my getting into workout clothes, walking the track once or twice and then sitting in the sauna for ten minutes before dressing and slinking back home—I'd never seen so many buffed out men and women. All of them tanned and smiling. But hey, I'd smile too if I looked like GI Jane, only with more hair.

"Want to jog the last couple of blocks?" said Malia. She must have flashed on *GI Jane* too—the part where Demi Moore does like four hundred one-arm push-ups.

"I'm carrying these darn onions."

"I'll take 'em," she said, reaching for the plastic bag. "You can carry the banana bread."

I traded the bulky onion bag for a bread bag that weighed next to nothing. We started off, and within a block my breath was coming in ragged gulps. I felt a stabbing pain in my side, and my pulse pounded so loudly in my ears I'm sure I qualified as legally deaf. Worried about a possible fainting spell, I slowed my gait.

"When we get to the corner..." I took a deep breath and blew it out like a kid learning to whistle. "...I'm going to walk the next block."

"That's fine. I'm going to keep going. You know the way, right? Turn left at Apua'a Street, then fourth house down." She wasn't even breathing hard.

"Got it."

I trotted the next block, then walked the final two blocks—chest heaving, perspiration popping out on my forehead and upper lip. I felt good, though. The ocean breeze dried my sweat and I ducked into Al's carport feeling refreshed rather than wilted.

Malia had left the side door open a crack which I appreciated since it answered the question of whether I should knock before coming in. I pushed against the door just as she flung it wide open from inside.

"Great news! Frank Jr. called."

"When?"

Malia looked at Lani, who must have been the one who'd answered the phone.

"I don't know," Lani said, shrugging. "Five, maybe ten minutes ago."

"Did he leave a number?"

"Yeah, I wrote it here on the front of the phone book."

The number wasn't one I recognized, but maybe Frankie had requested a new number when he re-established his cell phone service. Then, like one of those cartoon characters that skids to an abrupt halt—heels down, toes in the air, and a cloud of smoke billowing behind—it hit me.

"Are you sure he said he was Frank *Junior*?"

"Well," said Lani. "He said his name was 'Frank' and he said to tell you it was urgent."

CHAPTER 6

I never wanted to make my son a Junior. I believe every child deserves a unique name, but Frank insisted on immortalizing himself with his first-born. I prayed for a boy, cringing at the thought of a little girl named "Frankelina" or "Frankette." I'd mentioned "Francine" but he'd balked since it lacked the hard "k" sound.

Those were my halcyon days when I'd managed to convince myself nothing was more important than being a supportive wife and having a good marriage. Truth was, it was only good as long as whatever Frank wanted, Frank got. Looking back, pretty much every day of my married life had been a one-sided compromise. We'd have a difference of opinion, I'd offer my point of view, he'd point out where I was wrong, and then I'd concede. This went on for years. Decades, actually.

I checked my cell phone. It was turned off. I'd forgotten to turn it back on when we'd landed on Maui.

I fired it up and the phone did its little wake-up routine with a series of graphics, a little ditty, and finally a series of three beeps. When the ready screen appeared, I saw I eight phone messages. I took a deep breath and dialed the voicemail number.

Message one. "Hello, dear. It's your mother. I want you to call me the *second* you land in Hawaii. I'm nervous about you flying over so much water. They always put the life vest under the seat. Check your seat when you get on and make sure it's there, okay? Call me."

Next message: "Hi Nola, it's me, Frank. Call me when you get there. Something's come up."

Third: "Nola. Frank here. I mean it. You need to call me."

There were four more similar messages from him and then the final message:

"Hello, Nola. Frank again. I'm not amused by this passive-aggressive attitude you've adopted. I'm not leaving any more messages. I'll track you down at Malia's dad's house. I got the number from Jim."

Well, that answered the Frank Senior or Junior question. I punched in my mom's number, hoping she'd be out and I'd get her voicemail. No such luck.

"Oh my god, Nola. Are you okay? You had me worried sick. I can't believe you just got there. Didn't you leave yesterday morning?"

"I'm fine, Mom. Actually we got in yesterday afternoon but my phone was off. You know, you have to turn it off on the airplane."

"Well, yes, but you knew I'd be worried. I can't believe you lack the consideration to call your own mother. I thought I raised you better than that."

"I'm sorry. There was a big birthday party here last night. It was kind of loud and crazy."

Silence. My mom's catch-all response to hurt feelings—the silent treatment. I didn't want to burn up my cell minutes listening to her breathing so I picked up where I'd left off.

"Well, anyway, I'm sorry to worry you. We're doing fine. I'll send you a postcard. Good-bye, Mom."

I pulled the phone away and was about to punch the hang-up button when I thought I heard a faint stream of words coming out of the earpiece. Curious, I put it back to my ear.

"...and he said you didn't stick around to help him at all. You owe Frank an apology, Nola. Nola?"

On second thought, I guess I was mistaken. I didn't hear anything after all. I disconnected just as Malia came into the guest room.

"So? Which one was it?" she said. "Judging by the look on your face, I'm guessing it was Cowboy Frank." Malia had started calling him that in reference to the gay movie, *Brokeback Mountain.*

"Yeah, 'fraid so. His message said 'something's come up'. I'm dying to point out to him that if *something* had stayed *down,* or at least in his pants, we'd probably have avoided an ugly divorce. But his message didn't sound like he was in an apologetic mood."

"You going to call him?"

"I don't know. I sure don't want to. I just finished getting an earful from my mom. That's enough for one day. And here I was feeling good for the first time in weeks. But hearing his voice has me back to square one." I plopped down on the edge of the bed and stared at the phone. "I guess might as well get it over with."

"You want me to call him? He doesn't scare me."

"I'm not *scared* of him. I just don't want to talk to him."

"Sure, whatever. Look, let me make the call. I'll hear what he has to say and tell him you'll think about it. It's your turn to have a minion do the dirty work." She winked and held her palms up, as if to say, "at your service."

I punched in his number and handed her the phone.

"Hey, Frank. Good of you to answer," Malia knew about Frank's obsession with having someone else answer his in-coming calls. "What's up?"

I paced the room.

"She can't talk right now; she's in the shower. Whatever it is, you can tell me and I'll let her know when she gets out."

I popped my knuckles and stared out the window to the back yard.

"Listen Frank, if you don't want to tell me, you don't have to. But Nola won't be calling you back unless she knows what it's about. That's it. Either tell me, or stop calling."

A thrill of terror skittered down my spine imagining Frank's reaction to *that*.

"Fine, suit yourself. *Aloha.*" She tapped the disconnect.

"He won't tell me. Says he'll only talk to you."

"What should I do?"

"I can't believe you're really asking me that. For crying out loud, Nola, what do you care?" She tossed me the phone as if daring me to call him back. "He's a lying jerk who broke up your family and left you without a job or a home. Why the *hell* should you give a damn?"

It wasn't like Malia to swear. Her patience with my wimp behavior must have finally dried up.

"Sorry. It's just that I'm so used to..." I couldn't finish the sentence. I threw the phone down on the bed as if simply holding it might be too much of a temptation to revert to my old ways.

Malia sat down on the edge of the bed and patted the space next to her. I took a seat and she put a warm hand on my arm.

"Look, he can't get to you here. Besides, he's already taken everything he could take."

"But what if he's calling about Frankie?"

"It's not about Frankie. If it were, he'd have told me because although he's the biggest ass to walk the earth, he wouldn't keep something like that from you. And as sure as shootin' your mom would've said something. She didn't, did she?"

I shook my head.

"I didn't think so. The reason Frank wouldn't talk to me is because whatever it is, it's about him, or for him. He wants something and he knows I'd have told him to go straight to hell. Right?"

I nodded. "You're right on both counts. First, he wants something. And second, he *is* the biggest ass to walk the earth."

"Get in the shower, girl," she said. "You and I have a date with a naked sculptor."

Malia looked right at home behind the wheel of the *ohana*-mobile—dark hair flying, wrists twinkling with gold bangles. "*In Dis Life*" blasted from the boom box at our feet. She returned the shaka sign to everyone who waved as we drove down into town.

"You know everyone here."

"Not really, but when people see the *ohana*-mobile, they know it's my family so they wave. I gotta wave back or my dad will hear about some stuck-up girl who was driving his van. It's kind of like junior high. Being stuck-up is an unpardonable sin."

Aidan's studio was at the geographic middle of Lahaina Town. It wasn't on Front Street, the main drag along the waterfront, but a block inland. Al told me that commercial property anywhere in Lahaina sold for more than a thousand dollars per square foot. Since I'd been in the real estate business for a decade I was acutely aware of property values. I wondered how a local artist could manage a positive cash flow in such costly digs.

The spendy location didn't translate to the building itself, however. It was a clapboard box, two stories high, painted a shade of toad green that smacked of half-price paint from the 'mistakes' bin at the hardware store. Two sets of identical doors faced the street, making it appear to be a commercial duplex.

The windows on the main floor and in each of the doors were crusted over with steel-gray dust so thick it was impossible to see inside. Both doors were shut tight. From across the street, it looked like the entire building was vacant. On closer inspection, I spotted a small bronze plaque, etched with 'Aidan Lawson Bronzeworks' and the street number affixed near the first set of doors.

"Shouldn't we have called? He said he wanted us to phone first."

"Nah. Aidan's always up for company. It's lonely work."

"But what if he's, you know, got his clothes off?"

"So much the better, trust me." Malia shot me a naughty-girl grin and then stepped up to the door and rapped four times: two long, two short.

A few seconds passed in silence before we heard someone on the other side slipping the deadbolt. The door swung open wide and Aidan appeared in dusty low-slung jeans. He was stripped to the waist and barefoot. I stifled a gasp at his six-pack abs. I wasn't one to ogle men's bodies, but looking at him was like admiring the Hope Diamond, the Mona Lisa, or a perfect chocolate soufflé—in other words, extraordinary. He held one hand on the door handle and leaned back to grab a tattered plaid shirt from the back of a nearby chair. I almost mewed with disappointment as he slipped it on.

"I knew it was you. After all these years I still remember your knock."

Malia gestured for me to go first. When she entered, I turned and saw her give him a quick peck on the lips.

"What have you got to show us that we can't afford?" she said, glancing around the cluttered room.

"Everything I make you can't afford, my love. But looking's free." He stepped past Malia and caught up with me. "Great to see you again." He pecked me on the cheek and the heat from his lips seemed tangible, like a lipstick smudge. I reached up to rub it in.

"Don't like to be kissed?" he said, grinning at my involuntary response.

"No, it's fine. You're lips are really hot. I mean, warm. It's warm in here." A fourteen-year-old could have shown more poise.

"Not as hot as it gets when I'm pouring wax. Today I'm just doing some finish work. Come see."

He led us through the downstairs studio amid a forest of leaping dolphins, breaching whales, and diving turtles. All were smoothly crafted and amazingly lifelike, finished with a patina of aquatic colors—deep bottle green, pewter gray and watery blue.

"Look at my latest. I'm liking how this one's turning out." He stood next to a six-foot humpback whale, vertically arcing from a base of frothy waves. At the whale's side, a foot-long baby mimicked its mother's leap.

"How sweet," Malia said, running her hand along the furrowed sides of the larger whale.

"I call it 'Like Mother, Like Daughter'. What do you think?"

"It's beautiful," I said. "Do whales really look like this?"

Aidan turned. A slow smile progressed across his entire face—lips, cheeks, eyes—ending at uplifted eyebrows. I felt heat rise in my cheeks and neck as I waited for him to don his Frank persona and shake his head in pity at my ignorance.

"I like to think so," he said. "But they're quite a bit bigger."

"What's going to be in your show next month?" said Malia. "Except for this new one, most of these pieces look pretty familiar."

"The show is for a whole new line. Come upstairs."

We ascended a dark wooden staircase at the back of the room. The tread boards groaned in protest and the worn handrail wobbled when I grabbed it. But upstairs the windows were clean, letting in streams of sunlight and hinting at a possible ocean view.

"I've always loved it up here," Malia said, hugging herself and turning in a circle. "Can you open the doors and show Nola the *lanai*?"

"Your wish is my command." Aidan strode across the room and slid a tall stack of cardboard boxes out of the way. Behind the boxes was a set of French doors matching the ones we'd come in downstairs, but these doors were on the ocean side of the building rather than facing the street. He unlatched the deadbolt and pushed both doors open. We walked onto a spacious balcony running the full length of the building. It was like standing on the deck of a ship. The roofs of the one-story buildings of Front Street were below, and beyond was an unobstructed view of Lahaina Harbor with a sweeping expanse of ocean all the way to the horizon. A large island off to the left glinted golden in the sunlight. Boats tied offshore bobbed in inky blue water that sparkled in the sun like a well-cut sapphire.

"Wow!" Malia said. "This view never fails to take my breath away."

I didn't speak. I was busy mentally burning the postcard-perfect scene into my memory so on wet, dark winter days in Seattle I'd be able to vividly recall it.

"I wish I had a camera," I said. "It's the most gorgeous thing I've ever seen."

"Oh c'mon," said Aidan. "You look in the mirror every morning, don't you?"

"Aidan!" Maila punched him in the shoulder. "Back off, bruddah. Nola isn't one of your adoring art school groupies, so you can forget about laying on the BS."

Her remark irritated me. No one had blatantly flirted with me since high school and whether sincere or not, I was enjoying myself.

"The stuff for the new gallery show is up here?" she said. She turned and walked back into the almost empty room.

I glanced at Aidan and he shrugged. His expression was impossible for me to read. Then he smiled and placed his hand on the small of my back and guided me back inside.

"For this show, I'm working on a much smaller scale," he said, easing the balcony doors closed and setting the latch. "Still metalwork, but miniscule compared to my usual pieces."

He walked across the room and pulled a large tray from a bank of thin, wide drawers near the stairwell. He carried it to a rickety wooden table near the center of the space.

"Behold," he said using a fake Middle Eastern accent, "the treasures of Ali Baba." He nodded his head, gesturing like a rug merchant enticing us to enter the Kasbah bazaar.

The tray held an assortment of women's gold jewelry—necklaces, earrings, bracelets, and rings. The gold was smooth and shined to a high gloss, as if tempting us to run our fingers along the silken finish. Each piece was a simple graphic form. I recognized turtles, dolphins, and stick figures of people.

"Aidan, these are gorgeous," said Malia. "They're Hawaiian petroglyphs, aren't they?"

"Good for you. Most people compliment me on the graphic elements, but I ripped these designs off people who've been dead for hundreds of years."

"They're amazing. So smooth and shiny." I sounded like Dustin Hoffman in *Rain Man*. Why couldn't I manage an intelligent comment around this man?

"Thanks. The quality of the casting is my claim to fame. Gold and silverwork require a lot more precision than bronze. Let me show you some other things."

We spent the next hour looking at tray after tray of beautiful objects—mostly jewelry, but there were also a few gold and silver pieces meant for home décor or paperweights. In addition to the Hawaiian graphics there were pieces with Japanese symbols, pearl and shell combinations, and simple abstract designs.

We'd made our way back downstairs and out onto the street when I remembered the spectacular view from the balcony.

"Darn, I wanted to take a one more peek from that second story balcony before we left," I said as I opened the passenger side door.

"Don't worry," Malia said. "I've got a feeling Aidan will come up with all kinds of excuses to get you upstairs for another peek."

CHAPTER 7

The next few days flew by as we hit all of the tourist highlights. We started with the Maui Ocean Center, where we touched sea turtles and starfish in a tidepool before walking through an undersea acrylic tunnel. Sharks and manta rays glided overhead in a silent ballet; the spell broken only when three little kids came in and started hooting their approval. One exhibit featured a life-size model of a humpback whale. I marveled at how much it resembled Aidan's bronze sculpture only—as he'd pointed out—it was a whole lot bigger.

One morning we got up at three-thirty to drive up to Haleakala Crater to watch the sunrise. Haleakala was the mountain I'd seen when we arrived at the airport.

"You're going to need these," said Malia, pulling out a thick gray sweatshirt and fleece pants from a box in the hall closet. I caught a whiff of the bitter scent of mildew. The clothes smelled like they'd been packed away wet.

"Okay." I said, holding them at arm's length as if she'd handed me a sack of road kill.

"I know. They aren't very glamorous, but you'll be glad you've got them when we get up there."

We reached the summit two hours later. In the predawn gloom, the forest ranger station's big digital thermometer read 36° F. I snuggled into the musty sweats as if they were cashmere.

As Malia and I huddled together to keep our teeth from chattering, I saw a faint light peak over the cloud bank on the far side of the crater rim. Soon, streaks of pink, coral, and violet blazed against the indigo sky. As if someone had thrown a switch, shafts of yellow sunlight shot up from behind the fading colors. In a grand crescendo, a flat white disc ascended above the horizon. It wasn't hard to understand why ancient Hawaiians worshipped the sun as a living, breathing god.

"Wow."

"Yeah, wow," said Malia. "I've seen this at least a dozen times and I swear it gets better every time. Like celestial fireworks."

That afternoon while we napped in our swimsuits on a couple of creaky aluminum lounges in the back yard, I awoke to a woman's voice.

"Malia," I said. "I think someone wants you."

"Huh?" She lifted her head slightly, peering at the shaded back porch.

"Hi girls, it's me, Auntie Momi. Are you sleeping out there?"

"We're just resting our eyes, Auntie. I'll be right in." Malia turned to me. "You can stay here, but I've got to make an appearance."

"That's okay, I'll come too."

Wrapping towels around us, sarong-style, we went inside. At first I couldn't see a thing. The white sunlight pinched my pupils down to pinholes and the house was dark since they closed the heavy drapes every afternoon to keep it cool. Like a camera lens slowly coming into focus my eyes finally made out Auntie Momi sitting at the kitchen table. Her smiling face from the birthday party was nowhere to be seen. Instead, she wore a tight scowl.

"Hi Auntie, you remember Nola—Noelani—my friend from Seattle."

"Of course, nice to see you again." She seemed to force the sides of her mouth up. Then, as if it was just too much effort to maintain the strained smile, the frown reasserted itself.

"Auntie, you look upset." Malia placed her hand over Momi's trembling fingers.

"I am. I got bad news today."

No one said a word. I was used to long unsettling silences from both my mother and from Frank, so it didn't bother me. But judging from Al's crumpled brow, he was growing impatient to learn what was going on.

"So? What's the bad news?"

"I heard from that attorney about the store."

"Catch me up here, Auntie," said Malia. "What attorney? Is this about the Shore Store?"

"Yeah. You know, ever since your Uncle Koma passed on I've only been able to keep the store open a few hours each day. I thought I'd be able to do more; maybe find some help or get someone else to run, but it's too much. The ordering, the cleaning, standing on my feet all day. I just can't do it no more."

"It's a lot of work." Al said, glowering at the two of us as if daring us to disagree that a seventy-year-old overweight, arthritic woman might find it difficult to operate a store all by herself.

"Of course it is, Auntie," said Malia. Her tone sounded condescending to me, but Momi looked pleased with the unanimous vote of sympathy.

"But if I don't keep it open more hours, I have to close it down. I lose money every day. The lawyer said if I don't pay the taxes the government will come and take the building."

"Can they just take it?" Malia glanced at me, as if I might want to weigh in on the conversation since I'd worked in real estate.

"I guess so," Momi said. "But it doesn't make sense. My store's on crown land owned by the royal family. When the Kingdom of Hawaii was overthrown, the United States took the land. All of it; even the royal land. Now they say I gotta pay taxes on the land they stole."

She heaved a deep sigh. She looked like she might start crying. As the only non-native in the room, I fervently prayed I wouldn't be called upon to defend the state's right to sell property for back taxes.

"Actually, they didn't hand over the crown lands when they imprisoned our queen. That came later," said Al. "But it doesn't matter. You're still gonna lose your store if you don't pay the tax."

"I barely get by on my little Social Security check. It covers the rent on my cottage and my food, but not much more. Koma's medical bills and then the funeral took all our savings."

"When are the taxes due?" said Malia.

"They were supposed to be paid last August. After six months they say they can seize the store. That's the word the lawyer used, 'seize.' That gives me only until the first of the year—only a few more weeks."

"Couldn't someone else pay the taxes while you figure this out?" I broke in. With that, all eyes turned expectantly at me as if I'd whipped out my checkbook.

"I mean, couldn't your *ohana* help you with this debt?"

Al and Malia cast their eyes downward.

"It's a lot of money, Nola," Malia whispered.

"Oh," I said, feeling my cheeks warm as I sought to minimize the damage. "Maybe someone in the family could help keep the store open more hours to bring in more money."

"Momi has no children left in Hawaii," Al said. "Her boys went to the mainland and they aren't coming back." He said it as though Momi's sons were doing hard time for some unspeakable crime.

"The store's been in our family for generations," Momi went on, ignoring my measly attempt at problem solving. "If I let the government seize it I will have dishonored my mother. She gave me the family business, and then I failed to have a daughter who could take it over."

"Where is this store?" I asked. Everyone else at the table obviously knew where it was, but I was curious to know the location of this property that had once been owned by the King of Hawaii.

"You've been there," said Malia. "It's in the same building as Aidan's studio. The Shore Store's on the other side."

Huh? A multi-million-dollar view property that seemed out of place housing a dusty artist's studio also included a soon-to-be closed store? How odd.

"Why's it called the Shore Store?" I asked.

"Originally it was a store for sailors. Lahaina was a major port for whaling and cargo ships headed for the South Pacific and Asia."

"So the store sells sailor stuff? Like rope and maps?"

"No, no," said Malia. "During the Second World War it was converted into a convenience store for the downtown locals. It has a little bento lunch counter and you still sell beer and some household stuff, right, Momi?"

She nodded glumly.

Malia went on. "It's called Momi's Shore Store because whoever's running it always puts their name on the sign. But it was built in the mid-1800's, and nothing around here ever changes, so the locals still call it the Shore Store."

"Before me, it was called Wila's Shore Store. For my mother." Auntie Momi's voice dropped to barely a whisper.

"Maybe it's time to let some things go," said Al, squeezing her hand. "The boys are gone and Malia lives in Seattle now. Lani and the other kids have good jobs in Kahului. We can't expect them to drop everything to keep a West Side store going that's not even bringing in money."

"But that property's incredible," I said. "The view alone is worth a million dollars."

"Maybe," said Al. "But it's not worth nuthin' if she can't pay the taxes."

Malia leaned in and looked at her dad. "What will happen to Aidan's studio if they sell the building?" She'd finally asked the question I'd been dying to ask.

"He'll have to find someplace else," said Al. "I've heard he's doing pretty good. He doesn't have to pay rent now, but I think he could afford it if he had to."

I stifled myself to keep from screeching, *Aidan doesn't pay rent?* What kind of jerk doesn't pay rent to an elderly widow? I knew exactly what kind of jerk; I'd been married to one for more than twenty years. In his hard-charging pursuit of the almighty dollar, Frank never once showed a single qualm about screwing over a friend.

Malia had been half right. It wouldn't be Aidan coming up with excuses to see me again. It would be me finding an excuse to see him. And it wasn't to take in the view.

CHAPTER 8

As if echoing my cranky mood it rained the next morning. Poured, actually. I'd lived in Seattle all my life so I was used to rain, but this deluge was something else. Back home, an inch of rainfall in a day is considered a storm. But listening to the radio in the kitchen I heard that West Maui had gotten over two inches already and it wasn't even ten o'clock.

The radio was tuned to KPOA-FM, the Maui hometown station that routinely played a couple of Hawaiian-style re-mixes of popular songs followed by a string of low-budget commercials for local restaurants and businesses. The announcer said the Pali Highway—the only road to the airport—was closed due to rockslides. That tightly wound businessman from the first class cabin must've had a stroke when he learned he wouldn't be catching his plane. But I'd bet there were a lot more folks who'd cheered when given an ironclad excuse for telling the boss they'd be staying another day or two.

I was chafing to pay a visit to Aidan—by myself. I had a tough time coming up with a credible explanation for borrowing the *ohana*-mobile, but Al blessedly gave his consent without asking any questions. Wriggling free of Malia proved to be more of a problem. No way could I allow her to come along. In the past week it had become clear to me that many of the modern Hawaiian *kapus* or taboos dealt with money, so it went without saying that shaking down a friend of the family was probably on the list of no-nos. Since Aidan and I weren't family—or even friends, really—it seemed I'd be the best person to let him know he needed to help out Auntie Momi. I frankly didn't care how talented he was, how charming, or how sexy. He'd played in the free rent sand box long enough. Now it was time to pay the piper. I expected that after I explained her plight he'd quickly agree to pay her what he owed and hopefully more. But first I needed a few minutes of his undivided attention.

"I think I might go down to Lahaina today," I said to Malia as we were cleaning up the kitchen. I went for a casual, indecisive tone and even threw in a bit of a shrug for good measure.

"Great. I'll see if Dad needs the van. If not, let's do it."

"Uh. I already asked your Dad, and he said I could borrow it. I just want to walk around a little. You know, look in some of the shops. Maybe buy a few souvenirs." I drawled it out, hoping my morning plans would have the same allure as going to get my tires rotated.

"Sounds good," she said. "Nothing much else for us to do in this rain."

"Actually, I kind of want to go alone. If that's all right with you."

"Alone?" He face dropped into a disappointed pout and I felt sleazy for the shopping fib.

"Yeah. I feel like I need a little downtime, you know, just to think. I've got a lot on my mind." Well, at least that part was true.

"You're gonna call Frank, aren't you?"

"No!" I yelped a bit too quickly. "I mean, if I wanted to call him, I could do it from here. I just need some space. We've been here a whole week and I think both of us could use a break from each other."

"Okay. You're probably right. Tell you what. Why don't you let me drive you down to Front Street and then I'll go by and visit Aidan while you chill?"

Not the response I wanted *at all*. I steeled myself against being hit by a bolt of lightning and pushed on.

"So, what's the deal with you and Aidan?" I said. "Does Jim know about him?"

"What's that supposed to mean?" She pinched her eyebrows together, narrowing her eyes in a defensive glare. "I was just trying to help you out by driving you down there. I don't appreciate your insinuation."

I bit back the urge to apologize, since the accusation had served my purpose.

"Malia, I can drive myself the few miles to Lahaina. Why don't you relax here with your dad and Lani? I'll bet they'd like some alone time with you."

She blew out a breath in mute agreement. I pressed my lips together to avoid a triumphant smile. Rather than risk her seeing the truth in my eyes, I turned to go back to the guest room, mumbling that I needed to grab a jacket. Once there, I pumped the air with my fist, but then glanced quickly over my shoulder to make sure she wasn't following me.

"It's kinda hinky with the brakes," Al explained, demonstrating how he usually repeatedly tapped the pedal well in advance of a stop. "But take it slow and you won't have any problems."

He slid out of the driver's seat and I climbed in. He closed the door with a *thunk*, but the window was still open. The window crank hung from the door panel as limp as a broken bone.

"Oh, and, you know about giving aloha, don't you?" His voice dropped to a mumble. I had to replay the question in my mind for a few seconds to make sure I'd understood.

"Yes, Malia showed me how to do the shaka sign." I demonstrated my proficiency with an out-the-window shaka using my left hand. "No stuck up people can drive Al's car, right?"

"Good girl," he said. "You call me if you have any problem."

I hadn't received a sendoff like that since my own dad reluctantly handed me his car keys after I'd passed my driver's test. How odd that so many things in Maui reminded me of what it felt like to be a kid again.

"I'll be careful. Promise." A dead ringer for the farewell I'd given my dad.

I backed out of the driveway and waited for the cloud of blue-white exhaust to clear before throwing the transmission into Drive. Turning at Hono'apua Street, I slowly made my way west. The speed limit was only twenty miles an hour and the ohana-mobile puttered along nicely, keeping pace with the scattering of cars on the wet roadway.

Things turned ugly, though, once I hit the Honoapi'ilani Highway to go south. A local guy in a jacked-up white pick-up tailgated me even though I never strayed from the right lane and the left lane was wide open. I almost threw him a mainland version of the shaka sign—the one that featured a prominent middle finger—but at the last moment he roared around me. I chuckled as I read his bumper sticker, *Slow Down, This Ain't the Mainland.* That one, and the one that said *Live Aloha* were common bumper stickers on local cars and trucks. But I'd witnessed a definite lack of aloha on the roads around Lahaina. For some reason, impatience trumped courtesy in a kind of highway rock-paper-scissors game.

I turned right on Dickenson Street and then again on Lukulini, driving slowly as I peered through the sheets of rain. I was prepared to circle the block if necessary, but I located Aidan's studio on the first pass. And, as if signaling a good omen, there was even an on-street parking spot right in front. I'd hoped to take a few minutes to gather my thoughts before going in, but as I turned off the ignition, Aidan appeared at the front door. He closed the door and turned a key in the lock. He was carrying a soft-sided briefcase. I bolted from the van, not bothering to check if the door had shut tight behind me.

"Hey, Aidan."

He turned and squinted through the rain. His face softened a bit when he recognized me.

"Hey, what are you doing down here?" he asked when I'd gotten close enough to hear him over the sound of the rain hammering on the tin roof.

Then he added, "Are you alone?" He peered around my shoulder as if expecting Malia to pop out from behind the van.

I had a déjà vu feeling of being an unwelcome child at an adults-only affair who'd shown up without my mama.

"Actually, I came to talk with you," I said. "Just the two of us."

"I wished you'd called. I'm on my way to an appointment."

"No problem. I'll keep it short." I could tell by the shift in his eyes he knew I wasn't there to flirt and flatter. It reminded me of the look I used to get from my co-workers when I'd hit them up for their United Way donation.

"Okay, c'mon inside."

He opened the door and I walked inside. Glancing around the dimly lit room at the motionless yet lifelike creatures felt like some sort of underwater end of the world scene. Creeped me out.

"I'll get right to the point," I said, thrilled to hear my voice come out strong and unfaltering. "Why haven't you offered to pay Auntie Momi rent for your studio space here?"

"I don't see how that's any of your business," he said with a half-shrug that seemed to indicate, that for him anyway, the conversation was over.

He took a step toward the door, but I stepped into his path.

"You'll have to excuse me," he said nudging closer. "As I said, I have an appointment."

I faced him squarely, and put my palm up to signal *halt*. "That poor woman is fretting herself into apoplexy over not having any money. And now the State's threatening to sell the building for back taxes. I think it *is* my business to intervene when the obvious solution is for you to pay her a reasonable rent. It's called common decency, Aidan."

He glanced left, in the direction of the Shore Store, but didn't utter a sound.

"So," I said. "I guess my original assessment of you was correct. You're a jerk."

He offered no comment.

I continued. "That's it. You're a narcissistic jerk who's oblivious to other people and their problems."

"You don't know what you're talking about," he said. He scanned the room as if searching for an another exit. "But more importantly, it's still none of your business. I've got to give you points for chutzpah, though. Here you are poking your nose into Kanakoa family business when, from what I hear, you're not even on speaking terms with your own kid."

I reached over and slapped his face. No knockout punch or anything, but an open-handed *smack* that imparted both sound and fury.

Horrified, I ran out to the van. I pulled the driver door open and hopped in. Fumbling the key in the ignition, I glanced out the passenger-side window, half expecting him to jump in and grab me by my hair.

The studio door remained ajar but Aidan didn't appear before the engine roared to life and the van lurched away from the curb.

I turned at Lahainaluna Street and managed to make it to the traffic light at the highway before I killed the engine. I wasn't in any condition to drive, so instead of turning onto the highway I crossed over and went a few blocks beyond the rusting hulk of the old sugar mill. I pulled over. My heart thudded as if I'd robbed a bank. I glimpsed the familiar curling black splotches at the edge of my vision.

Part of me wanted to call Malia for help but another other part wanted me to turn the van around and go back and apologize. I resisted both urges and instead sat in the driver's seat, watching the raindrops trickle down the windshield. My thighs stuck to the wet vinyl seat, and my fingers gripped the slick plastic steering wheel as if it were a life preserver in open water, no land in sight.

A few minutes passed and my heart rate slowed. The rain had let up, so it seemed like a good idea to get out and walk around for a few minutes before going back to Al's. In my mind's eye I heard Aidan calling Malia and filling her in on my outrageous behavior.

"She slapped me."

"No!"

"Yeah. She's nuts. Your friend is totally nuts, *Malia."*

I got out and climbed block after block of Lahainaluna Road. The road was steep; the ascent like a stairway to heaven. My thigh muscles burned in protest and my breath came ragged and shallow. I forced myself to inhale deeply through my nose. At the corner of Ikena Street I turned into a pocket-sized park and walked to the edge where it faced the ocean. I took in the expansive view of West Maui as the wind lifted my hair and a few straggler raindrops wetted my cheeks. Something stirred in me that I hadn't sensed in a long time. If I'd been home in Seattle I might have pegged it as fear. It felt a little like fear—dangerous, jumpy, with a dash of suspense. But I was pretty sure it wasn't fear because I didn't feel one whit of shame or weakness.

I started walking down the hill, and as the van came into view, I identified the feeling. It was *courage*. I'd made the effort to set something right. The execution of my new-found assertiveness had been a bit unsophisticated. I mean, I'd never spanked Frank Jr. for bad behavior, so what on earth caused me to slap Aidan? But I figured I should cut myself some slack. Being daring was totally new to me. Throughout my life I'd been described many ways: I was considerate, sweet, friendly, bubbly, modest, and generous. The whole 'good girl' smorgasbord. But, to my knowledge, *courageous* or *daring* never made the list.

Wearing my new mantle of fearlessness I trudged to the van determined to face whatever awaited me at Al's. I'd apologize to Malia for lying about where I'd gone, but when I considered apologizing to Aidan, all that came to mind was something my grandma used to say: *If you're gonna make an omelet, you gotta break a few eggs.*

CHAPTER 9

Sunlight streaming through the van windshield nearly blinded me by the time I turned onto Al's street. The clouds had tamped it down all morning, but now that the sun had broken through, it seemed to be ferociously working to make up for lost time.

I pulled the van into the driveway. I wasn't looking forward to explaining myself to Malia, but summoning my newfound courage helped still my inner chatter as I went into the house.

She looked up from her book and a tight smile played across her face. I nodded hello, waiting for her to speak first.

"That was quick. I thought you'd be down there for hours."

"No. That was enough for me." I laid the keys in the catch-all basket on the counter.

"So, how about this afternoon?" she said. "You up for going to the beach? It looks like the rain's stopped and with all the humidity this house is going to get stifling."

Good move. Anything we had to say to each other would be better discussed away from Al's eager ears.

While she gathered up towels and beach gear, I packed a light picnic lunch. We headed for the van and Malia hopped into the driver's seat. I took my customary shotgun spot and waited while she slid the seat forward and adjusted the mirror.

"So, I didn't see you carrying any bags. Didn't you find anything you liked?"

I couldn't detect whether she was being sarcastic or sincere, so I sucked it up and dived in.

"I didn't go shopping, Malia." I said, watching her face, trying to read her expression as she pulled out into the street.

"Oh? What *did* you do?"

One vote for sarcasm.

"I went to see Aidan."

She turned and gave me a long stare, running onto the gravel shoulder in the process. Okay, one vote for sincerity. The van nearly stalled as she jerked the steering wheel hard left to get back on the pavement.

"That's why you didn't want me to go?" She grinned and punched me lightly on the thigh. "You dog. You're hot for Aidan. Why didn't you just say so?"

"That's not why I went to see him."

We pulled into a tiny street side parking lot for the Honokawai Beach Park, but after circling once we found no open spots. A visitor would probably have given up and gone to a different beach, but it seemed locals don't let mere paint stripes deter a good time. Malia backed up and humped the van over the far curb, bringing it to a stop on a ragged patch of park grass.

"Won't you get a ticket?"

"Nah. And even if I did, my cousin's a deputy sheriff, remember?"

She grabbed the tote bag out of the back seat and took off toward the sand, leaving her cell phone in the cup holder between the front seats. I didn't point it out to her because I didn't want Aidan calling while we talked.

"Do you want me to lock my door?" I shouted as I climbed out of my side.

She turned and laughed, then waved for me to hurry and catch up.

We unrolled flimsy bamboo mats and laid them out on an open spot on the beach. This took some doing because the mats caught the breeze and flapped like sheets on a laundry line. We wrestled them to the sand, anchoring them with the picnic lunch bag, beach towels and our bodies to keep them from lifting up and scuttling away.

"Go on," she said once we'd settled. "You went to see Aidan, but you're denying it was out of lust for his scrumptious body. I'm dying to hear what it *was* about. Have you decided to become an art collector?"

"I went there to ask him why he didn't pay any rent to Auntie Momi."

Malia's lips formed a tight O. She nodded, her entire upper body slightly rocking with the motion.

"Oh, boy. So, what'd he say?"

"He blew me off. Said it wasn't any of my business."

"Which it's not."

"Yeah. Well, maybe not, but it's just like something Frank would do. I can't watch that poor woman lose her property when there's an obvious fix. If he'd pay her rent, then she could pay the taxes and keep her store going."

Malia pursed her lips and shrugged. It made me only a bit less annoyed than I'd been with Aidan's rude dismissal.

"Am I right or not?" I went on, my voice cracking in indignation. "So Mr. Celebrity Artist who's got his work in fancy hotels and government buildings all over the island can't pay rent to an old lady? What gives with that?"

"Okay, so Aidan said it was none of your business and then what happened?"

Big score for sarcasm; game over.

"He called you, didn't he?"

"Yeah. But all he'd tell me was that you'd come by the studio and slapped him and then left. I tried to get the whole story, but he said I needed to ask you. I figured maybe he'd tried to grope you or something."

"It's embarrassing. It just exploded out of me. Now I know how people commit crimes of passion."

"Well, I'm sure you didn't injure him—bodily anyway. But he seemed pretty flipped out. Claimed he couldn't understand why you were so mad."

"That's pure BS. He not only refused to consider helping out Auntie Momi, he also made a snide comment about Frank Junior being gone. That's what made me snap. So what's wrong with me, Malia? Why do I keep throwing myself under the jerk bus? First Frank and now this guy. You'd think I'd learn."

"I'm not going to take sides. You two need to work this out on your own. But I will say this: I've known both

Frank and Aidan, and trust me, they're two different species. Probably not even from the same planet."

"I don't want to work it out. I've only got three more days here," I said. "I think my best bet is to simply avoid him. And, although I'll admit it's a little embarrassing, I'm not all that sorry I slapped him."

"Suit yourself. Now let's eat."

I unwrapped silky, cool papaya slices and placed them in a star pattern on top of the vanilla yogurt I'd divided into two small bowls. Then I sprinkled homemade granola from the farmer's market on top and finished with a light dusting of chopped macadamia nuts.

"Oh, yum," said Malia, digging into her yogurt. "This is fabulous. You may be scary when you're pissed, but you're a goddess with food."

We finished lunch and settled back on the beach mats until the sun's heat and the gritty sand won out over any effort to pretend we were enjoying ourselves. We packed up and headed back to the van. Even with the open driver side window, the car seats had heated up to oven temperature. We rolled down all the windows and laid our towels across the seats.

As I snapped my seat belt I heard Malia's cell phone peep to alert her she had a message. She picked it up, glanced at the caller ID, and then slipped it into her shorts pocket. She threw the transmission into reverse and we bounced over the curb and back out to the steet.

The heat, coupled with the emotion of the morning's events, caused my eyes to droop on the ride home. By the time we pulled onto Apua'a Street I was within seconds of drifting off.

"Oh, boy," said Malia, rousing me out of my stupor.

"What?"

"That's Aidan's truck." The enormous black truck took up most of the curb in front of Al's house.

"I guess your plan to lay low for the next few days is blown," she said. "Do you want me to drive around for a while until he leaves?"

Old scaredy-cat me silently said, *Hell, yes.* New daring-dog me mutely shot back, *Bring it on.*

"No, go ahead and pull in. If he wants a showdown, I guess he's making it my business."

She pulled the van into the driveway and we lurched forward as she slammed on the brakes. For all her feigned nonchalance, she appeared nervous about the unpleasant exchange about to take place.

Auntie Momi peered out the kitchen window, her ashen face drawn into a mask of tragedy. Maybe Aidan had upped his ante with regard to claiming jerk-of-the-hour status and had chastised her for not paying the taxes. As we went in, I looked around the house but couldn't see him in the kitchen or the family room.

"Oh, girls, where have you been?" Momi's whispery voice hovered at the edge of tears. "We've been trying and trying to get a hold of you."

"What's wrong, Auntie?" said Malia. "What's happened?"

We heard the wail of the ambulance before Momi could tell us the whole story. All we got from her was that Al had fallen and he couldn't get up. She'd called Aidan before calling 9-1-1.

Two paramedics banged into the house after a quick rap on the doorframe. I stayed with Momi in the kitchen while Malia directed them to the back bedroom.

After half a minute of pretending our panic was under control, Momi and I slipped down the hall to see what was happening. We stood in the doorway, watching, as one paramedic inserted an IV line while the other contacted the hospital in Wailuku to say they were bringing in a cardiac patient. Seconds later, they bundled Al onto a gurney and as they passed by, I caught a glimpse of his pallid face. It stunned me to see how much older he looked without his ever-present smile.

Aidan walked alongside the gurney until they folded down the wheels and slid it up into the back of the ambulance. He gave Malia a quick hug and whispered something in her ear.

The older-looking paramedic told Malia they'd take her father the fastest way possible, with lights and sirens, but the trip to Wailuku would still take at least thirty minutes, maybe longer with the rockslides and washouts along the Pali Highway. He offered her the choice of following them in her own car or riding along with her father.

"Are you joking?" she said, getting into the ambulance. She reached a hand down to grasp mine. "I'm so sorry, Nola, but I've got to go."

"Of course you need to go. I'll drive the van over later." I waved good-bye as the younger paramedic hopped in back. The older guy shut the doors and then sprinted around to the driver's side. Within seconds, the engine roared to life, spewing a plume of exhaust.

The ambulance pitched out of the driveway—siren keening, red lights strobing. As it turned on Apua'a Street, I turned to say something to Auntie Momi, but she was gone. So was Aidan's truck.

I stumbled back to the house and sat down hard on a kitchen chair. My earlier jolt of courage dissolved like a spoonful of salt in a cup of hot water. I rubbed a tear from the corner of my eye with the back of my hand. Then I dug out my phone and called Frank.

CHAPTER 10

I hadn't been a steady churchgoer for years, but still I considered myself a spiritual person. Therefore, it was with sincere and profound gratitude that I later thanked God that Frank didn't answer. Alone in Al's house, I'd panicked after the ambulance pulled away. Suddenly, I missed Seattle. I longed for my son, my house, even— heaven help me—the familiar companionship of Frank.

When Frank's voicemail picked up and I heard his voice asking me to leave a message I had the presence of mind to hang up before I made a fool of myself. He had caller ID, so I expected my stab of homesickness would probably garner a callback. But after a few deep breaths, I'd gotten a grip and decided when he called back I'd say I'd called to tell him Malia's dad had been taken to the hospital. Just a newsy call. Nothing more. .

Having dealt with that, I turned my attention to how I'd get to the hospital. Wailuku was about twenty miles from Al's house but, as the ambulance driver warned, it could take more than an hour to get there due to the earlier highway closure.

I didn't know where the hospital was, so I looked up the address up in the phone book. Luckily, there was only one hospital on the island, Maui General. The address didn't mean much to me but I figured I'd stop and ask directions, if necessary. That was something Frank would never allow, so maybe I'd stop and ask just for the heck of it.

Once on the road, the ride became a blur as I stared at the back bumper of the car in front of me. I listened to cars swishing by coming from the other direction and I mumbled continuing divine appeals to spare Al's life. I didn't call Malia because I didn't want to bother her, and I didn't want chance my reaction to bad news while trying to negotiate the twists and turns on the Pali Highway.

Wailuku isn't for tourists. It's a locals' town, with drab beige government buildings punctuated by an old stone church here and there and a few schools with scrubby playgrounds. The hospital sat on a small rise, giving it an open feeling as it looked down on Kahului Harbor off in the distance. I was relieved to see there were parking stalls on all sides and a few visitor spaces were still available.

I parked the van and made my way to the main entrance. With each step I said a trio of prayers in cadence to the rhythm of my stride—*Please make him be okay; please makes his heart strong; please let him come home soon.*

The woman at the information desk was chatting on the phone, so I glanced around for a directory. They would have taken Al to either the emergency room or straight into the cardiac unit. I found both departments on the hospital map.

I went first to the ER, even though it seemed unlikely he'd still be there. The waiting room resembled an airport where all flights had been grounded for a couple of days. Parents shushed screaming babies, sullen-eyed teenagers pounded the heels of their oversized sneakers into the scuffed linoleum floor, and bowed-back old couples huddled shoulder to shoulder, gripping onto each other as if they could only survive as a matched set.

The ER admitting nurse looked up Al's name on her computer and said he'd been taken to the cardiac care unit. She gave me detailed directions on how to get there, apparently relieved to reduce the population of her overcrowded waiting room by one.

I threaded my way through a maze of corridors and elevators by following the green arrows as I'd been instructed. In addition to green, there were also red, yellow, blue, and white arrows. How could a color-blind person navigate such a labyrinth? But before I could reflect on the question further, the elevator door pinged. I got in and punched the button for the third floor.

The elevator doors closed behind me with a hushed *thunk* as I stepped out into the cardiac unit. The place smelled like rubbing alcohol and freshly starched laundry. The nurses' station lay straight ahead—a buzz of activity corralled inside a high semi-circle counter. I glanced around, hoping to see Malia. Patients in the unit were in glassed-in private rooms, but I couldn't see any visitors in any of them.

I stepped up to the counter. "Would you please direct me to Al Kanekoa's room? When I asked in the ER they said he'd been taken up here."

The nurse in front of me pointed to a colleague sitting at the other end of the counter. I walked over and stood directly in front of her. She was tiny, with a massive white nurse's cap that looked as if a swan had landed on her head. Eyes down, she was engrossed in working on a complicated-looking form. She'd positioned a ruler across the form to mark her place. When she'd filled in one line she moved the ruler down to the next line. I cleared my throat. She looked up and scrunched her face into an expression that reminded me of a baby who needed to be burped.

I asked her for directions to Al's room.

"Are you family?"

"I'm a friend of the family."

"Mr. Kanekoa's condition is guarded. Only family members will be allowed to see him until seven this evening. Sorry." She said it with a smirk that made her look anything but sorry.

"Can you just tell me which room he's in? I won't go in, but I drove a car over from the West Side and I need to give the keys to his daughter. She came in with him in the ambulance."

"You'll be escorted out if you attempt to go in the room before seven."

She'd obviously pegged me as some kind of hospital rabble-rouser.

"No problem. I only need to see his daughter."

"Room 3-B, to your right." She hardly got it out before dropping her head to resume filling in boxes on the form.

I glanced inside the other patients' rooms as I made my way to 3-B. In each room, tubes ran from white-sheeted patients who were connected to machines that blinked, peeped and whirred. The patients' faces all shared the same ashy pallor. In room 3-D, the body of a man three times Al's size was pressed against both sides of the bedrails. In room 3-C the shades were drawn, but as I passed the door I heard the low rumble of a man's voice chanting a refrain I couldn't make out.

Malia's sister, Lani, stood just inside the doorway to her dad's room. When I caught her eye, she waved. She left for a moment and soon Malia came out to the hallway.

"How're you doing" I said. I meant to simply use my 'inside voice' but it came out sounding more cringing than polite.

"I'm okay," she said, "But Dad's not so good."

I held out my arms and we hugged.

"I brought you the van. I'll get a ride back to Lahaina with whoever's going back later. I figured you'd need a car."

"Thanks. I don't know if I'll be able to leave him, though. His heart rhythm is still irregular. They want to do a bypass as soon as he's stable."

"That sounds good."

"It does?"

"Sure. They're already talking about next steps. That means they expect him to get better."

"You're so great," she said. "I didn't think of it like that. I just thought about my poor daddy lying here with a broken heart and they're just itching to cut him open."

"Your dad's a Medicare patient, Malia. The hospital wouldn't consider operating on him unless they felt he was a good candidate for a full recovery."

I had no idea what I was talking about, but I thought it sounded reasonable.

"I called Jim, but he's still in surgery. He'll probably call when he's out." She massaged her temples as if trying to rub away the creases of anxiety in her brow. "Well, c'mon in and say 'hi'. He's pretty looped up on sedatives but I know he'd like to see you."

"I can't. Nurse Ratchet over there said family members only until seven."

"Well, Noelani," she said, using her dad's island dialect. "I be pretty sure *kahuna* Al already make you a member of the Kanekoa *ohana*, yeah?"

I weighed the cost-benefit ratio of offending Al or getting kicked out by the crabby gatekeeper in the swan hat. Al's side won.

"Hey, Al. It's me, Noelani. I can only stay a minute, but I want you to know that the worst part is over. From now on it's all the red Jell-O you can eat and pretty nurses at your beck and call."

Al's stony appearance didn't offer even a twitch of recognition. His sedated haze must have rendered my droll attempt at solace meaningless. Then one eyelid quivered and he peered at me as though trying to recall my name.

"I like *ghee*," he murmured in a slurry voice, his dry lips barely moving.

"What's that, Dad?" Malia put her ear close to his face, her eyebrows knit together in a tense scowl. "Are you in pain?"

"I like *green*," said Al, his voice a bit stronger than before.

"What?" Malia looked up at me. Her eyes darted around the room as if looking for someone who could translate.

"Green. I think he's saying he likes green Jell-O, not red." I said.

I reached over and patted Al's hand just as the Big Hat Nurse flew into the room.

"I said no visitors until *seven*," she hissed. "I can get Security here in less than a minute."

"She's *ohana*," said Malia in a steely voice. "Now please leave. You're interrupting a family prayer vigil."

I caught a ride back to the other side of the island with Lani. She had to go to work in the morning but she'd be able to leave if her dad was taken to surgery. When I got back to Al's the house was spooky dark and deathly quiet. I went from room to room turning on every light as well as the television and the kitchen radio. I checked my cell phone for messages but there weren't any.

I collapsed on the sofa. About four in the morning a noise woke me up. It was the sound of a key turning in the lock. I bolted upright and my heart rate shot up. I felt a flutter of fear, but I was elated by the idea of someone else in the house.

"Hey, sorry to wake you." said Malia. She had that disheveled look my grandma used to call *ten miles of dirt road and runnin' outta gas.*

"No problem," I said. "How's your dad?"

"They'll do the bypass tomorrow afternoon if he stays stable. I came home to pack some things. I'm going to be crashing at my cousin's house in Kahului for a couple of days until Dad's out of the woods."

She plopped down in a kitchen chair and leaned her elbows on the table. She dropped her face into her hands and her shoulders began to quake. I got up and scooted a chair next to her.

"You know he'll be fine," I said. "He's strong, he's got a great spirit for life, and he's been doing his tai chi so he knows how to quiet his mind. I'm thinking this is like my car. I got the transmission replaced last year and I swear it drives better than it did when it was new."

My hand flew to my mouth. Had I really just compared Al's heart attack to a faulty drive train?

"Sorry. That didn't come out right," I said.

She lifted her head. "No, I like it. It's true. The surgery is going to make him better than before. I'm so glad you're here, Nola." She paused and blew out a breath as if she'd just been able to set down a heavy sack she'd been lugging around. "But I feel bad leaving you in this empty old house all by yourself. Do you want to come over stay in Kahului with me? I'm sure my cousin wouldn't mind. But I'll bet we'll get stuck sleeping on a sofa bed."

She shot me a grin.

"If it makes you smile, I'll take the grief over dissing your sofa bed," I said. "But I'm going to stay here. I think your dad would feel better knowing someone's watching the house. And besides, as everybody knows, I'm a sucker for a good mattress and box springs."

"Well, don't stay here on account of my dad. The neighbor lady next door watches this place like a hawk. I was surprised she didn't come running over when I pulled in. I know she's dying to get the scoop on what happened to Dad."

We both looked at the windows, as shiny as black obsidian in the pre-dawn hour.

"Maybe she's lurking out there but we can't see her," I said.

"Well, if she is, she'll have to wait. I'm beat and I'm going to bed."

We went to our respective bedrooms. After a couple of hours I awoke to the sound of Malia dragging a suitcase down the hall.

"I hate it that I can't take all my stuff," she said. "But my cousin's place is really small. There's no way it would all fit.

"If you think of anything you can't live without, I can bring it over later."

"Thanks. And don't be shy about asking for a lift," she said. "There are no strangers here. Just stick out your thumb and tell anybody who stops that Al Kanekoa's in the hospital. They'll probably drive you right up to the front door."

"Thanks. But I'll see if I can hitch a ride with Auntie Momi."

"Then be prepared to deal with Aidan," she said. "Auntie Momi doesn't drive. Aidan's her chauffeur."

"Okay. In that case, I'll ask to tag along with your sister Lani."

Malia was pacing the floor, apparently anxious to get back to the hospital. I talked her into having a quick cup of coffee, but couldn't sell her on the idea of breakfast. When she got up to leave it was a few minutes after seven.

"I'll call tonight if I don't see you before then," she said, heaving two large suitcases into the back of the van. "I really hate traveling so light. What if I need my good black sling-backs, or my snorkel gear?"

"Snorkel gear?" I echoed, and we both laughed. "I already told you. If you need anything, let me know and I'll bring it over." We hugged and she climbed into the driver's seat.

I stood in the driveway waving good-bye as if she was going off to war. Tears formed in the corners of my eyes but I blinked them back until Malia made the turn off Apua'a Street and was no longer in sight.

The past few months had roughed me up so much it seemed I was holding back tears almost every day now. For twenty years I was immune to tears. Oh, I'd choke out a few stifled sobs at a sad movie or maybe dab away a couple of blissful tears at a wedding. Nothing major. But the year was drawing to a close. The holidays were only weeks away. I'd lost so much since I found Frank's stupid misplaced floral card. There was no denying the obvious: Christmas and New Years were going to be brutal.

I pulled the drapes in the family room and plopped down on the sofa. I felt my eyes welling up, but again, I held back. It felt familiar to hold back. Frank scoffed at crying. He claimed it indicated weakness; and weakness was the mark of a loser. Well, to hell with Frank, and to hell with holding back. I clutched a throw pillow to my chest and began to bawl like a baby.

CHAPTER 11

Momi called around four that afternoon to ask if I'd like to go with her to visit Al. I wanted to go. The whole day had dragged; each hour stretching out longer than the one before. But the thought of sitting next to Aidan for the hour-long journey across the island was more daunting than staying home alone.

"I'm sorry, Auntie, but I think I'll wait and go tomorrow. Al's still probably pretty groggy from the surgery."

"Okay," she said. "Then we'll pick you up tomorrow. I sure liked that onion pie you made the other day for Al."

I recognized a thinly veiled request when I heard one.

"Would you like me to make you one?"

"Oh, would you? How sweet. You're a good girl, Noelani." She hesitated, making a little humming sound that let me know she wasn't finished. "So, tomorrow we'll come over for a bite of onion pie, and then we'll all go over to visit Al. Is six o'clock a good time?"

Masterful. She left me no wiggle room whatsoever.

"That will be fine. I'll see you then." I played it straight. "I guess Aidan will be coming with you?"

"Of course, *ipo*. He's my driver. So kind of him."

I heard the smile in her voice as she signed off with her *aloha*.

The next morning I was about to head out to the farmer's market for Maui onions when my cell phone chimed. I answered, certain it was Malia checking in to make sure I'd survived another night alone in the house. We'd talked after Al's surgery and she'd said he was looking better already and all signs pointed to a rapid recovery. I'd let down my guard and let it slip that I was feeling lonely and would be thrilled when they were back home. She'd promised to check in more often now that her dad was on the mend.

"Hello." I chirped, looking forward to hearing a friendly voice.

"Hi, sweetheart. It's me, Frank."

I fumbled the phone, resisting the impulse to hang up.

"Oh. Hi, Frank. What's up?"

"You tell me. I've been trying to reach you for over a week now."

"I called three days ago. You didn't answer."

"Oh? I didn't get a message."

He knew damn well I'd called. Frank had a Ph.D. in guy toys, with a major in cell phone management.

"Didn't you check your missed calls? You always tell the agents they need to call back any missed calls—whether or not they leave a message." A few months earlier I would've let it slide. I probably would have even apologized for not leaving Frank a message. But that was then. It felt good to call his bluff.

"I guess maybe I did see your number. But my message clearly stated I needed to talk to you. You should have tried again."

"What do you want, Frank?"

"Why do you think I want something? I was calling to see how things are going."

"You left four messages, you called my mother, and then when Malia called you back you refused to give her a message. I'd say all that doesn't exactly add up to a 'how ya doin' call."

"I'm not a big fan of your friend Malia. If you want to know the truth, I've always considered her a bad influence on you."

"Yeah, well you're not exactly topping her chart either."

"Nola," he said, drawing out my name as if he were about to break into song. "I think there's a possibility I may have made a big mistake." His voice had dropped to barely a whisper.

I wanted to roar back a sarcastic, *Oh ya think maybe having a sexual fling with a boy barely older than our son might constitute a big mistake?* but I held back, itching to hear the rest of his sorry excuse for an apology.

"Babe," he continued, "This has been really tough, you know? I walk through our house and that little chiming clock I bought you on our tenth anniversary is still on the mantle. I wind it every week, like you always did. And I'm taking good care of the plants and all of your other things, too. I don't know, Nola. I think we should give it another shot before the divorce is final."

Was he nuts? That was his best shot at expressing regret—winding a clock and watering some plants? Maybe he'd been diagnosed with AIDS and given only a few months to live and he was looking for cheap nursing care. Well, whatever he was selling, I wasn't buying.

"Frank, our divorce will be final in four and a half months. I have every intention of seeing it through and getting the money I'm owed from the sale of the house and the business."

"That's another reason why I called. I haven't been able to put the house on the market."

"Why not?"

"I need your signature on the listing form. You know, Washington's a community property state."

"So send me the damn form. Does it need to be notarized?"

"I was hoping we could meet in person and discuss it."

"Two problems, Frank. Number one, I'm in Hawaii. Number two, there's nothing to discuss."

"I know you're over there. But won't you be coming home in a day or two?"

"I was supposed to come back this weekend, but I may have to stay a little longer. Malia's dad had a heart attack and he just got bypass surgery."

"So?"

Frank wasn't the kind of person who'd inquire if Al's surgery went well, or even bother to offer condolences.

"So," I said, dragging it out as if I were talking to a dim-witted person, "we're staying a little longer to make sure he's okay."

"You don't need to stay. It's *her* father, not yours."

"Frank, I'm hanging up now."

"I'll call again in a few days, Nola. I think once you stop meddling in other people's business you'll realize we've got a lot to talk about."

I didn't say good-bye before I hung up. My stress level had torqued into the danger zone and although I didn't see any black splotches yet, it was a short journey from the back of my skull to my eyeballs.

The walk to the farmer's market seemed like a huge effort after dealing with Frank, but duty called, so I slipped on my sandals and headed out. The sun glinted off the ocean and the air held the soft fragrance of plumeria blossoms. Within a couple of blocks I started trotting at twice my normal walking speed. By the time I turned into the market area I'd increased my heart rate to the point that a healthy pulse hummed in my ears.

Frank was nuts. He probably had had a falling out with his boyfriend and expected me to pick up the pieces. He'd come out of the closet, for crying out loud. Did he really expect me to just shrug it off like that time he brought home a boxer puppy that chewed shoes, furniture, and even the down comforter on our bed before Frank ordered me to get rid of it? I'd found the little guy a good home with a family out on acreage, but I'd had to put an ad in the newspaper, answer dozens of phone calls, pay a hundred-dollar vet bill for shots and a well-puppy check-up, and then endure a two-hour ride out to the far reaches of Enumclaw with a howling puppy that kept trying to crawl into my lap.

I put Frank out of my mind and focused on selecting good quality onions. I didn't really know how to pick a good onion from a not-so-good one, but I looked for firm ones with no bruises or soft spots and no mold. I bought more than enough, just in case. I also bought a few red peppers, a pineapple and two green papayas.

The walk back up to Al's house with three bags of produce was certainly more strenuous than the walk down, but my legs felt strong. Something about getting out in the sunshine and the warm ocean-scented breeze made exercise less tiring. To tell the truth, it felt almost enjoyable.

I took in a lung-filling breath before going back into the house. It was probably my imagination but I felt calmer and healthier than I had in years. My serenity vanished, however, when I remembered I'd soon be facing Aidan for the first time since the slap-down. I did a few shoulder rolls and reluctantly went inside.

I pulled out ingredients and cookware for the onion tart and spread them out on the counter. The onions glared at me from their plastic bag. They knew I was planning to chop them up but they'd get the last laugh. Sweet Maui onions are allegedly tear-free, but my initial experience didn't support that claim. But so what? The tears were quickly forgotten as I inhaled their fragrant aroma as they baked.

Al's phone rang just as the timer on the stove started dinging. I grabbed the handset and cradled it on my shoulder while I opened the oven door to check on the tart.

"Hey, Nola. It's Aidan."

The phone slipped from my chin grip and clattered across the tile floor. The crust wasn't quite done, so I closed the oven door before picking the receiver back up.

"Oops," I said. "Sorry. The phone fell."

"Wow, that was loud. Got a grip on it?"

"Yeah. It slipped. I'm trying to do two things at once here."

"Like walk and chew gum?" He chuckled, and I visualized Frank's sarcastic grin on Aidan's gorgeous face.

I bit back a response.

"Nola? You still there?"

"Um-hmm."

"I was calling because Momi said we'd be picking you up tonight when we go to visit Al and I wanted to make sure you were okay with going with me."

"Yes. I didn't go yesterday and I told Malia I'd come by tonight."

"Okay, I just wanted to check. We didn't get a chance to iron things out after our last meeting. You know, the one where you assaulted me?"

"You mean the one where you *insulted* me?"

"Look. Let's call a truce. You're way too cute to hold a grudge. I'm sure it causes frown lines or something."

Apparently Aidan wasn't just an accomplished metal sculptor, he was also talented in the art of the backhanded compliment.

"I'm not holding a grudge. But I still don't understand why you won't help out Auntie Momi."

"Tell you what. We'll all go visit Al and after I drop off Momi we can talk. I'm not the bad guy you think I am. Believe me."

"Okay. I'm making a little dinner for us. Momi says you're going to be here around six, right?"

"Sounds good."

I hung up feeling better—until I saw the smoke oozing from the sides of the oven door. Darn. I pulled the rest of the onions out of the refrigerator and started peeling.

Momi came into the kitchen first. She'd tamed her mass of black hair into a complicated braid she'd wound around her head. She wore what appeared to be her Sunday best *mu'u mu'u* and she carried a colossal white patent-leather purse that looked big enough to hold a blanket and pillow, with maybe a change of clothes thrown in.

"Auntie Momi, you look so nice."

"You think so? I hate to show up at Al's hospital looking like a bag lady, so I dressed up a little."

I flicked my eyes toward the outsize handbag, but just nodded and again commented she looked lovely.

Aidan strode in carrying a bundle of tropical flowers and a bottle of white wine. When he held out the flowers to me, I didn't know how to respond. Were the flowers for Al or for me? Maybe he just wanted me to put them in water to keep them fresh until we left for the hospital.

"Does Al have a vase we could put these in?" he asked.

That didn't help clear up my confusion.

"I'm sure there's one around somewhere. Let me look." I dug through the clutter under the sink and came up with a dusty two-quart Mason jar.

"I don't think that'll work," said Momi. "It will be top-heavy."

"Maybe we could get a vase at the hospital," I said.

They both shot me a bewildered look.

"What? No, these are for here," said Aidan. "For you. I have another batch for Al out in the truck."

"Oh. Well, thank you. They're beautiful." The spray included three protea, which look like large furry rose-colored artichokes; a few stalks of fragrant white freesia, and two stems of canary yellow orchids. Each stalk of blooms was stunning in its own right, but together the colors and shapes created a spectacular arrangement. In Seattle, such an exotic bouquet would cost more than a hundred dollars, but here on Maui I'd seen similar flowers for less than a twenty dollars at the farmer's market.

"I'll find something to put them in," said Momi. She rummaged through the cupboards and came up with a tall plastic pitcher. "This will do until you can get something nicer."

Aidan didn't offer to open the wine so I tucked it away in the refrigerator. I set the table with glasses and a carafe of water from the water cooler on the back porch and called them to come in and sit down.

We started with a Kula greens salad with fresh herbs and homemade papaya seed vinaigrette. Then I brought out the onion tart. I didn't mention making the scorched tart I'd wrapped in newspaper and buried at the bottom of the garbage can.

"This is *good,* Noelani," Momi said, swallowing a big bite. She looked over at Aidan, as if expecting him to chime in on my culinary skills.

"Huh?" he said. "Yeah, it's real good."

"More, anyone?" I asked. I got up from the table and noticed Aidan's eyes follow me as I stepped to the kitchen counter.

"Can I have a nice piece to take home with me?" Momi said. She smiled a toothy grin that crinkled her eyes into a man-in-the-moon face.

"How about you, Aidan?" I said, cutting a thick wedge of the tart and covering it in plastic wrap for Momi. "Would you like to take some home?"

"Maybe later." He winked at me.

"You two are so cute together. I think you should take Noelani out to dinner sometime, Aidan. Don't you think she was nice to have us over like this?"

I wanted to mutter *Forget about taking me to dinner, pay this woman some rent* but this wasn't the time or the place. Although I'd promised myself I'd keep my hands to myself and not smack him around anymore, I wasn't done making my case to him about helping auntie pay the back taxes.

Aidan offered to wash dishes while I tidied up the kitchen. While we worked, Auntie Momi entertained us with stories of Al's childhood antics. She paused after a tale of Al climbing to the top of a palm tree to make good on a bet and then not being able to get back down.

"He was such a good boy. A *pono* older brudda. No one on this whole island had a better big brudda than my Kailealoha."

Aside from Malia's quick introduction at the airport, I'd never heard anyone use Al's complete given name, not even on his birthday. Momi stopped talking. She cast her eyes upward and pressed her lips tight. I hurriedly wiped down the counter so we could leave for the hospital.

The ride to Wailuku passed more quickly than when I'd driven it alone. Aidan's truck had a king cab with two sets of doors and a wide back seat that turned out to be pretty comfortable. He pulled up at the front entrance, presumably to let Momi out before looking for a parking spot. But then he parked the truck in the handicapped parking space right by the door. Before I could point out his error, he whipped out a blue plastic tag from under his seat and hung it on the rearview mirror.

"You're not handicapped," I said.

"I'm Momi's sole means of transportation. She needs to be close to the door."

"Yeah, but *you* don't need to be."

"You think I'm gonna leave her standing out here all by herself while I cruise the lot?" He shook his head. "You're quite the little rules follower, aren't you?"

"I just think an able-bodied man ought to leave the handicapped spaces open for people who really need them."

"Well, welcome to Hawaii. Land of da free, home of defiance."

He ran around to Momi's door and helped her out. I waited for her to be settled on solid ground before I got out. I reached for the door handle, but Aidan had already popped it open. He held out his palm to assist me as I climbed down from the back seat. Momi winked at me as

Aidan double-timed it so he could hold the hospital door open for us.

Al looked tired, but a lot better than I'd expected. His cheeks were pink and his trademark grin was back in place. He pulled the sheet down to show off a wide swath of bandages on his chest.

"I got more bandages on my thigh where they took a vein, but I don't think none of you girls wanna see that," he said with a laugh.

"I do," said Aidan.

Al smiled but didn't lower the sheet.

Malia announced that she'd been told Al would be released from the hospital the next day.

"Really? So soon?" I said. "Seems kind of quick after radical surgery."

"The doctor says it's not considered that radical anymore," Malia said. "They do about three or four bypasses a week now."

"So, you're coming home," I said to Al. "I'm so glad. Your little house is way too empty without you."

The nurse came in to take Al's vitals and Malia cupped my elbow and steered me out into the hall. "I'll probably need to change my airline ticket," she said. "I don't think I should leave Dad alone so soon."

"No problem," I said. "If you like, I'll stay with you. I'm not that anxious to get back to finalizing my divorce. And I don't even want to *think* about looking for a job or a new apartment."

"You'll stay? Thanks, Nola. I'd really appreciate it." She hugged me. "Dad has to be out of here before noon so we can reschedule our flights when we get back home."

We visited for another half hour before Auntie Momi announced that Al needed his sleep. Aidan pulled in front of Auntie Momi's rented cottage and while he saw her to her door I moved to the front seat. When Momi unlocked her door her yappy little dog dashed outside and started going bananas.

Aidan returned to the truck and climbed back into the driver's seat. He hung his head, unmoving.

"Are you okay?" I asked. "You want me to drive?"

"No, I'm good," he said. "You know, I worry about her. She's taken this thing with Al pretty hard."

"Speaking of worrying, can we revisit her losing the Shore Store because she can't pay the back taxes?"

"You're like a little terrier. Like that crazy mutt of Momi's. You get your teeth into something and you don't let go. Tell you what. Let's go back to Al's house and have a glass of wine and I'll tell you my side of the story. You can't hit, though. Promise me—no matter how much you want to, there's no hitting allowed."

I rolled my eyes the way I'd watched Frankie do it a thousand times. Then I did a little cross-my-heart, hope-to-die sign.

"Good," he said.

After turning off the truck in Al's driveway, Aidan pulled another bottle of wine from behind his seat. He walked around the truck and offered me his hand once again as I climbed out of the cab. I looked into his eyes, which were more gray than green at night, and I saw a gentleness that pulled me in.

"I never did apologize for slapping you the other day," I said.

"Forget it. I deserved it."

"No, really. I'm not a violent person. And I don't condone violence in any form. I—"

"Would you mind?" he said, handing me the bottle of wine.

I took it with both hands, one hand around the neck, the other cupping the bottom, so I had no defense when he scooped me into his arms.

"Huh?" I said. An astonished gasp slipped out before I could hold it back.

He carried me to the kitchen door. He nudged the unlocked door open with his elbow, and once inside, bent his knees to allow me to slide my legs down to a standing position.

"I always wanted to do that," he said, grinning.

I stood in the middle of the kitchen—stunned.

"Let me guess," I said when I finally found my voice, "Is there some odd Hawaiian custom involved here?"

"No, like I said, I just always wanted to do that. And you're so tiny I thought it'd be fun to give it a try on someone I knew I wouldn't drop."

I felt heat gather at the base of my neck. Usually people get attractive flushed cheeks when they're embarrassed. Not me. I get a nasty red splotch that blooms in the cleft of my throat like an angry rash. I didn't need to see it to know it was there.

"Red or white?" he asked. For a split second I thought he was referring to my splotch. Then he plucked the bottle of red wine from my hands and I made the connection.

"Oh. I like them both. But probably the white. It's already chilled."

I reached in and pulled the white wine out of the refrigerator. As I turned back around, he stepped up to me, his scent emanating from his firm warm chest. He took the bottle from my hands and set it on the counter.

"You're an amazing woman, Nola." His voice dropped to a husky whisper. "I'm aware you've got a solid right hook so I'll back off if that's what you want. But I swear, I could just eat you up."

I wanted to slump forward against him. I wanted to feel his massive arms around me, his unyielding chest muscles hard against my cheek. But I had questions, concerns. I didn't want to get involved with another handsome, self-centered man. Forget pectorals, what about integrity? Okay, maybe a little fun now and then could be nice for a change, but overall I was looking for a guy who navigated life with a moral compass.

I looked into his eyes, but the fading light made them difficult to read. He stroked my cheek with his finger, lingering at my jawbone a moment before lifting my chin. As my eyes closed and my mouth yielded, a pang of guilt snapped through me. What kind of woman sets aside ethical concerns for a few moments of pleasure? Certainly not me. I'd never put passion before duty and I wasn't about to start.

Oh, no. His warm mouth felt enveloping and tender. Like hearing a familiar voice after years of solitary confinement. I responded to his kiss as if we were long-lost lovers meeting again after years of painful separation.

CHAPTER 12

Aidan's lingering kiss left me gasping for air. My knees sagged and once again he lifted me into his arms. He turned toward the hallway.

"I can't," I mumbled into his shirt.

"Can't what?"

"Can't go back there with you until we talk about Auntie Momi."

"You're kidding," he said. He dumped me, butt first, on the sofa in the living room.

The obvious bulge in his pants alerted me he wasn't in a mood to chat. But on the other hand, I wasn't in the mood to crawl into bed with a guy who ripped off old ladies. A line had been drawn.

"What do you want to know?" He leaned forward, his crossed arms resting on his thighs, acting about as nonchalant as possible for a man with a major hard-on and no relief in sight.

"I want you to explain why you'd allow this poor woman to lose her family's store to the tax man before you'd help out by paying her some rent."

"I don't pay Momi rent because she'd consider it an insult. The way the Kanekoas view the world; friends don't charge friends rent. They expect payment in other ways. Think about it: I haul her to the store. I take her to visit family members. And I go with her to her doctor's appointments. I buy her groceries every week and I pay her phone and light bills. If she needs her toenails cut, who do you think she calls?"

"You cut her toenails?"

"She can't reach," he said. That didn't help me shake the image of him hoisting her gnarled foot up into his lap like a blacksmith shoeing a horse. "That's our arrangement. And that's why it's none of *your* business."

"But she needs money. The taxes are due and she's going to lose her building. Why won't you just give her some money?"

"I could give her a million dollars, but she still wouldn't pay the taxes. I've talked to her lawyer about sending the tax bills to me. But he said until she gives me a power of attorney I have no rights in the matter." He put a fingertip between his eyebrows and rubbed. Then he continued. "Get this. I secretly paid the taxes the year before her husband Koma died and when Momi found out she threatened to burn the place down."

"What?"

"How much do you know about native Hawaiians and the whole sovereignty issue?"

"Not much. I've heard the word mentioned, but they all stop talking about it when I come in the room. I asked Malia but she just shrugged."

"I doubt if Malia's as into it as the others. But the rest of the Kanekoas are rabid. They're part of a group that wants the United States to return the islands to the native people. It's a big thing over here."

"What does that have to do with Momi paying her taxes?"

"She refuses to give any money to the State because she claims the crown lands were illegally seized from the Kingdom of Hawaii by the United States."

"Well, from what I've heard, that's pretty true."

"Absolutely. But refusing to pay your taxes isn't the smartest way to prove your point."

"So, what should we do?"

He put his hand on my shoulders, kneading my tense muscles and working his way up to the back of my neck.

"It's up to you," he said. "You want to discuss local politics or get naked?"

I choked out a nervous laugh. Although I welcomed an opportunity to see him in the buff, I shuddered at the thought of returning the favor.

He held his ground. Then he upped the ante with a kiss that hinted he wasn't afraid to throw in a little tongue.

I shifted my hips and leaned against his shoulder.

"Hmm?" He mumbled. "You need to say what you want. I've heard about these 'yes' means 'no' things, and I'm not playing."

"What are you suggesting?"

"Anything your little heart desires. Soup to nuts, I'm the full buffet."

I thought about brunch sex with Frank, and Aidan's comment made me smile. My nether region had grown damp in anticipation, but my upper region was silently screaming, *Are you crazy? You're a not-yet-divorced, pudgy, middle-aged soccer mom. Get real.*

My bottom half mutely shot back, *Oh, get over yourself. You're on vacation. You're in the middle of a demoralizing divorce and here's a gorgeous man who's talking about giving you some pleasure. Lighten up, already.*

Decades with Frank had taken its toll. My brain prevailed.

"I can't, Aidan."

"Okay. Suit yourself." His scowl betrayed his seeming acceptance.

He stood, arched his back, and stalked back into the kitchen. As I watched his sculpted ass disappear through the doorway I let out of huff of disappointment.

The clock showed a few minutes past midnight. I nestled into the sofa cushions, unable to get up and drag myself down the hall to the guest room. I didn't even hear Aidan's truck start up before I succumbed to the anxiety of the past few hours and drifted off.

I dreamed someone was throwing rocks at me while I tried to dodge out of the way. *Boom-boom-boom*, the rocks landed with such force they exploded on impact.

When I awoke, someone was pounding on the kitchen door.

I sat up and staggered through the kitchen. I opened the door a crack and there stood Aidan, hair like a wild man, rumpled shirt from the night before.

"Are you going to let me in or wait until the entire neighborhood's gawking at me?"

I glanced next door. It was six-thirty in the morning, but Kilia was out watering her lawn, smiling and doing the pageant-wave like a girl on a parade float—elbow, arm, elbow, arm. I gave her a half-hearted smile and wiggled my fingers. She flexed her bicep, pointing at Aidan. I recognized her 'hunky guy' gesture, but I chose to pretend I didn't. I stepped back to let him in.

"What are you doing over here so early?"

"Truck wouldn't start last night."

"You stayed out there?"

"I considered checking into the Ritz in Kapalua, but it's a five mile hike." He tossed me a glare that could liquefy glass. "Damn straight I stayed out there. What the hell else could I do?"

I started to chastise him for playing the martyr, but then caught myself. He was right, I probably wouldn't have bought his car-won't-start story last night.

"How about coffee? You want some?"

"Absolutely." He slumped into a kitchen chair.

I went to work getting the coffee maker set up and then I pulled coffee mugs out of the cupboard. Looking up, I glanced out the window and saw Al's van pulling to the curb in front. Aidan's truck took up most of the driveway.

"Malia's here," I said. Dread pinched my throat.

"Whoa!" she said, bursting through the door. "I leave you two alone for a couple of days and look what happens."

"Aidan's truck wouldn't start."

"Oh sure. Nothing like the old stand-bys: flat tire, car won't start, we just cuddled all night." Her voice had the fake cheerfulness of an also-ran Oscar contender telling a reporter it was an honor just to be nominated.

"No, really," Aidan broke in, "I brought Nola back here last night and when I went to leave, the engine wouldn't turn over. I slept out there."

"You two check your drivers' licenses lately?" she said. "Because last I looked you were both way past the age of consenting adults. Please spare me the teenager excuses."

Aidan and I said nothing.

"Anyway, I'm here to pick up some clean clothes for my dad," she said, flouncing down the hall to the bedrooms. "Since he's coming home today I hope you limited your nasty business to the guest room. I'm in no mood to change the sheets."

Aidan followed her down the hall. I wanted to plead my case, but he'd been dealing with her moods for a lot longer than I, so I let him handle it. A few seconds later, Al's bedroom door slammed shut.

Exactly six minutes later—but who's counting?—they came out laughing. Malia carried a change of clothes for Al; Aidan held a short stack of baseball caps.

"Well, I'm off again." She nuzzled her head into Aidan's shoulder. "Want to come with me, Nola?"

The last thing I wanted to do was ride shotgun on the nearly hour-long drive back to Wailuku in early morning traffic. But voice tone suggested it was more a command than a question, so I meekly nodded.

"Good." She turned and gave Aidan a peck on the cheek. "See ya, sweetie. Tell Kiwi I said 'hi', okay?"

We climbed into the van and I waited until we were out on the street before I spoke. "Who's Kiwi?"

"He's my second cousin from my mom's side. Knows everything about cars. He'll help Aidan get his truck running."

"You know, he really did get stuck here last night."

"I know." She shot me a sunny smile. "Kind of mean of you to make him sleep in his truck."

"He didn't tell me he was having trouble."

"And you complain about my sofa bed."

"So," I said, taking a deep breath, "How's your dad doing?"

"He's good. He's being pretty cooperative. Since his incisions look good, they said he could be released to home care."

"What's that mean, 'home care'?"

"Means we need to do a bunch of stuff they'd do if he was in the hospital. Clean the sutures, change the dressings, take his blood pressure. Sort of do-it-yourself nursing."

"For how long?"

"I guess until he's better. Maybe a month or so."

"Are you planning to stay a whole month?"

"I don't know. I talked with Jim this morning. My principal's having a hard time finding substitutes to take my class. I've got some rowdy kids who really give the subs grief when I'm gone. I guess I'll just take it one week at a time. When I cancelled our airline tickets I left the return date open."

When we arrived at Al's room he looked more robust than any man should three days after open-heart surgery. His doctor arrived a few minutes later. Malia dazzled the doc with her knowledge of hospital-speak, finally confessing her husband was also a heart surgeon.

"Good. I feel better about releasing your dad so soon after surgery knowing he'll be in capable hands."

I stifled a snort. There was a world of difference between talking the talk and walking the walk. I'd seen Malia swoon over a paper cut.

We got Al up and dressed in his khakis and Hawaiian print shirt. He was a little unsteady but cheery—an Aloha Joe version of Bypass Patient of the Month.

"You're my best girls," he said. "I'm gonna be good. I'm gonna do everything the doctor says. No more smoking, no more drinking."

"Dad, you never smoked."

"No, but if I did, I wouldn't do it no more."

"And I'll bet you won't pass up a beer if the boys bring some over."

"I'll have a few beers, but no *real* drinking."

She wagged her head as she helped him into his sandals.

I offered to go down to the parking lot and pull the van around to the front entrance. After sitting out front for more than ten minutes, I rolled down the windows. It was getting hot. Soon after, the glass doors whooshed open and Al appeared in a wheelchair, Malia pushing from behind. She nudged it across the threshold to the covered portico. As she hesitated at the top of the handicap ramp, Al bounded out of the chair, pushing free from the armrests like a Olympic swimmer going for the gold.

"Dad, sit back down." Malia hissed, tugging on his shirt and glancing into the hospital lobby as if expecting wailing sirens and uniformed guards with guns drawn.

"I'm done—*pau*," he said. "This place is for sick people. I'm not *ma'i*. And I'm done riding in that cripple-mobile like a feeble old woman."

"Shhh. Dad, they're letting you out early because you promised to cooperate. Now if you're planning to act up and make yourself sick, then I'll take you back upstairs. No problem." Malia folded her arms tightly across her chest and they glared eye-to-eye.

He let out an irritated sigh and plopped back down in the chair, grumbling loudly in Hawaiian, punctuating his rant with a few well-placed English expletives.

Malia and I each took an arm as we helped him into the back seat and buckled him in. She shut the side door and I hopped up into the passenger seat. I took out my lip gloss thinking I'd apply a fresh coat while I waited for her to trundle the chair back to the hospital lobby.

A few seconds later, the back doors of the van opened. Al and I both twisted around as Malia lifted the wheelchair into the van.

"What are you doing, girl?" Al's face flamed in outrage.

"I'm putting your wheelchair in the car."

"*My* wheelchair," he roared. "No way. Get that damn thing outta here."

"Dad, here's the deal: it's my way or the highway. You can have homemade *haupia* pudding at home or institutional green Jell-O here. Your choice."

Overhead, a commercial airliner roared out of Kahului Airport in a steep climb, heading east toward home. I didn't have much to go back to, but paradise had certainly started to fray around the edges for me. Malia was committed to staying on, taking it week by week. But maybe it'd be better if I went on home. I'd spent twenty years avoiding my own family squabbles, I wasn't going to get caught up in someone else's.

I'd tried to help Auntie Momi get her taxes paid and I'd been unsuccessful, and now Al was safely on his way home. The situation with Aidan was precarious. I couldn't afford another trashing so soon after Frank.

Yep. My mind was made up. I needed to score a seat on a mainland-bound jet before anyone noticed I was gone.

CHAPTER 13

The next morning both Malia and Al slept in. I figured they were both worn out from the trauma of Al's sudden heart attack and hospital stay, not to mention anticipating the thirty-day power struggle that lay ahead.

I slipped out the kitchen door before even grabbing my first cup of coffee and headed down to the farmer's market. I didn't have a grocery list in mind, but I longed for a bit of fresh air before the others got up and the bickering resumed.

My shorts felt a bit loose around the middle, but I attributed it to wear and tear. I'd only packed for ten days, and even light at that. So my poor khaki shorts had been worn and washed more in the past week than in the previous three years. No wonder the waistband sagged.

The market was just starting to take shape. A stack of tattered cardboard boxes in the parking lot tilted at a wild angle like a kid's Leaning Tower of Pisa project for social studies class. I drifted over to look at a large platform scale—the kind used to weigh boxes of fruit bound for the mainland.

"Hey," one of the market workers called to me. "Hop up there. If I can guess your weight, you have to buy a pineapple. If I guess wrong, you get it for free." He was tall and thin as a reed, with curly brown hair sun-streaked to almost blond. I shot him a quick smile, but no way was I going to step on a scale in front of a dozen strangers. Heck, I wouldn't step on a scale in front of a goldfish.

"No thanks. I'm not here for pineapple today." I waved him off as I moved along, pretending to be enormously interested in a clump of fresh garlic.

"C'mon," he said. "I don't have anything to do until these bruddas get the tables up. Go ahead. Step on the scale." His persistence was beginning to annoy me, like the pushy panhandlers who used to follow me out to my car in Seattle.

"Tell you what," he said, winking conspiratorially. "I'll give you a free pineapple even if I get it right."

Dread clenched my chest as I fought for an acceptable excuse why I didn't want to play along. I had lots of genuine reasons I'd never tell him: I was touchy about my weight; I didn't like being the center of attention; and worst of all, this guy bore a striking resemblance to my mental image of Frank's home-wrecker boyfriend.

"One hundred twenty, give or take three." He crowed like a carnival barker.

I glared at him as if he'd yelled out my birthday, social security number and mother's maiden name at a seminar for identity thieves. But I said nothing, slowly picking through the garlic.

"No really. We do this every morning." He dashed in front of me, waving his hand in an old-fashioned 'howdy' greeting. "I'm Josh, by the way. I'm good at this. One-twenty-five, right?"

Truth was, he stunk at it. I hadn't weighed less than a hundred and forty for years. Still, I had no intention of crawling up on the scale to prove him wrong. Twenty-some years with Frank taught me the power of not needing to win an argument.

"Tell you what. I'll throw in a couple free papayas if I'm off by more than three pounds."

That comment earned him a shout from one of the guys setting up the papaya table.

"No really," Josh insisted. "Two ripe papayas. If you want I'll throw this tarp over the scale so you're the only who can see."

Did the guy suffer from some kind of obsessive-compulsive disorder? I got a vision of being tackled and hauled up onto the scale like a big floppy tuna. I shrugged a glum acceptance, if only to shut him up.

"But I want the tarp."

He draped a sheet of worn olive-drab canvas over the scale read-out and I stepped onto the two-foot-square weighing platform. Once he'd stepped back, I lifted the canvas and ducked under it like an old-fashioned photographer. The cover smelled like a camping tent—earthy, oily—and beneath it the green gloom was so dense I could hardly make out the digital numbers.

One hundred twenty seven? That couldn't be right. I threw back the tarp and squinted in the bright light. Yep, the scale numbers read one-two-seven.

"See? I was right. Guess you don't get the papayas," he said. "But I'll still give you the free pineapple." He bent over and ripped the top off a pineapple box.

Then it dawned on me. They must have adjusted the scale to weigh light. It would only take a minute to recalibrate it once the market opened for business. The 'guess your weight game' was just the type of odd marketing ploy that a bunch of doobie-smoking island hippies would come up with while loading produce into the back of a truck at five a.m.

"Thanks. I need to pick up a few other things too." After all, the whole idea of the false flattery was to drum up business, so I felt obliged to play along.

He smiled, hefting a pineapple in each hand.

"Do you know how to pick out a sweet one?" I asked.

"Well, duh, I work here," he said. "You look for the ones with the big eyes. Like Little Red Riding Hood, you know?" He pitched his voice into a falsetto, "Grandma, what big eyes you have!"

"Big eyes?" I wasn't following the link between a fairy tale and tropical fruit.

"Yeah. See these things here," he pointed to the scaly round bumps on the pineapple skin. "They're called 'eyes'—like potato eyes. The bigger ones mean sweeter fruit inside."

"Huh. I thought you were supposed to sniff the bottom."

"Nah," he laughed. "Bottom sniffing's for dogs."

I took my free pineapple and went over to select a couple of mangos. Everything looked wonderful—the tomatoes, the fresh Maui corn, the homemade guacamole. I grabbed a shopping basket and loaded up.

At the check-out table I couldn't get a good grip on my four bags of groceries. The pineapple bag alone took one hand.

"Hmm," I said, glancing down at my bounty. "Could I maybe leave a couple of bags here and come back for them later? I live up the hill and I'll need to make two trips."

"You local?" The thirty-ish woman who'd added up my purchases had a sun-splotched face, with frizzy hair pulled back in an off-center ponytail. Her eyes were the color of pale blue topaz.

I wrestled with the lie and then gave a bobble-head nod. I'd watched Malia in action enough to know that the right answer to the 'local question' was always *yes*.

"Well, then go ahead and take the basket home. Bring it back next time you come down."

"Thanks—uh, I mean *mahalo*." Nothing like blowing my cover by forgetting the local pleasantries.

I chugged back up the hill, switching the basket from arm to arm with every block. By the time I got to Al's kitchen door my arm muscles were twitching. I'd swear the load had packed on another couple of pounds on the trip up.

"What'cha got there?" Al said as I heaved the basket onto the counter. He was sitting at the kitchen table reading *The Maui News*. The wheelchair was nowhere in sight.

"Just a few things from the farmer's market. They guessed my weight and I won a free pineapple." I almost clamped my hand over my mouth. Why'd I tell him that?

"They got it wrong? They're usually pretty good at it." He dropped his head and went back to reading. Thankfully I didn't feel compelled to dig myself any deeper by giving him the details.

I put the groceries away and poured myself a cup of the coffee I'd been craving for the past hour. I listened for Malia, but aside from the ticking of the kitchen clock and the rustle of Al's newspaper, the house was quiet.

Finally, Al folded the last section and looked up. He seemed surprised to see me still standing at the counter.

"You girls going to the beach today?"

"I'm not sure. Is Malia still in bed?"

"Nah. She left in a huff about a half-hour ago. I thought you might have seen her at the market."

Malia wasn't one to slink away quietly. I was pretty sure there was more to it than he was letting on, but I'd wait and get the story from her.

I went back to my room and puttered around. I wondered what time it was in Seattle, and that got me thinking about calling Frank. Why on earth did he come to mind whenever I felt stressed? Maybe I was a stress junkie and knew Frank could always supply a good fix.

Any thoughts of Frank were usually replaced with anxiety about Frank Junior. I took in two quick breaths in an attempt to quell the tears. It was as if I'd come up with a mathematical equation: anything related to Frank equaled thoughts of Frank Junior which, in turn, equaled a crying jag. I couldn't grab onto a happy memory of my son long enough to override the wave of anguish and dread I felt at not knowing where he was. And, every time I cried, my loathing of Frank Senior increased by the same factor as the additional pain I felt from missing my only child.

I'd managed to book flight to Seattle for Thursday, only two days away. I planned to tell Malia on Wednesday night after dinner. No sense in dealing with her getting all moody until it was absolutely necessary.

I stared out the window into the empty back yard for a while and then checked my watch for the tenth time in as many minutes, but still no sign of Malia. Time to go find her.

Al hadn't moved from the kitchen table, but a scowl replaced his usual impish grin.

"Al, did Malia make you any breakfast?" I asked.

"Nope. She just stomped outta here. No toast—no nothin' for me."

"Let me make you a little something before I go out to find her. How about some papaya and lime to start?"

He nodded, his smile returning. I cut a buttery-ripe papaya into halves and scooped out the seeds. Then I cut a lime into quarters and drizzled the juice across the fruit. The tart contrast of the lime enhanced the soft-peach taste of the papaya.

A few minutes later, I slipped a three-egg green onion and fresh tomato omelet—made more heart-friendly by using one whole egg and only the whites of the other two—onto Al's plate. I added a stack of whole-grain toast buttered with cholesterol-free margarine. I braced myself for wails of protest about the dietary substitutions, but he simply thanked me. Then he tucked into his food while I cleaned up the kitchen.

"I'll take a walk down toward the market again and see if I can find her. She probably met an old friend and got caught up in *talking story*."

He nodded, his eyes focused on his plate, his fork stabbing at the last of the omelet. The back of his left hand bore bruises from where they'd inserted the IV needle, and the plastic hospital wristband still dangled from his bony right wrist.

"Do you want me to wait until you're done here? I can help you back to your room if you like."

"No. I'll stay out here. Maybe watch some TV."

"Why don't I get you a pillow and some blankets, just in case you want to rest your eyes?"

He didn't answer. I slipped down the hall and grabbed a pillow off his bed and a spare blanket from the closet.

"Let's get you situated before I leave, okay? It may take me a while to find her."

He mumbled something I couldn't understand.

"What's that?"

"Bathroom," he said in a low growl. He grimaced and I saw how hard it was for him to ask for help.

"Oh. Well, how about I help get you in there and then you take it from there?" I hoped he didn't want me to stay for the whole show.

"Good," he said. "Malia thinks I can't even wipe my own ass."

"No problem with me on that. I figure you've wiped your own ass for seventy years so I expect you're probably pretty good at it by now."

He chuckled and nodded. But when I took his arm to steer him into the tiny half-bath, I felt the hesitation in his step and the weakness of his grip.

While I waited, I listened to the clock on the wall. I didn't want to rush him, but I didn't want him falling, either. *Tick tock, tick tock.* Four minutes passed as slowly as thirty. Finally, I heard the toilet flush and then water running in the sink.

"How're you doing in there?" I called through the door when the water stopped.

"Good. But I'm resting a bit."

"Can I give you a boost back to the sofa?"

"Come on in. I'm decent."

I went in and found a very pale, shaky old man sitting on the closed toilet seat.

"I'm sorry," he said. "I got a little light-headed." He put his bruised hand up to cover his eyes. A stab of pity shot through me as I recognized how humiliating it must be for this once robust man to have become so feeble.

"No worries," I said. "We'll get you set up on the sofa with the TV remote and then I'll get out of your hair for a while."

As soon as I'd made him comfortable, I sprinted out the door to find Malia. It didn't seem reasonable she'd leave her infirm father alone in the house for so long. What if I hadn't come back and he'd needed to use the bathroom?

I nearly tripped over her as I rounded the corner of the carport. She was crouched down, chin resting in her palm.

"Jeez," I said, my hand flying to my throat, "You startled me."

"Sorry," she said. "I was watching through the window. You're really good with him, you know? With me, he's horrible. Uncooperative, belligerent, rude—"

I figured the list would go on and on, so I interrupted, "But he hates this, Malia. Can't you see? He's used to being the top dog, the head of the household, the big *kahuna*." I had my own long list for her.

"But he's suffered a heart attack," she whispered. "He could be dying. I can't think about losing him so soon after my mom." Her face crumpled into a wad of pain.

"I know," I said, leaning down to put my arm around her. "But his ego's taking a beating that's at least as severe as his heart problem."

"Will you stay here with us? He'll listen to you, Nola."

"I'll stay as long as you need me," I said, patting the back of her hand as if I'd just offered to make her a nice cup of tea. "It's the least I can do after everything you've done for me."

Funny, how some people never learn. Just a day ago I'd made plans to be on the next thing smokin' back to Seattle. And yet I blithely tossed it all aside when Malia asked for help.

For as long as I could remember, I'd made choices that served everyone's interests but my own. As Dr. Phil would say, *How's that workin' for ya?* Well, let's see—I was homeless, jobless, and for the foreseeable future, childless. The bigger question was, *What kind of crazy, pathetic, pony-in-there-somewhere mentality made me believe this time things would turn out differently?*

CHAPTER 14

It was six days until Christmas. With Al's surgery and Auntie Momi fretting over losing the Shore Store we'd all kind of blown off preparing for the holidays. But when Malia's husband, Jim, called and offered to bring their daughter Leila over to spend Christmas in Maui we all revved up into Martha Stewart mode.

The local supermarket had real evergreen trees for sale in the parking lot. Dried out and forlorn, they were a far cry from the elegant noble firs I was used to in the Pacific Northwest. They'd arrived on ships from the mainland tightly trussed like bristly green mummies. Once cut free of the wrapping twine, those dried-out Charlie Brown trees shed their needles in the tropical heat like a Marine getting a boot camp haircut. But the locals went nuts over the unfamiliar piney smell and the promise of a *real* Christmas tree like the ones they saw on Currier and Ives greeting cards.

"Eighty bucks?" I gasped at the price tag on the droopy Douglas Fir Malia picked out.

"You think it's too much?" she asked. Obviously, she hadn't been their family's primary Christmas tree buyer back in Seattle.

"It's outrageous. And that thing is just one string of lights away from sparking a two-alarm house fire."

"But Leila will hate it if we don't have a real Christmas tree."

"Suit yourself," I said. "Personally, I think a string of twinkly lights wrapped around that palm tree in the front yard would be much more festive than a desiccated doug fir propped up in the living room."

She bought the tree.

I wouldn't be looking at it much anyway. After much discussion we'd come up with an arrangement where I'd stay overnight at Momi's to allow for more room at Al's while Malia's husband and daughter were in town. Momi seemed to like the idea because she missed her sons on the mainland and, once again, neither one of them was coming home for Christmas. Also, this would be Momi's second Christmas without her beloved Koma. He'd died a year ago November, so last year she'd still been in shock.

The first night I went over to Momi's I brought my little black suitcase, a few plastic containers of leftovers for her refrigerator, and a tiny nod to Christmas décor—a synthetic body-double of the ratty fir tree in Al's living room.

"Here's a little fake tree I found at Long's Drugstore," I said as I hauled the four-foot bogus shrub from the back of the van.

"Oh, you didn't need to fuss," said Auntie Momi. She was the kind of lady who'd be bestowed honorary

Southern Belle status if she ever went to Georgia. She always had the perfect line of sweet talk on the tip of her tongue, and she routinely displayed faultless admiration for all things social.

I'd bought a few dozen Maui-themed tree ornaments at the local crafts fair. I'd picked surfing Santas in papier-mâché, clear glass globes filled with sand and tiny shells, and a bevy of angels made from dried palm leaves and seashells. My favorites were glass balls hand-painted from the inside. Some featured dolphins and whales. Two were beach scenes with black palm trees silhouetted against pink and orange sunsets.

After my third night, I got into a rhythm of Aidan picking me up at Al's every evening to take me to Momi's cottage and then coming to get me in the morning to take me back to Al's. Most mornings we'd stop for coffee before he dropped me off, but we managed to keep the conversation light and the displays of affection to a minimum. A couple of nights I'd almost gathered the courage to lean over and kiss him good-night when we got to Momi's, but he'd always leapt out to open my door before I had the chance. Besides, as soon as we'd pull up, Auntie Momi would be out on the porch to greet me with the security light blazing and her ancient little dog, Pookie, yapping nonstop and running NASCAR circles around her feet.

Over at Al's we'd decorated and cooked and cleaned for five solid days. On Saturday, the twenty-fourth, Malia took the van to pick up Jim and Leila at the airport. I looked around the house. In short order we'd managed to pull together a pretty holly jolly look.

On Christmas afternoon, while everyone else was watching the World Series of Poker on TV, Jim came into the kitchen where I was washing lettuce for a salad.

"I brought you something," he said.

"Oh, you didn't need to do that. I don't have a gift for you."

"It's not from me." He handed me a battered post card with a generic beach scene on the picture side.

I turned it over and immediately recognized my son Frankie's handwriting. The large stamps looked foreign. I gasped and looked up at Jim's face, as if hoping he had more to tell.

"Go ahead. Read it."

Dear Jim, I'm OK. I'm in Cabo San Lucas working at a timeshare condo. Tell my mom I'm fine and I hope she's OK. Feliz Navidad, as they say. He'd signed it "Frank Stevens Jr." which I thought was cute, as if he thought Jim might not know who it was if he'd simply signed it "Frankie."

"Thanks so much for bringing this." I could hardly get it out; my voice had evaporated. I handed back the card, but he waved it away.

"No, keep it. It means a lot more to you. At least now you know where he is."

"You can't imagine what a relief this is. It's the best Christmas present ever." I pressed the postcard to my chest and leaned in and gave him a hug.

"Okay, now it's your turn to help me," he said. "What the heck's going on with those two?"

He didn't need to elaborate. I knew exactly which *two* he meant. I'd learned in the past week I should never leave Malia and Al alone together for more than fifteen minutes unless I planned to come back brandishing a whip and a chair.

"I think they're both afraid," I said.

"Well, it's a good thing you're here."

"I can't referee forever."

"I know," he said. "Thing is, Malia needs to come home. Her principal called and said if she's not back in her classroom on January third she'll be in violation of her teaching contract."

Malia hadn't said a word to me about going back to work.

Al's sutures were healing nicely and his strength was returning, but the thought of leaving him alone to care for himself sent a chill down my spine. And that's saying something since it was eighty-degrees outside.

"I guess I could stay until he's a hundred-percent," I said, my mind whirling while my stomach clenched. "He's doing better every day, but he's still not able to shower and shave without help. And cooking? I don't think Seven-Up and pork rinds exactly cover the four food groups. But I'm worried about staying here if Malia has to go home."

"What do you mean?"

"Well, it's *her* dad, after all. She might get jealous."

"Yeah, it's her dad. And she'd have killed him by now if it weren't for you. Nola, trust me, she's well aware of how much you've helped out. And she sincerely appreciates it. I think she'll be beyond pleased to hear you're willing to stay a little longer."

And so it was decided. On December thirtieth—the day before New Year's Eve—I drove Malia, Jim and Leila to the airport to catch their flight back to Seattle.

"Are you going to be okay?" Malia said as I waited with her in the baggage check line.

"Sure. I expect I'll be home in a couple of weeks if your dad keeps improving. He's doing really good."

"I'll never forget this, Nola. You truly are *ohana* now." She lifted one of the sweet-smelling lei from around her neck and draped it over my head. Then she gave me a quick hug.

"*Mahalo,*" I said. I lifted the lei to my nose to inhale the spicy scent. "Al will be fine. I'll call or email you every day to let you know how he's doing."

"I'm not worried about him. I want an update on how *you're* doing. Dad can be a little tyrant and I don't want you letting him take advantage of you."

Actually, Al and I worked well together. We used euphemisms and vague language to avoid embarrassment, and we managed to judge each other's moods and act accordingly. Above all, we maintained our physical distance. If Al wanted fresh air, I'd wheel him out to the back porch and then I'd make up an excuse for me to go back inside.

He spent more and more time in his orchid shed every day. I'd have enjoyed hanging around out there with him learning how he coaxed those spindly spikes to explode into glorious blooms but I knew Al liked his space. Although he'd always been a social animal with his family, his infirmity had heightened his need for personal boundaries.

At dinner that night, I asked Al about how we should handle our living arrangement now that his family was gone and the guest room was empty.

"Would you be okay if I still went to Momi's every night? I'll come back every morning, just like we've been doing. But I think Auntie Momi likes the company."

He made a big show of pondering my proposal, but I could see in his eyes he was thrilled at the thought of having his house all to himself for at least part of the day.

"That'd be good. I think you're right. Momi's been real lonely ever since she lost Koma."

And that's how I became the nomad caregiver. I kept most of my personal things at Momi's because I showered and dressed there, but I did most of the cooking at Al's. Within the past few weeks, his kitchen had become as familiar to me as a well-worn pair of *rubba slippas.*

Aidan called mid-afternoon the next day, New Year's Eve.

"Everyone get out of there okay yesterday?"

"Yep. I stayed until the plane took off and then Malia called when they arrived in Seattle. She said it's raining and about forty degrees and there are more showers forecast for New Year's Day."

"You got plans for tonight?" He'd blown off commenting on my up-to-the-minute Doppler radar weather report for Seattle.

Was he asking me out on a date? That seemed odd. We'd been acting nonchalant regarding our mutual attraction for the past few weeks. I'd pretty much written him off to 'just friends' status.

"No plans. Just going over to Momi's later."

"Tell you what. How about I bring her over to Al's and get the two of them some nice takeout and a little bottle of champagne. Then she won't feel like she needs to wait up for you."

I'm no math whiz but I can put two and two together. "You mean you're going to suggest that Momi spend the night at Al's?"

"Yeah, why not? The guest room's available and that way she and her brother can ring in the new year together."

Smooth, very smooth.

"So, you and I are going out to celebrate New Year's?"

"Or, stay in and do it," he said.

...stay in and do it? That got points for honesty, but demerits for coming up a little short on subtlety.

"I'd like to go out, if that's okay," I said. "I've been playing nursemaid for weeks now, and, to tell you the truth, I could use a little New Year's cheer."

"Just say the word. How about I pick you up at Momi's around seven? And don't eat beforehand. I've got a great place for dinner."

I told Al about Aidan's suggestion for New Year's Eve. I watched his face, looking for signs of disapproval.

"Aidan's bringing dinner? What's he gonna get us?" Al zeroed in on his dining options, seemingly oblivious to the evident ploy at work here—to give Aidan and me some privacy.

"Why don't you call and tell him what you'd like?" I followed up by slipping in a little request of my own. "Do you mind if I borrow the van so I can get ready over at Momi's before Aidan shows up? He's taking me out to dinner."

"Sure," he said. "I think I want some of those good barbecue ribs they got up there in Napili."

"Sounds good," I said, stifling a comment about pork not exactly making the heart healthy top ten. "Oh, and one more thing. I may be a little late getting back here tomorrow morning. Is that okay?"

"Or maybe I want some of that *ono* mahi-mahi from the *okazuya* down in Honokawai."

"Whatever. You two have fun tonight." I gave him a hug. "I'll see you next year!"

Getting into the van for the trip to Momi's made me feel like a teenager sneaking out to meet up with a boy my parents disapproved of. The only boy I'd ever sneaked out with had been Frank. To say I was unschooled in the art of romance would've been an understatement. I'd never seriously dated anyone but Frank and that had been more than a quarter century ago.

Thinking in terms of centuries really drove home the point. I'd gone from living in my dad's house to living in Frank's house. Not only was I completely clueless about romance, I didn't know diddly-squat about being independent. I'd never applied for a job, never earned my own money. I'd never had a personal checking account or even a credit card in my own name. Frank Junior was more self-sufficient than I was. I resolved in the year ahead I'd get up to speed. I had no choice. As Leila put it, *It's time to put on the big girl panties and get 'er done.*

When I arrived at Momi's, I told her about Aidan's plans for the evening and then went in to take a shower.

Afterward, I was rummaging under the sink for my moisturizing lotion when I came across an old bathroom scale. I flashed back to the scale at the farmer's market. One-twenty-seven. Yeah, right.

I pulled out the scale and stepped on it. The needle jiggled back and forth, finally settling on a number. One-twenty-five? Unbelievable.

I did it again. Same number.

I wiped the fog off the full-length mirror on the back of the bathroom door and took a long look at myself—front and rear. I hadn't really looked at myself in months. *Damn*, I thought. I look pretty good. My thighs were toned and my fanny actually had a pleasant roundness to it I'd assumed had been lost to the ages. My upper arms were firmed up. I no longer sported the droopy bat-wings that had made me throw out every sleeveless blouse I owned back in Seattle.

Hauling groceries up the hill from the farmer's market every other day seemed to have turned my physical clock back ten years.

"So, Noelani," I said to the smiling reflection in the mirror. "No doubt about it. You're starting to look like one hot *wahine*."

"You all right in there?" It was Momi, calling through the door.

I squirmed at the idea of her hearing me make a fool of myself.

"I'm fine, Auntie."

And for the first time in years, I was.

CHAPTER 15

It took me ten minutes to pick out underwear. Not that I had a vast assortment to choose from, but I figured I might not be the only person seeing it that night so granny panties and anything ripped was out of the question. I settled on pale pink bikinis and an almost matching bra. The bra had a bit of lace that I hoped would pass for sexy.

I slipped into an above the knee black shift with large tropical flowers printed at the hem. I'd bought it at a tourist shop on Front Street. It wasn't haute couture by any stretch of the imagination, but it skimmed my body and showed off my newly tanned and toned legs.

I pulled my hair into a plastic comb clip. It looked cute from the front, but slapdash messy in back. I took out the clip and brushed out my now sun-lightened curls. Maybe a simple black grosgrain ribbon could tame it into a ponytail that I could release with a flourish at just the right moment.

I felt like I was getting ready for the prom. The anticipation, the fantasy, the ache for perfection. My old self was still very much alive—nagging, telling me I was pitiful, pointing out the crow's feet and strands of gray.

But my newfound confidence drowned out the irksome chorus. After all, I was becoming svelte and I was physically stronger than I'd been in high school. I might not qualify as a total hot mama, but chances were, most men would at least think twice before kicking me out of bed.

Aidan pulled up in a silver Porsche Carrera.

"What's this? A friend's car?" I said.

"No, it's mine. I don't drive it a lot." He squinted, looking a bit uneasy, as if expecting me to accuse him of owning a mid-life crisis car. "It's not much good for hauling stuff."

He opened the passenger side door and I had to do a little duck and dip to get myself lowered into the low-slung black leather seat.

"You look fabulous," he said. "I'm rethinking our reservations at Mark Allen's."

I gasped. Mark Allen's was a Lahaina culinary landmark. A very spendy, trendy restaurant I'd been dying to try, but hadn't had the occasion—nor the ready cash—to consider.

"I've always wanted to go there," I said. "They were voted 'Best Restaurant on Maui' for the past *ten* years."

"Actually, it's been twelve now, but who's counting?" Aidan shrugged. "Lech is a friend of mine."

I'd read that although the name of the restaurant was Mark Allen's, the owner's real name was Lech Gorelczenko. I supposed the name Lech's wouldn't have the same cachet with the gourmand-set as Mark Allen's. I didn't care what it was called. I wanted to touch the hem of the chef's coat, if only to vicariously bask in the creative culinary glory of someone so famous and talented.

"What a great way to start the New Year." I tried to throttle back my enthusiasm a bit. I didn't want Aidan to think I was some hick who'd never dined at a restaurant with a decent Zagat rating. But I couldn't stop my hands from doing the little clapping thing I involuntarily do when I'm excited.

"Know what I like about you?" he said. "You're like a little kid. Boundless enthusiasm." He reached over and squeezed my hand. Then he popped the gearshift into first and we took off like a shot.

We pulled up outside Mark Allen's in downtown Lahaina and a valet appeared at Aidan's door before the tires stopped rolling.

"Good evening, Mr. Lawson. Nice to see you again."

"Hello, Enrico. Put this someplace safe, won't you?"

"Your spot's waiting. Lech's here tonight, but only until eight."

We went in and I was captivated by the casual yet elegant ambiance of the dining room. The dazzling space, complete with snow-white tablecloths, glistening silver, and luminous crystal stemware could have been anywhere—New York, San Francisco, Dallas—but it was just a half-block from the waterfront in West Maui. Outside, people shuffled by in oversized tee-shirts emblazoned with *I survived the road to Hana!,* but inside this magnificent oasis of tranquility everything was luxurious and sophisticated.

We were seated at a prime table in the front corner.

"That's Lech over there," Aidan said. He raised his hand in greeting and the celebrity chef nodded and smiled. Then he excused himself from the couple he was chatting with and made a beeline to our table.

Aidan stood and the two men gave each other a brotherly hug.

"Lech, this is my friend, Nola. She's almost as good a cook as you are."

"Really?" Lech raised an eyebrow. "So what have you fixed for our friend here that he would make such an assertion?" His slight Eastern European accent turned his "t's" into "d's."

I stumbled to form a coherent reply. It came out sounding like, "I'm glad to meet—not anything really."

He had the good manners to just smile.

The meal was spectacular. Everything was fresh, crisp, and cooked to full flavor. I enjoyed an elegantly presented pyramid of mahi-mahi with a truffle oil finish. It was perfectly balanced between sweet and savory. Three triangle wedges of fish were positioned against a mound of couscous studded with almonds and bits of lemon peel. Aidan ordered a small cut of filet mignon. A moat of smooth tarragon-tinged béarnaise sauce surrounded it.

Frank and I always shared bites of our entrees, but I didn't want to come across as ill-mannered so I simply commented on his steak's excellent presentation.

"It's fabulous. Here, try a bite." Aidan extended his fork across the table and a drop of béarnaise landed on the pristine white linen.

"Uh-oh," I said. "It made a spot on the tablecloth."

"Yeah, I see. Well, for what Lech owes me for artwork, I could dribble on every piece of linen he owns and I'd still be in the black."

I looked around the room searching for Aidan's sculptures, but all I saw were vivid oil paintings on the walls.

We lingered over dessert and coffee. I ordered their special rendition of bananas Foster, with a sprinkling of coconut and a luscious liqueur that tasted like mangoes. We shared bites, adding even more artful splotches to the tablecloth between us.

"This was so wonderful, Aidan. How can I ever thank you for such a treat?"

He looked over his shoulder as if checking to see if anyone was listening.

"You really want me to answer that in public?"

I didn't have time to think of a reply before I felt heat flood my cheeks and settle at the base of my throat.

We went to Momi's and Aidan parked in back, out of view of the neighbors. I didn't mention the obvious implication of hiding the evidence, but my pulse spiked at the thought of what came next.

"It's not even ten yet," I said. "We've got more than two hours until midnight."

"Yeah," he said. "Two hours and nothing to do; nowhere to go." He set the parking brake, his eyes reflecting the glimmer of Momi's back porch light. "I brought some champagne. It's got a different label than the stuff Al and Momi drink."

From behind his seat he pulled a bottle of Moët and Chandon.

"It'll take an hour or so to chill it," he said. "You got some ice in the house?"

"Sure."

"Then let's do it."

For some odd reason, that line caused me to flash back on Frank's "We Do 'Em All" trademark line. A shudder flashed through my body.

"You cold?"

"No, just thinking about other New Year's nights."

"These holidays are killers, aren't they?"

We went inside and I pulled a foam picnic cooler out from under the sink and filled it with ice. I crunched the bottle down into the ice and filled the cooler with water. I'd read somewhere that ice water chills wine faster than ice alone.

"This will have to do for a bottle chiller. As you probably know, Momi isn't exactly an aficionado of fine wine."

"I know. That's why I got Al and her that cheap stuff. They prefer wine with a nose like Karo syrup."

The champagne was chilling, the car parked out back, and the warm night air swirled around us as we pulled two wicker chairs close to each other on the concrete lanai. We turned off the outside light to discourage any light-seeking insects and I inhaled the scent of plumeria blossoms from the trees in the yard.

"You're the best thing that's happened to me all year." Aidan said, reaching over and taking my hand in both of his.

I almost said, *Me too,* but inwardly chuckled at how absurd that was. Oh yeah, you're much better than a gay cheating husband, a lost son, a divorce, no job, and being homeless. What a compliment.

"This has been a tough year for me," I said instead.

"Next year will be better. I promise."

With that he leaned over and placed his fingertips under my chin. It was so dark I didn't see his face before I felt his lips on mine.

After a few kisses he stood and pulled me up to him. I leaned against his solid chest and felt his heart thudding in rhythm to mine.

"Let's go in," he said. "I think we've got some time until that champagne's drinkable. And what the heck. Most of this year wasn't so great, so let's bid it farewell with something to celebrate."

I considered putting up some kind of coy defense of my reputation, but then let it go. Our lovemaking was inevitable so what was the point of putting on some prim and proper act? I thought about protection, though.

"Umm. I hope you have—" I didn't even get it out before he pressed a foil-wrapped condom in my palm. "Well, well," I said. "You're quite the little Boy Scout, aren't you?"

"I hope your referring to the 'be prepared' motto and not some kinky den mother fantasy you've got," he said.

We laughed, easing the tension as we made our way through the dark house into the guest room where I'd been staying. The rock hard mattress I'd been battling since I'd moved to Momi's felt luxurious with Aidan's arms wrapped around me.

"How long do you think until the champagne's ready?" I asked as we wiggled out of our clothes.

"As long as it takes."

It was so dark he wouldn't have been able to see my underwear even if I'd been wearing boxers and an Ace bandage for a bra, but I didn't care. Fine with me to skip the preliminaries. The skin on his upper arms was cool and smooth, but the furry patch in the center of his chest caused my fingers to linger.

He stroked my back and then tenderly moved to my breasts, lightly circling each one until my nipples were at full salute.

Through a haze of desire, I heard music. I cocked an ear. It sounded like Bruce Springsteen's *Born in the USA*. A radio? A passing car?

"Oh, shit," said Aidan. "I've got to get that."

"That's your cell phone?"

"Yeah. I like that song. It really grinds the locals."

He got up, padding naked across the room to where he'd dropped his pants. I squinted to catch a glimpse, but could only make out his broad shoulders.

"Hel-lo." There was a long pause. He blew out a breath and walked from the room, shutting the door behind him as he went.

My jaw clenched as I pushed back thoughts zigzagging from my head to my heart. Why did this feel so familiar? Then I remembered Frank's shutting the door to his office as he took an incoming call. I slid off the bed and slipped on my dress.

I quietly opened the door and went down the hall to the living room. I stopped when I heard Aidan's urgent whisper.

"No, it's *not* okay. Just get it done, dammit. I think I've been more than patient." A pause. "Look. I gotta go.

No more drama, Claire. You know what you need to do."

I heard the phone dropped on a table and then a creak as he got up from Momi's prehistoric sofa.

"What was that about?" I said.

"Nothing."

"Didn't sound like nothing."

"Okay," he said. "Let's just say it's nothing that concerns you."

"Well, since I was lying in bed naked with you less than two minutes ago, I'd say I have a somewhat vested interest."

He stopped moving, and I could sense the gears turning in his brain.

"It's a voice from my past—my distant past."

"Gonna have to do better than that, buck-o."

"It was my wife, okay? Now are you glad you asked?"

A fist of nausea pushed against my stomach and I envisioned my beautiful Mark Allen's dinner spewing across Momi's living room floor.

"You need to leave now," I said.

"It's not what you think, Nola."

"What's there to think about? You're married. End of story."

He paused, and then blew out an irritated snort.

"So, is this the part where I get to remind you that you're as married as I am?"

CHAPTER 16

They say how you spend your New Year's Day provides a glimpse of the year ahead. If that's true, I should have opted for a twelve-month coma.

I drove the van back to Al's at around seven in the morning. Aidan had left in a huff right after the *you're married; yeah, well you are too* showdown. Not eager to welcome in the New Year alone, I'd crawled in bed and called it a night. But by daybreak I'd decided a lousy New Year's Eve could be set right by surprising Momi and Al with a fabulous homemade brunch.

Pulling up to Al's I saw Momi's normally manic little dog, Pookie, lying in the middle of the driveway. He was probably twenty years old, and I wasn't sure if his hearing had gone bad or what, but when I beeped the horn, he didn't move. But my little tap on the horn brought Al's neighbor, Kilia, racing to her window.

I carefully navigated the van halfway up the driveway, stopping just short of the belligerent dog. I muttered to myself I'd become so pathetic I couldn't even get respect from a yappy hairball like Pookie. The stupid dog refusing to budge seemed to sum up my dealings with all the males in my life—human and canine alike.

I turned off the engine and got out and slammed the door, hoping the noise and vibration would startle him awake. As I rounded the front of the van he was still on the pavement; he hadn't moved a muscle. I bent down for a closer look. His glassy eyes shined like a pair of black Tahitian pearls.

Kilia marched over, arms pumping, hands in fists. "Now look what you've done," she said. "You killed Momi's dog."

"No, no. He was just lying here. I didn't touch him."

"I saw you pull in to the driveway."

"He was *already* dead when I got here. Look, he's not squished or anything."

She shot me a sneer and then sprinted back to her house. I'd no doubt made her day; she'd be on the phone for hours.

I looked back down at Pookie and remembered Auntie Momi's trembling hands and quavering voice when she'd told me about her husband dying. Now her beloved dog was gone too. And since I was the one who'd found him, it fell to me to break the bad news. More than ever I wished I'd been on that plane when Malia went back to Seattle.

Wanting to spare Momi the sight of her cherished pet's body broiling in the Maui sun, I began looking for something to use as a shroud. The green tarp I'd ducked under at the farmer's market came to mind. I walked into the carport hoping to find something similar.

"*Aloha* Noelani," Momi said, startling me as I rooted through dusty boogie boards and plastic flower pots. "I heard you pull up. What are you looking for?"

"Hi, Auntie. It's nothing. I'll be in shortly."

"Do you need some help?"

"No," I said, with a bit more vigor than the question called for. "Really, it's fine. I'll be right in."

"I'm making Al breakfast. Are you hungry?"

I squirmed at the thought of forking Momi's home cooking into my mouth while casually mentioning her darling Pookie had been summoned to Doggie Heaven.

"Uh. No, not right now, thank you. Maybe I'll have something later." I planted myself between her and the van, hoping to block any glimpse of the deceased.

"Well, okay, then. We'll just go ahead and eat if that's all right." She went back into the house.

Al's carport was a jumble of hoses, shovels, buckets, old car parts and black plastic garbage bags stuffed with aluminum cans for recycling. I couldn't find a tarp or an empty bag anywhere. I finally settled on an empty cardboard box with the words 'Baby Clothes' scrawled on the side in felt-tip marker.

I didn't want to touch the dead peek-a-poo, cock-a-poo or whatever kind of 'poo' the dog was, but I summoned the mind-set I use when I pull the sack of entrails from a raw Thanksgiving turkey. I squinted my eyes nearly closed, reached down, and got a good grip. I made sure I had a hand under both ends so I wouldn't drop him. Then I gently laid him in the box.

Although his tiny body had already stiffened a bit, he actually looked pretty good resting in his makeshift casket. His unblinking stare was a bit unnerving, but he looked at peace.

After sliding the box into a shadowy corner of the carport, I turned toward the kitchen and took a deep breath. What's the best way to tell a seventy-year-old widow she's lost her last remaining companion? He'd been her loyal friend; the one she'd counted on to comfort her as she lived out her days without a husband or children. Now she was all alone. I couldn't help but note how disturbingly similar our circumstances were.

"Happy New Year!" Al said as I pushed through the kitchen door.

"Did you and Aidan have a good time last night?" Momi chimed in. Her face was aglow with the hope she might be in store for some juicy gossip.

"Uh. Yes, it was a nice dinner. We got in early, though. I was asleep before midnight." Like *two hours* before midnight, I thought, wincing as I remembered the sound of Aidan slamming the back door and revving up the Porche.

"Can I talk you into a banana-macadamia muffin? They're pretty *ono,* if I do say so myself," said Momi. She held up a plate of gigantic muffins studded with chunks of the costly nuts.

"No, thanks. I'm not very hungry." I searched for a way to break the news. The longer I delayed, the more agonizing it would be. "Al, I need to talk to you for a minute—alone. Do you mind, Momi?"

"Of course not. I hope everything's okay. You feeling all right?"

That was a question I'd leave unanswered. But I nodded to be polite. She took her coffee cup out to the back patio.

"Al, something horrible has happened," I said.

His forehead crinkled up, so I moved right to the point before stressing him into another heart attack.

"I found Auntie Momi's dog lying in the driveway."

"It does that. It's kinda stupid."

"No, I mean, he was...well, he wasn't moving."

"Dead?"

"Yeah."

"Did you run over him?" He clenched his teeth in a grimace.

"No! I was very careful and avoided him. He was already...you know."

"Dead." Al didn't dodge the truth. He was the kind of guy I'd want to have around if I ever got washed ashore on a desert island. Lots of laughs; very little BS.

"No worries," he said, "I'll handle it."

"I don't want to dump this on you. I'm the one who found him."

Just then, the kitchen phone rang. Al reached over and picked it up. He listened a bit and then said, "No, no. It was old. Besides, it was dead already."

He listened some more, rolling his eyes my way. A minute later he signed off.

"That was Kilia, wasn't it?" I said.

"Yeah. She says she saw you run over the dog."

"Well, she's *wrong*." I said. My defensive tone veered dangerously close to too much protest.

"I know," he said. "That's what I told her."

I thought his response didn't exactly qualify as a rally to my defense. But this wasn't the time to quibble over semantics.

"Where's the dog now?" He peered out the kitchen window.

"I put him in a box in the carport. To get him out of the sun."

"Good," he said. "Well, I'm gonna tell Momi before Kilia yells something over the back fence. You gonna be okay?"

"Yeah, I'm just sad. She really loved that goofy dog."

Al asked me to get an old sheet from the closet to wrap up the dog. Then he shuffled out the back door. I thanked God that Jim had brought me the postcard from Frankie at Christmas. I don't think I would've been able to keep it together seeing Pookie's lifeless little corpse if I hadn't known my own little boy was alive and well.

Momi blamed herself for Pookie's death.

"I shouldn't have let him out alone." She held her hand over her mouth so it was hard to make out her words. "He wasn't used to this house. He was always afraid over here."

Her anguished sobs stabbed at me, making me second-guess if maybe I should have attempted doggie CPR.

"I'm so, so sorry."

She went down the hall and holed up in the guest room. I ducked out into the orchid shed to be alone for a few minutes. The pungent smell of the soil was in sharp contrast to the beauty of the boisterous blooms. Even though orchids are a feast for the eyes, most varieties have very little scent.

"Beautiful, aren't they?" Al said. He'd slipped in behind me.

"Yes, they're gorgeous. I hope you don't mind me being here. I'm hiding out."

"This is the best place to be in times like this. I'll take her and the dog back to their place so she can grieve."

"Al, I don't know what to do. I feel so sad for her, but I don't know what to say to make her feel better."

"Sometimes it's best to say nothing." He picked up a spray bottle and started misting a canary yellow cattleya orchid. "Mainlanders spend a lot of money on sympathy cards and sending fancy flower bouquets. Over here we believe it's best to just sit with the person. Some people bring food and flowers from their garden, but mostly we just show up to share their pain."

"Do you think I should go to her house with her?"

"Not yet."

"When should I?"

"You'll know." He held my gaze so long I felt as if he were hypnotizing me. Then he patted my shoulder. "Remember, we're *ohana*. We feel each other's love and pain as if it were our own."

About a half-hour later, Al loaded the small sheet-wrapped bundle into Momi's arms and helped her up into the front seat. I stood outside, giving a small wave as they left. I felt Kilia's eyes on me and when I turned toward her house I saw one of the slats in the blinds drop down. Al examined Pookie's body carefully and declared he'd died of natural causes. He assured me when he got back home he'd talk to Kilia and squelch her story about seeing me run over the dog.

When I went inside my cell phone was chiming. I flipped it open before even looking at the caller ID. I continued to hold out hope Frankie would call.

"Hi, Nola." Unfortunately it wasn't Frankie. It was his father. Probably the last person on the planet I'd hoped to hear from right then.

"Hello Frank." I said it with the tone I'd use if I'd just discovered dog poop on my shoe.

"Hey, what's with the sour attitude? I called to wish you a Happy New Year."

"I still haven't received the papers for the sale of the house."

"I know. That's because I haven't sent them."

"What's the hold-up? I thought you were anxious to get it on the market. You know we only have four more months until the divorce is final."

"I think we should talk about that."

Why was it every time Frank wanted to talk, I got the urge to scream?

"Nola? You still there?"

"Uh-huh. What's there to talk about?"

"I miss you, Nola. I mean it. And, don't worry; I'm not blaming you for taking off. Really, I'm not. But it's time for you to come home. If you come home I know we can work on this together. We need to get things back to the way they were."

I couldn't get my lips to move. Unfortunately, he must have taken my silence as a tacit form of encouragement.

"Yeah," he went on. "I'm thinking of buying you that little red Mercedes you've always wanted. That is, as long as you'll agree to put my realtor sign on the door, heh-heh." Frank's lame attempt at humor sent a chill down my spine.

It dawned on me I'd trained Frank to treat me the way he did. He'd be cruel or inconsiderate, and I'd be hurt and pout. But all would be forgiven once he'd bought me off. I couldn't blame him for giving it one last shot—it'd worked for more than twenty years.

"Frank, I can't talk right now. I've got to go." I clicked off the call and threw the phone on the counter. Our little *quid pro quo* arrangement had always been a little short on the *quid*, and I was no longer willing to let him off so easy.

It wasn't even noon on New Year's Day. But in the past twenty-four hours I'd learned my Sir Lancelot on a white horse was instead Jane Eyre's Mr. Rochester—the guy with the wife hidden in the attic. Then, I'd stumbled on the dead body of Auntie Momi's adored companion and the whacko next door had accused me of murder. And for the three's-a-charm finale, my gay ex-husband had attempted to buy me off with a spendy piece of German engineering.

I had nine more hours to go before I could reasonably call it a day. If there was a killer meteor hurtling toward planet Earth, I was pretty sure where it would hit.

CHAPTER 17

I laid low the rest of New Year's Day. I kept the TV on all afternoon but it was just one football game after another, so I never sat down and watched it. At about four o'clock I fell asleep on the sofa and only awoke when Al came back home at dinnertime.

"I don't know if I should go over to Momi's tonight or not," I said. "What do you think, Al?"

"I think she'd like some company. And besides, isn't Aidan coming by in a little while to pick you up?"

Oh joy. I'd pushed the Aidan mess to the back of my mind. I didn't know if he'd be picking me up or not, but I didn't feel like discussing it with Al.

"What would you like for dinner?" I said. I'd been charged with nursing Al back to health. Feeding him definitely fell into the 'must do' category.

"I don't care. I didn't get any lunch over at Momi's. She was crying and carrying on, so no food for me. Whatever you want to fix is fine."

I made saimin noodles with snow peas, shredded chicken, and little hunks of fresh ginger root. It came together quickly and Al ate with gusto.

"I don't suppose we get dessert," he said. "Even though it's New Year's and all." His face resembled a kid who'd brought home a good report card and was angling for a reward.

"I'll go to the store and get something if you like. Do you think they're open?"

"Sure," he said, his face brightening. "They close on New Year's Eve, but on New Year's Day everyone's hung over and hungry so they'll be open. The store clerks are probably hung over too, but it's time-and-a-half, so they show up."

Al was right, the supermarket was bustling. I picked up some low-fat strawberry ice milk and put it in my cart. Then I went to the cookie aisle and got some cellophane-wrapped sugar-free, reduced fat vanilla cookies. I got in the checkout line behind five people. When it was almost my turn I asked the guy behind me if he would please back up and let me out.

"You want me to hold your place?"

"No, thanks. I need to pick up some things I forgot."

I put the ice milk back in the freezer and pulled out the extra creamy chocolate macadamia nut ice cream made in Honolulu. It's fattening and expensive, but worth every bite. Then I replaced the gritty good-for-you cookies with a package of humongous coconut macaroons from the in-store bakery. Al deserved a splurge after the crummy day he'd had dealing with his grief-stricken sister. And since he'd promised to clear things up with Kilia, I owed him.

"I got us ice cream," I said as I dropped the grocery bag on the kitchen counter.

"That icy milk stuff?"

"Nah. I bought the yummy kind that's really bad for you."

"Good girl," he said.

I handed him an overflowing bowl and he took it and held it aloft like a fine glass of wine.

"Let's toast to the memory of Momi's ratty mutt. May we all rest in peace now that we don't have to put up with that racket anymore." His eyes darted toward the door as if half-expecting the yapping ghost of Pookie to fly in and latch on to his ankle.

I had two good reasons for wanting to avoid going to Momi's that night. The first one was sitting in the driveway.

"Isn't he gonna come in?" Al said. He peered out the kitchen window at Aidan's truck.

"I don't think so. We had a spat last night."

"So? I didn't. He's supposed to come in; not sit out there like a taxi driver."

I went out to the truck and stood next to the driver door. Aidan took his time lowering the window. The engine was idling.

"You ready to go?" he said. He stared straight ahead out the windshield.

"Al wants you to come in."

"Why?"

"I'm just the messenger. It's been a bad day around here. I'd appreciate it if you'd just come in for a minute to be polite."

"By 'bad day' are you referring to you flattening Momi's dog into a Frisbee?"

"How'd you hear about the dog?"

He turned and shot me a look that said, *You still don't get it, do you?*

"For the record," I said. "I had nothing to do with Pookie's death except I was the one who found him in the driveway. He was already quite dead."

"That's not what I heard." He leaned back and stiff-armed the steering wheel. "Anyway, you ready to go?"

"I didn't run over Pookie. Come in and talk to Al. He'll vouch for me. I'm afraid there aren't any leftovers from dinner, but I've got some killer chocolate mac nut ice cream and some big macaroons from the bakery."

He turned off the engine and slid out of the driver's seat.

"With all this commotion over the dog, I missed the UH football game," he said. "You owe me, big time."

"Yeah? Well, you owe me too. Like an explanation regarding your marital status."

"Okay, that's fair." He grinned and slipped an arm around my waist. "So tell me, was Momi's mini-Cujo really DOA? Or are you claiming self-defense on grounds the loony dog was driving you nuts?"

I didn't dignify the question with a response.

Aidan ate a big bowl of ice cream and then we left. We didn't talk much on the ride over. I was unclear about what I should say to Momi, and my jaw was sore from clenching my teeth all day. What if I said something that made it worse? I felt relieved when Aidan offered to come in.

"Hi, Auntie." I said. "How're you doing?"

She hadn't come out on the porch to greet us like she usually did. It probably didn't feel right without Pookie causing a ruckus and doing his whirling Dervish routine. She looked up from the sofa, her eyes red and watery. Her hands were folded into a brown knob.

"I didn't know if you'd come over tonight or not," she said.

"Oh, Auntie, I'm so sorry for your loss. I couldn't wait to come over and be with you." Good thing Pinocchio was just a fairy tale; my nose would have grown six inches on that one.

"Do you want to see his grave?" She pointed toward the back yard.

"Of course." I held the back door open as Aidan helped her get up off the sofa. Glancing outside I saw a mound of earth up against the back fence. It seemed Al had been pressed into service to dig a dog-sized hole in the rocky soil; definitely not on his cardiologist's list of approved activities.

But Momi cleared it up for me.

"This dear young man dug Pookie's grave while I took a hot bath," she said. She patted Aidan's cheek. "See? He put him over by the fence where my baby boy liked to dig."

She dabbed her eyes with a balled-up tissue, then leaned into Aidan's brawny arm. It seemed those muscles were magnets for all women—young and old alike.

The three of us walked to the little gravesite. It was ringed by maroon-colored lava rocks and covered with plumeria blossoms from Momi's trees.

I remembered when I'd first come to Maui and I'd remarked to Malia about the sad-looking cemetery on the road to Lahaina. Had it only been a month ago? It seemed like years.

"Did you eat dinner, Auntie?" I said. "I can fix you some soup or maybe a salad."

"No, child. *Mahalo*, but I think I'll go to bed early. It won't be the same without my Pookie to keep my feet warm." Her tears started up again and she excused herself and went inside.

When she was out of earshot I turned to Aidan.

"Should I help her get a new dog?"

"I'd give it a couple of weeks."

"Well, I'm worn out from this whole thing."

"Yeah, nuking an old lady's pet requires some pretty heavy labor."

"Can you let it go? Kilia was mistaken. She saw me pull in and Pookie was lying in the driveway. She just sort of connected the dots. But she's wrong and Al's promised to set her straight. Besides, you and I have more pressing issues to discuss."

"Talk about heavy labor..." He ran a hand across his stubbly chin. "Okay. Fire away."

"You're married, right?"

"Twenty-five long years," he said.

"Twenty-five? Really?"

"Don't go buying me a silver anniversary present. We've been separated for twenty-three of those years."

"Why?"

"Why are we separated, or why haven't we gotten divorced yet?"

"I think both answers could be enlightening."

"Claire lives in Vermont. She's got her own thing going on back there and I'm definitely not a part of it."

"That doesn't explain why you aren't divorced."

"She comes from an old New England family. Old money, old attitudes, old everything. Our so-called marriage lets her keep up appearances and it keeps her folks off her back." He blew out a breath. "But it's getting irritating. I've been playing along all this time, but I've had enough."

"Why'd she call last night?"

"I sent her divorce papers a week ago. I was kind of expecting a call. I knew she'd pitch a fit."

"I'm not following this. Why would she want to stay married if you've not been together for over twenty years?"

"You remember when I said I liked you because you're such a kid at heart?"

"Yeah."

"Well, this is a time where it'd be better if you'd look at the situation like a cynical adult."

I was stumped. "Is it money?"

"No, she's a trust fund baby. Money's not an issue. I'll give you a hint: one of the reasons I was anxious to meet you is I'd heard about what you'd just gone through with Frank. I know how it feels."

"Oh my gosh. Your wife is *gay*?" My mouth flew open and stayed that way. If there'd been a flying insect within ten yards it would've had ample time to cruise on in and make itself at home.

He nodded. "I thought mentioning Vermont might've been a clue."

"I don't know anything about Vermont."

"They were one of the first states to allow gay civil unions."

"But how would that work? She's already married."

"Bingo. She lives with her lover in a tolerant community but because she's already married to me, her parents assume they're just roommates. Claire and her partner have even come to Hawaii on the pretense of her visiting me."

"Get outta here. Really?"

We both sat silent for a minute.

"Why'd you decide to ask for a divorce after all this time?" I said.

"I've met someone. Now it's my turn to get what I want."

"Well, good for you." I gave him a quick smile. I didn't want to appear presumptuous. He hadn't exactly come out and said *I'd* been the reason for his change of heart.

"That's all you've got to say? I was hoping for a little more of that child-like enthusiasm."

I stepped forward and wrapped my arms around his waist. He pulled me in tight. His shirt smelled like iron-rich earth and plumeria blossoms.

As Malia had promised, Aidan turned out to be a good guy after all. But Al was improving day by day. In no time he'd be back to his pre-hospital vigor and it would be time for me to head home. A rebound romance—no matter how tempting—was bound to end badly. I'd just finished a year of 'sad endings.' I wasn't about to embark on another.

CHAPTER 18

On January fifth I learned Momi's tax situation had been resolved. Not without a touch of deception, to be sure, but at least threatening notices no longer littered her mailbox. Without telling anyone but me, Aidan went to the tax office in Wailuku and paid the bill in cash. He claimed Momi couldn't drive—which was true—so she'd sent him on her behalf—which was not so true. While there, he'd asked a guy he knew who worked there to slip him a few sheets of county letterhead and an envelope. Together, he and I devised an *'oops, our mistake'* letter which explained that the taxes were rescinded after the county confirmed the property was on Kingdom of Hawaii Crown Land.

I invited Momi to dinner at Al's to celebrate her good news.

"I knew those people made a mistake," she said, waving the letter under Al's nose.

"That makes no sense," he said. "All land has taxes."

"Not *Crown* Land," Momi argued. "This is our land. We don't pay taxes to the State of Hawaii for our own sovereign land."

I stayed discreetly out of the discussion as they hashed it out. Finally, they tired of talking politics and moved on to Momi's excitement over getting a new dog.

I'd offered to help her find a new purebred puppy, but she wanted to go to the animal shelter and rescue a homeless mutt, preferably one who'd been there a while.

As I drove her across the island to the Humane Society, I used the opportunity to clear up any lingering doubts.

"I know you may have heard talk about me hitting Pookie with the van but it's not true. I found him in the driveway. He'd already passed away."

"It's okay, Noelani. I know it wasn't on purpose."

"I didn't have anything to do with it. Kilia happened to look out her window and saw Pookie lying there and assumed the worst. He didn't get run over."

"Don't worry about it," she said, patting my shoulder. "What's done is done. And he was getting pretty old anyway."

I wanted to rant on and force her to acknowledge that Kilia was a half-blind old busy-body who liked to stir up trouble. But instead, I kept quiet. *Living aloha* isn't about placing blame and demanding justice. As a philosophy, *living* a*loha* is more along the lines of *let it be*.

"Well, I hope you can find a new dog today. One who'll be as good a companion as Pookie."

"My Pookie was a special boy," she said. "I'm worried about leaving this new puppy at home by himself while I work at the store. I'd bring him with me but it's not allowed. No dogs in food stores, you know."

I could take a hint.

"Do you want me to watch your dog while you're gone?"

"Then he'd think you're his mommy, not me."

Ah. Wrong hint.

"Well, then maybe I could work at the store for you for awhile," I said. "If you'll help Al during the day, I'll be happy to take your place at the Shore Store. I don't think we should leave him alone yet."

"The puppy?"

"No, Al."

"Oh. That's a good idea," she said. "I can't pay you, though. I barely break even."

"No worries. I want to do it." I wanted to say that helping out at the store proved I was innocent of Pookie's death, but even I could see it looked like quite the opposite.

"Will you make us lunch and leave it in the refrigerator every morning?" she said.

The price of forgiveness was rising.

"Sure, no problem."

"You know, Aidan's studio is right next door. He comes over sometimes." Her eyes twinkled.

We went into the animal shelter and walked up and down the rows of chain link cages. There were dozens of different dog breeds, but all I saw were the liquid-brown eyes pleading for a pardon. I knew exactly how they felt: they were simply guilty of misplaced loyalty, yet they'd been tossed out like yesterday's trash.

Momi picked out a fluffy tan-colored dog with close-set beady eyes. The dog was stubby and bow-legged, with a squished-in face that made him look like a kid about to throw a tantrum.

"His name is 'Furby'," said the shelter volunteer. "He's been here for more than a month. No one's sure, but the vet thinks he's about five years old. He was found near the highway; probably dumped there by people going back to the mainland. He needs to get adopted soon, or..." She didn't finish the implied threat.

Momi seemed to ignore the volunteer's hardball pitch. "What kind of silly name is 'Furby' for a *nani* little sweetheart like this?" she said.

"We just make up names for the abandoned ones," the volunteer said. "We go alphabetical, like hurricanes. It's not his real name."

"Auntie, you can give him a new name later," I said. "I'm sure he'll come to whatever you call him."

"I'm naming him '*Hulu hulu*,'" she said. "That's Hawaiian for 'furry.' See how fluffy he is?"

Momi filled out the paperwork and I insisted on paying the fee, even though I knew my cash had 'guilty as charged' written all over it.

"Hulu," as he became known, turned out to be a better match for Momi than Pookie had ever been. He wasn't a yapper, and no matter what was going on he remained calm. He was mellow almost to the point of lethargy.

He and Momi would take a leisurely walk around the neighborhood every afternoon. Hulu would sit quietly while his mistress chatted with every living soul within four blocks. In the evening she'd haul him onto her lap while she watched TV in the living room. He'd make like a tree sloth until bedtime when she'd drag him up onto the foot of her bed where he'd remain until morning.

I began working at the Shore Store the following Monday. Momi unlocked the door and I was hit with a smell that reminded me of the tack room in my grandparents' barn. Ancient wood walls and floors, dusty cans and boxes, and crumbling cardboard disintegrating in the tropical humidity all blended to create an odor that hardly encouraged customers to load up a grocery basket.

In the back corner was a refrigerated glass case stocked with deli goods and cold lunches to go. Next to it was a serve-yourself refrigerator packed tight with bottled beer and canned pop. Momi had a loyal cadre of working folks who'd stop in to pick up a sandwich and chips or a take-out carton of salad during the lunch hour.

"I know what everybody likes," she said. "No mustard for Keoki. And Kona likes two pickles. I don't charge him for the extra one."

"I'll do the best I can, Auntie. If I make a mistake I'll just make the order over again."

"Oh, no. Don't waste food. Just tell them you'll get it right *next* time."

Al drove her back to his house and I wandered through the tiny store. It was like a trip back in time. The prices were hand written on little stickers. I found items like laundry bluing and sugar-free candy made with saccharin; things I couldn't imagine anyone in the twenty-first century actually buying.

At about ten, I went over to see if Aidan was in his studio. He lived in a tiny *ohana*—the Hawaiian word meant 'guest house' as well as 'family'—in back of a lovely waterfront home in Lahaina. Aidan parked his Porsche in a tumbling-down garage about five blocks from the studio and usually drove his truck to work.

The front door to his studio was locked so I didn't bother knocking. I went back to Momi's store, but after an hour I grew bored waiting for a customer to show up. I crept up the back stairs allegedly searching for cleaning supplies.

The second floor on Momi's side of the building was downright scary. The windows were filmed over in red dirt and paper bags littered the floor. The humid air swirled with dust moats kicked up by my intrusion. After poking around for a few minutes, all I found was a battered plastic bucket, some petrified Bon Ami cleanser and a sour milk-smelling sponge.

I couldn't resist cracking open the French doors to steal a peek at the spectacular view. It was the same glorious sight I'd seen from Aidan's side. In fact, since the lanai stretched across the full length of the building I could've entered the second floor of his studio if his upstairs doors were unlocked.

I was gazing at the ocean toward the island of Lana'i when I heard a bell tinkle downstairs. Finally, a customer!

I stepped carefully down the dark stairwell. The light didn't work and the last thing I needed was to fall ass over teakettle and break a leg. Frank's insurance company would probably question a three thousand-dollar ambulance ride to the Wailuku hospital. And besides, knowing Frank, he'd already cut off my coverage.

"Hello?" I didn't see anyone at first.

"*Aloha*. Where's Momi?" A short, powerfully built man with tea-colored skin and short black hair that looked like he'd cut it himself stepped from behind a row of dusty canned goods.

"She's taking care of her brother today. I'm filling in for her."

"You the one who killed her dog?"

"No," I said. "I'm the one who *found* her dog when it died. From natural causes."

"You know," he said. "She loved that dog. Treated it like her baby."

"Yes, she did. What can I get for you?"

"Momi knows what I eat."

"Well, if you'll tell me, I can make darn near anything."

He sighed, as if placing an order would take a lot more energy than he wanted to squander on lunch.

"Turkey on one of those long buns. No mayonnaise. I *hate* mayonnaise. Just butter and a few of those pickle slices. The yellow ones, not those sour green ones."

I nodded. I wanted to write down his order, but there wasn't a pen or pencil in sight.

"Oh, yeah," he said, seeming to gather steam. "And I want you to cut it sideways. You know? Not straight across, but crooked-like. Make it pointy on each side of the bun."

"Got it. Anything else? Chips or pop?"

"You mean 'soda'?"

My patience was wearing thin, but I kept my smile plastered in place.

"Yeah, soda. Want a cold can or a bottle to go?"

"Momi usually just puts one in there."

"So, I guess you want the whole plate lunch—sandwich, chips and soda?"

"That's what I said."

"Great. You go pick out your chips and soda and I'll get your sandwich made up right away."

It went like that all morning. Everyone who came in accused me of killing Momi's dog. Then they'd grumble about having to tell me their standing order. It seemed these people must eat the same lunch every day.

Although business was steady, it was by no means brisk. By one-thirty I'd clocked twenty minutes since the last customer had come through the door. I began counting up the day's receipts. There'd been eighteen customers for a grand total of one hundred eleven dollars and change.

I stayed until four, although it was a waste of time. In the final two hours I sold four cans of soda—the word *pop* was stricken from my vocabulary—a small bag of pork rinds, and a bar of hand soap. So the entire day's receipts for the Shore Store was less than a hundred and twenty dollars. I felt like I was running a roadside lemonade stand.

I'd heard Aidan crashing around on his side of the building during lunch, but I'd been so busy getting the 'no mustard' versus 'heavy mustard' sandwiches to their rightful owners I hadn't had time to go see him.

As I wiped down the counter for the last time, I heard the bell tinkle on the door.

"I'm sorry, we're closed," I said, not even looking up. My thighs ached from standing and I felt as if I'd spent the previous four hours satisfying the elaborate demands of an entire busload of pop star divas. I was beat.

"Good," said a familiar deep voice. "Then I'll lock the door."

Aidan walked back to the deli area and, without saying a word, filled the sink with hot water. He added a couple squirts of detergent from a bottle he pulled from under the sink. Then he expertly broke down the meat slicer and put the blades and hand guard into the sudsy water.

"You've obviously done this before."

"Like five days a week for the past four and a half years." He smiled and held up soapy hands, cherry red from the scalding water. "It's a great way to get sculpture wax out from under my fingernails. See? It's a win-win."

"Business was slow today," I said. "I hope Momi won't be upset."

"What'd you bring in?"

I told him.

"Are you kidding? That's a kick-ass day for her. I think you got some curiosity business because people wanted to get a look at the woman who snuffed her dog."

"You know, I'm really getting tired of being accused of that."

"Well this is a small town, Nola. Everything's news, especially gossip. And it stays news until the next big thing comes along. I imagine Momi's dog dying ranks right up there with a soldier from Maui getting killed overseas or Taylor Swift tossing out the latest boyfriend. It's all fair game."

He went on. "You know, everyone thinks of this island as a big, overcrowded tourist trap. Kind of like Las Vegas with a beach. But it's not crowded. In fact only about 120,000 people live here. Maui's landmass is over seven hundred square miles. That means there's just a hundred and seventy people per square mile. That's pretty rural, when you think about it."

"Did you do all that math in your head just now, or have you memorized your little Chamber of Commerce speech?"

"I've said it a few times. But my point is: welcome to small town America."

"Or small town Kingdom of Hawaii. Take your pick."

"Yeah," he laughed. "Well, that's another story. Anyway, when we're done here, are you gonna need a ride somewhere?"

"That'd be great. Al brought me here this morning and I told him I'd walk back to Momi's, but after standing all day I doubt I could make it. I need to take a shower and then he'll pick me up so I can fix him dinner."

"Whoa. Sounds like you're pulling a double shift, don't you think?"

"Yeah, but tell that to Momi. I think I'm going to be playing 'indentured servant' for a while until this Pookie thing blows over."

"Tell you what," he said. "How about I pick up some take-out tonight? Al and Momi love the chicken from that barbeque joint up in Napili. You take your shower and I'll be back by the time you've finished."

I reached up to give him a kiss on the cheek but he turned and met me straight on with his lips. Even with my thighs throbbing from standing all day, I felt the warmth gather in my crotch. I leaned in to avoid breaking contact. It wouldn't have taken much convincing to get me to sign on for six months at the Shore Store in exchange for one uninterrupted evening with Aidan. But duty called in the form of two elderly siblings waiting for their dinner. I ended the kiss and got back to work.

When we were done cleaning up, I flipped off the lights. "By the way," Aidan said as he held the door open for me. "I've got a big favor to ask you."

CHAPTER 19

Aidan's art show was coming up and I didn't have a thing to wear. I'd been relieved to hear that the big favor he'd asked didn't include food preparation because I was in no mood to make two hundred mini crab cakes. I'd dodged chow duty, so I readily agreed when he asked me to co-host the event with him.

I'd never attended a function at an artist's gallery. Frank's idea of high culture was being first in line on opening night for a superhero action film. So what one wore or how one acted at an art gallery reception was as foreign to me as high tea with the queen.

But since arriving on Maui I'd learned to adapt quickly, so I started throwing out feelers and gathering clues, fully expecting to rise to the occasion.

"I guess this gallery reception is a pretty formal affair?"

"Not really," Aidan said. "Just sort of dressy, you know."

I didn't know. I tried a different source of information.

"Auntie Momi, have you ever gone to one of Aidan's art shows?"

"Oh yes," she said. "They have those little wasabi cheese puffs. Those are so *ono*. My mouth waters just thinking about them. They serve wine, too, but I don't drink it. It's always the sour kind."

"What do you wear?"

"My *mu'umu'u*. Usually the good one I save for church."

Momi pretty much lived in *mu'umu'us*. She had a closet-full, from ratty cotton housedress types to glorious hand-painted silks. I took her comment about wearing her church *mu'umu'u* as a sign I needed to buy a new dress.

Three days before the show, I closed the Shore Store promptly at three to give me time to drive to Kahului to shop. All the big stores were on that side of the island. I had to find something fast, so I checked out the malls first. I sprinted around the Queen Ka'ahumanu Center, the Maui Mall, even Wal-Mart and the discount stores, but I came up blank.

Everything I found resembled matronly mother-of-the-bride dresses. They might be a hit in Omaha, but they were laughable on a tropical island. Lavender polyester crepe? Black wool gabardine—accented with gold braid? What were these retailers thinking? Most probably the buyers selecting the merchandise weren't within three thousand miles of Hawaii. They were sitting at desks in Los Angeles or Boise. If they *were* local, it was hard to imagine the sense of humor it would take to order thick black wool sheaths with matching jackets knowing the customers would be wearing them in eighty-four degree weather with seventy-five percent humidity.

I drove home in rush hour traffic keeping my nothing-to-wear panic at bay by switching my gaze from the road ahead to the nearly flat ocean. The water was ablaze from the reflection of a fuchsia and tangerine sunset. As if choreographed just for me, the sun plunked below the horizon the moment I pulled into Al's driveway.

"Show me what you bought," said Momi as I came into the kitchen. I held up my palms to show her I was empty-handed.

"You didn't find nothing?" Her forehead creased in concern.

"Nope. Unless I'm willing to wear something even the Queen of England would turn down as too matronly, it seems I'm out of luck."

"Did you try everywhere?" she said. She started rattling off the store directory for the mall. "Macy's, Island Girl, Blue Ginger, and Coconut Company? How about Sears, or—."

I interrupted, unwilling to review my entire list of strikeouts. "I went to them all, believe me."

"Hmm. Well, maybe you should wear something of mine."

Now, Auntie Momi was a delightful lady and she'd been more than generous to me, so I didn't want to disrespect her offer. But the woman had at least a hundred pounds—as well as almost thirty years—on me.

"That's sweet of you, Auntie, but I don't think—"

This time she cut me off.

"No, that's it. I've got some special things that would look wonderful on you. They're boxed away and I'll probably never get a chance to wear them. We'll find you something tonight after dinner."

Why, oh why, couldn't Macy's have stocked one measly dress in a color other than funeral black?

For dinner I served Asian-style chicken wraps I'd concocted from ingredients we stocked at the Shore Store. Al and Momi raved about them.

"These are really *ono*. You should sell them at the store," Momi said.

"I don't know," I said. "I doubt if the folks who eat the same thing every day would give them a try."

"You'd be surprised. I think they get tired of what they eat but they're just too lazy to order something different. You should give away little samples. Not too much; just a tiny bite."

Aidan came over and picked us up for the ride back to Momi's. When we pulled in front of her cottage, she asked him to come in and help get some boxes down from the attic. I felt my chest tighten with dread. I'd have to find a nice way to sidestep wearing whatever was in those boxes. I visualized a mothball-infused *mu'umu'u* with big pink cabbage roses. Or, maybe a 1980's plus-size dressy suit with thick shoulder pads and a half-pleat skirt.

"Auntie, I really haven't given up on shopping. I should look around a little more."

"No," she said. "I've got some lovely things that would look beautiful on you. You'll see. Leave it to Auntie. You'll be the best dressed *wahine* there."

Aidan climbed the pull-down stairs. He turned on the attic light and then let out a low whistle.

Momi shouted at him from the base of the ladder. "Why you making that noise? You've seen those boxes before. You're the one who put them up there."

"Yeah, but I never really looked. You've got one heck of a fire trap here, Momi."

"Well, forget about that. Get me the boxes with the Japanese writing."

Japanese writing? I sat down on the sofa, expecting the black blotches to come marching into view at any moment.

"You mean these?" Aidan handed down a tattered yellowed cardboard box with Japanese characters running vertically down one side.

"Yes, that's them. There should be three or four up there."

I heard him rummaging around for another minute before he handed down two more cartons.

"That's all I could find." He thumped down the creaking ladder, brushing cobwebs—real or imagined—from his eyebrows.

"Okay, sweetie," Momi said to Aidan. "Now you go home and leave Noelani and me to find the perfect outfit for your show on Friday. She's gonna look good, for sure." She grinned and nodded in my direction.

I looked over at the crumbling cardboard boxes festooned with foreign lettering and cringed as I imagined what lurked inside.

Aidan's truck roared away from the curb and Momi went to work cutting through decades-old yellowed strapping tape.

"Those boxes look pretty old, Auntie."

"Oh, yes. They're very old."

From the first box she pulled out a shiny fabric in brilliant scarlet. She held it up. A pattern of cranes and bamboo had been intricately embroidered on it in gold and black.

"Wow. That's beautiful. Is it silk?"

"The best kind. My Koma brought these home for me after the war."

"You mean the Second World War?"

"The Big War. We haven't had a good war since that one," she said. "He was stationed on Okinawa for a year during the occupation. I was just a girl, but he gave me these later on when we got married. He felt sorry for those people there. They were practically starving after Japan surrendered, so the soldiers bought their treasures for cash. It was sad, really."

"I'll bet. So are these Japanese kimonos?"

"Kimonos and some silk shawls. But only the best. Most are antique. See how smooth and heavy they are?"

The fabrics were astonishing. I'd always leaned more toward cooking than sewing, so I was no expert in appraising antique textiles. But even with my untrained eye I could see these kimonos were works of art.

"Pick one and try it on," she said. "You need to see how you look."

I picked a deep shade of coral, with a pattern of willow trees and a flowing stream embroidered on the back. But I had no idea how to put it on.

"Ah. I've never worn one either," Momi said. "We need to get Mrs. Fujioka over here."

She called her neighbor. The tiny woman was at the front door in a flash. She looked Momi's age or maybe slightly older. She wore her black hair, tinged with gray, in a tight bun at the nape of her neck.

I followed her lead and bowed during our introduction. Mrs. Fujioka seemed totally at ease with the gesture, while I felt self-conscious. Straightening, she headed for the kimonos. As she pulled them from the boxes, tears welled in her eyes.

"My mother had kimono just like this one," she said in a soft voice. She reverently held a folded cobalt blue and ivory silk in her upturned hands as if it were the widow's flag at a military funeral. "It was her favorite."

Momi hesitated only a second. "Perhaps this one is from your family?"

"Oh, no. My mother lived in Nagasaki..." She didn't finish.

"Well, it's yours now," said Momi. "It's probably from the same bolt of cloth. It's important to keep such things in the family."

Mrs. Fujioka's eyes opened wide. She bowed deeply to Momi and muttered something in Japanese. When she stood back up, she'd regained her placid composure. She picked up the precious kimono and ran her hand across it, smoothing the fabric.

"You are a great and true friend, Mrs. Anakua."

"So are you, Mrs. Fujioka."

Mrs. Fujioka assisted me in stepping into the coral-colored kimono I'd picked out. She wrapped the sash around and around my waist. She told me the Japanese words for all the different pieces and wraps, but I quickly forgot them in my eagerness to see what I'd look like once I was encased in the elegant costume.

I felt a little awkward in the kimono, but vowed to get over it. It was an exquisite look—graceful and charming. I couldn't wait to see Aidan's face when he picked me up to take me to the show.

On Friday, I spent two hours getting ready. I didn't need a lot of make-up because my tanned face looked better with only a light dusting of blush than a coat of full-blown foundation, but I did give some attention to eyeliner, mascara and deep amethyst shadow to make my eyes stand out.

I pulled my hair into a sleek knot at the top of my head, with a few curly tendrils at my brow and wisps along the sides. Momi helped me smooth the back and then she coated my head with hairspray until it felt as stiff as shredded wheat. I wasn't crazy about the texture, but I knew it would hold tight for the entire three hour affair.

Mrs. Fujioka appeared at just the right moment to help me don the kimono. She tugged and wrapped and cinched me until I felt like a swaddled infant.

At exactly six o'clock, Aidan pulled up in the Carrera.

"Oh, no," I said, as we all peeked out the front window. "I forgot. How am I supposed to get into that sports car?"

"He'll place you in it," Mrs. Fujioka said. "That's how it's done in Japan."

I glanced over to see if she was kidding. She looked dead serious.

"Wow," Aidan said, as I stood in the open front door. "You look fantastic." Then his voice dropped and he ran a hand across his forehead. "But I can't let you go looking like that."

"Why? Do you think it's too goofy?"

"No. You look great. But I'm supposed to be show-casing *my* art tonight. You're going to steal my thunder."

I wasn't sure what to do. "Do you want me to change?"

"Of course not. That was a compliment. I mean it, though—you'll steal my thunder. But that's okay because I just got a great idea."

He didn't elaborate and we needed to leave to avoid being late.

As Mrs. Fujioka predicted, Aidan simply lifted me up and hoisted me into the low-slung car. It took a little effort for me to reach around and get my seat belt on, but soon we were on our way.

Getting out wasn't nearly as difficult as getting in. I walked in baby steps once I was vertical because the kimono was very confining. But I probably would have walked that way anyway because the little shuffling steps added a certain authenticity to the look.

Aidan unlocked the rear gallery door and we went in. The caterers had already set up an eye-popping buffet of *pupus*, or appetizers. Free-standing ice buckets holding champagne bottles were placed strategically around the three-room space.

"Here," he said, moving quickly to a locked display case. "This will help me regain some thunder."

He pulled a gold necklace from the case. It was a smoothly fashioned Japanese symbol on a short gold chain.

"It's perfect," he said, clasping it around my neck. "It's the character for 'peace'."

I gazed at myself in a small oval mirror on the display case. The necklace lay across the silk of the kimono in just the right position.

I felt like a starlet at the Oscars in borrowed Henry Winston diamonds. Oh sure, everyone knows it's a "Queen for a Day" moment and the jewelry has to be returned the next morning, but for one night, I was swathed in silk with a glinting gold necklace around my neck.

Even though Aidan had numerous other jewelry models positioned around the room—all of them half my age—he never left my side.

The gallery show was a huge success.

Aidan's designs and craftsmanship got high praise both from the attendees and from the review the next day in *The Maui News*. Of course, the Maui newspaper has a soft spot for locals. I'd never read a cranky opinion of any local artist's work.

They printed a picture of Aidan and me talking with the gallery owner and his wife. In the photo caption they called me Aidan's 'colleague' and they described my apparel as a 'stunning antique kimono'.

I'd never been in the newspaper before. I always figured my obituary would be my only shot.

CHAPTER 20

My goal for the next week was to memorize every finicky whim of my lunch regulars at the Shore Store. That involved solving riddles such as: Why did Momi keep a sticky jar of Major Grey's mango chutney in the deli refrigerator? Answer: A housepainter named Moki considered chutney a critical element in his thinly-sliced chicken breast on rye. Some of the wild flavor combinations demanded by the customers gave me hope. Perhaps these folks might be willing to try a bit of culinary innovation after all.

As Momi predicted, the Asian chicken wraps were a hit. I pushed the envelope by using spinach tortillas, which gave them a jade green hue. Still, even with the unusual color, they flew out of the deli case at a rate that made late-comers go wanting.

After my success with the wraps, I introduced an assortment of cold salads. I started with a spinach salad with walnuts, dried cranberries and tangy raspberry vinaigrette. Emboldened by my victory in getting some iron and fiber into their diet, I plied them with a mélange of baby bib lettuce from the cool green hills of Kula in upcountry Maui, tart green apple slivers and blue cheese. It took a leap of faith to foist apples and blue cheese on people raised in the tropics, but bless their hearts, they were willing to give it a go.

Soon I'd filled the refrigerated case with all types of salads. Even if the regulars ordered their usual—and truthfully, most still did—I'd throw in a tiny plastic cup of whatever salad I was featuring that day as an incentive to expand their gustatory horizons.

Week by week I watched my customer base grow. I now served women who worked in the Front Street shops along with my usual clientele of tradesmen and taxi drivers.

"I didn't know you had these great salads," said Jennifer, from the Quicksilver Surf Shop. "My boss is a vegetarian. She'd really like these."

Sure enough, the next day, Jennifer came in with her boss. Jennifer ordered a sesame noodle salad with chicken and mandarin oranges. Her boss eyed it hungrily but stuck with a hearts of romaine with avocado and grapefruit sections.

Lahaina was fertile ground for culinary inspiration. With four Michelin-rated restaurants within a half-mile of the Shore Store, I'd often run into celebrity chefs—both local and from the mainland—while checking out the wholesale produce warehouse.

One early morning I heard a voice off to my left as I sniffed a fragrant bouquet of fresh basil.

"Nola, is that you?" he said. Like being able to identify a familiar song after hearing only a few notes, when I heard him say my name I immediately recognized the distinctive accent of Lech Gorelczenko from Mark Allen's.

"Yes," I said. "I'm amazed you remember me."

"How could I forget such a beautiful face?"

"Thank you," I stammered. Bald-faced flattery unnerved me a little. I waited for the *just kidding* follow-up, but his countenance remained serious, so I let down my guard a bit.

"What are you doing here?" he said. "Have you decided to open a restaurant and make the rest of us nervous?"

"Oh, no. I'm just helping out Momi Anakua. She's the lady who owns the Shore Store next to Aidan's studio. The store has a little deli counter in back and I'm buying provisions."

"Of course. I know Momi," he said, smiling. "Aidan has brought her to my restaurant many times."

"Well, good. I mean, that's nice. Anyway, I'm helping her out for a few weeks."

"Are you doing this because you ran over her dog?"

It'd been more than two months since Pookie's death, but unlike Momi's dog, the accusations refused to die.

"I didn't hit her dog. That was a misunderstanding. He was old and died of natural causes. She has a new dog now."

He nodded. "How is she doing?"

"She's great." Dragging up my Pookie defense for about the hundredth time made me lose all interest in swapping recipes or commiserating with him on the scarcity of papayas at this time of year. "I guess I better get back to the store."

"It was good to see you again," he said. "Come by the restaurant sometime and I'll fix you a plate."

I perked up. For me, Lech's offer to fix me a plate was like having Donald Trump offer to take you for a spin in his helicopter.

"Thanks, I'd really like that."

I walked back to the Shore Store vowing to come up with something that would really put the deli on the map. The mangoes had looked good, but what I was really in the mood for was a fabulous tomato salad. I love Italian *caprese* salad—fresh buffalo mozzarella, aromatic basil, succulent tomatoes splashed with balsamic vinegar and extra-virgin olive oil. But I'd never made it because I hadn't been satisfied with the tomatoes I'd found at the market. It might be worth it to try growing some of my own. The upstairs lanai would offer late afternoon sun and no one could pilfer them when I wasn't looking.

I tapped on Aidan's door a few minutes before our normal quitting time.

"C'mon in," he said. He was wearing low-slung, threadbare jeans and rubber sandals. That's all. The jeans were shredded at the hem, making him look like an aging Adonis trying out for the role of Scarecrow in the *Wizard of Oz*.

"Hi," I said, "I've got a proposition for you."

"Why is it I already know my answer's going to be 'yes'?"

"No, really." I stepped back as he reached to pull me in for a kiss. "I'm serious. I'd like to set out some tomato plants on the lanai."

He blinked—twice.

"I'm waiting for the punch line," he said.

"That's it. I just wanted to be sure you wouldn't mind. We share the space so I thought I should ask."

"Sweetheart, you can keep a pony up there for all I care. Say, do you have one of those chicken wraps left?"

"You know those are the first to go."

"True. But what I don't know is why you never set one aside for me. It's not like I'm going to give up asking, or haven't you noticed?"

I found a crack on the floor and suddenly found it fascinating.

"Sorry," I said. "I'm just so busy over there I can't think straight."

"How many people today?"

"I don't know. It's impossible to keep track anymore. The daily till is averaging over a thousand dollars."

"Whew," he whistled. "That's great for Momi."

"Yeah, well, what's great for Momi is pretty much killing me."

"You know, I bet it would be easier if it wasn't all take-out."

That puzzled me. I waited for him to go on.

"Think about it," he said. "If you had a few tables and chairs, you could hire some help and make more money. Dine-in is a lot slower pace than takeout, and the prices are higher."

"But it's a store."

"Oh, c'mon. How many bags of groceries have you sold lately? You're a cook, Nola. Not a shopkeeper."

"But what about when Momi comes back?"

He laughed. I felt myself flush. He was right. She was never coming back. It would probably fall to me to find someone to take my place when I went home to Seattle.

"Back to the tables and chairs," I said. "You think I should ask her?"

"I think you should just do it. You know what they say: it's better to beg forgiveness than ask permission. She doesn't care what you do. Ever notice the first thing out of her mouth is, 'What was the till today'? I don't remember the last time she asked what you sold. All she cares about is how much money she made."

Again, he was right. Auntie Momi, former champion of the downtrodden masses, had become a raging capitalist now that she had an unpaid employee. She never asked me who'd stopped in; or if so-and-so's wife had had that baby yet. It was all about the money. Still, I felt I should ask before I made any big changes. It seemed only right.

That evening I made an attempt to broach the subject.

"You and Al seem to be doing pretty good together. Do you want to keep going over there during the day?"

"Uh-huh. We do okay."

"Do you sometimes miss going to the store?"

"Not so much. Hulu doesn't like it at the store."

To the best of my knowledge, her new dog had never been to the store. I'd finally caught on how first Pookie, and now Hulu, functioned as Momi's alter ego. If she didn't want to do something, it was always the dog that had a problem with it. If she wanted to go to bed a little earlier than usual, then Hulu had had a tough day and needed to hit the hay. If she wanted me to fix a steak for dinner she'd comment how Hulu wished he had a bone to chew on.

So it seemed Momi wasn't all that interested in discussing the store. Probably Aidan was right. I should just do what I wanted and mention it to her later.

I spent the next weekend cleaning the first floor and tossing ancient grocery items into garbage bags. In two days I'd completely filled the dumpster in the alley. I started cramming the overflow bags into the back storeroom. When that got full, I asked Aidan if he had any extra space I could use until I could haul it away.

"Sure, but you'll need to get the stuff out of here by the end of the month. I'm doing a commission job for a big hotel chain and this place will be filled to the rafters by early March."

I was dying to ask how much he'd make for such a big job. I was slaving away for mere room and board, but I figured Aidan probably got a thousand dollars or more for his sculptures.

"Yeah," he said, smiling as if he'd noticed the gears turning in my head. "This contract is worth big bucks. I'm getting kind of tired of making these guys," he patted the flank of a spinner dolphin, "but the higher the price goes, the more people want 'em. It's weird."

"If I may ask, what does a piece like this cost?"

"The price for this contract is fifty thousand."

"You have a *fifty thousand* dollar contract?" I was horrified to feel some spit fly out of my mouth with the 'f's' in 'fifty'.

"Whoa." He stepped back as if I'd showered him, but I saw the gleam in his eye that he'd managed to impress me. "It's fifty grand *per piece*, but please hold your spit. I don't want you getting dehydrated."

I glanced around for a chair to fall into.

"How many pieces does the contract call for?" I plopped into an old rattan rocker.

"Six."

"Whew. Three hundred thousand dollars? I'm stunned."

"Now I guess you're gonna make me pay full price for that chicken wrap you'll be saving for me."

"Damn straight, brudda. And don't forget to tip."

That night I went to bed pondering how I could ask Auntie Momi for a raise.

CHAPTER 21

Some people believe they're more powerful than they are. They think they can summon the rain and it will pour. Or they can wish bad luck on someone and bring on a pox. It's a function of mind over matter, which I tend to accept as having some validity. But sometimes, events, both bad and good, just happen. Without reason, and with no earthly or cosmic cause propelling them into motion.

"What do you mean, you want me to pay you?" said Momi. "I'm just a poor old woman. I don't have money to pay you for helping me out."

"But Auntie, your till from the store is ten times what it was before I started. You don't have to give me a lot of money, but I need at least a little. My divorce isn't final and I won't get anything until it's settled."

"How much do you need?"

"Could you feel comfortable paying me, say, seven dollars an hour? That's less than minimum wage. It would come to about fifty dollars a day."

"Fifty dollars a day! When I was a young girl, I worked at my father's store for fifty dollars a *month*! I think maybe I could give you fifty dollars a week, but that's all."

I let it go. Momi was generous with her love but not with her money. I'd spent almost all the cash I'd brought with me, and Frank had closed the only credit card account with my name on it. Even with my room and board covered, living on Maui was expensive. Shampoo, clothing, the little bit of make-up I wore. Everything cost nearly twice as much as back home. I had to get my hands on some money or return to the mainland. And Al's final check-up was more than a week away.

With my back against the wall, there was no other option but to call Frank. Maybe he'd agree to give me an advance on the sale of the house and business. I waited until Momi was out walking Hulu. It was four o'clock in Lahaina, but already six in Seattle.

"Well hello, stranger," he said, answering his cell on the third ring. "I wondered when you'd get tired of coconuts and palm trees and finally come home."

"Frank, I'm calling to ask a favor."

I felt him silently start up with the fifteen-second countdown. I waited patiently, mentally counting along with him.

Sure enough, when I got to *fifteen-thousand*, he spoke, "You have the temerity to ask me for a favor after I've humbled myself to you and you've been nothing short of spiteful in return?"

"Look, Frank. I'm not asking for a kidney. I just need you to send me something that's already mine."

"What is it you want? Money?"

"Yes." This wasn't going well. I mentally kicked myself for not calling my lawyer and asking him to shake down Frank. "I've run out of cash."

"Nola, I don't have any to give you. Do you have any idea what they're saying my business is worth? One and a half *million* dollars. It's outrageous. I'm having another valuation done, but if the next one comes in at anything over a million I'm screwed. There's no way I can get my hands on that kind of cash to pay you off."

I did my own counting to fifteen before I replied.

"Frank, you're the one who had the affair, not me. Maybe you should've checked with your CPA before sticking it to that boy at your health club."

I clicked off the call. Had I really said that? And had I really just hung up on Frank? I stared in the mirror over Momi's dining room table. The last time I'd looked so smug was when I was four months' pregnant and pretty darn proud of it.

But pride goeth before the fall. I couldn't afford even a pinch of pride. I'd pissed off Frank, my only potential source of funds. The irony of the whole mess was once my divorce was final I'd be awash in cash, but until then I'd be holding out my hand every week while Momi begrudgingly counted five ten-dollar bills into my palm.

My marriage to Frank had hardly been a model of gender equity. But I'd never had to play *Mother may I?* for pocket money. I especially resented it since I was putting in long, exhausting hours at the Shore Store.

"Auntie, I'm afraid I'm going to have to go back to Seattle."

"You aren't happy here? I thought you and Aidan were, you know, boyfriend and girlfriend. You can't leave."

"I don't want to leave. But I'm broke."

"How can you say that? I give you free rent and Al pays for your food. Are you going back to be with your husband?"

"No. I'm going back because I need a job that pays me a living wage."

She stared me down, but I held her glare. I hoped she'd reconsider and offer me a bit more cash, but it wasn't to be. I went to bed that night feeling sad to leave, but relieved I'd made my decision. Limbo's a lousy place to hang out.

As I took my shower on Friday morning I mentally prepared for my return to Seattle. In another week Al would go for his ten week check-up. He'd resumed his morning tai chi, and had added a brisk walk every evening before dinner. I felt fairly certain he'd be fine living alone again, but I hated not keeping my promise. I hadn't discussed finding my replacement for the Shore Store with Momi, but I figured if she needed my help she'd ask.

I dried off and slipped on one of Auntie's old *mu'umu'u*'s that she'd given me to wear around the house. As I passed her closed door I heard Hulu whining. It sounded as if he needed to go out. It wasn't like Momi to ignore the slightest peep from the normally quiet little dog.

I tapped on the door.

"Momi? I think I hear Hulu. Do you want me to take him outside?"

Silence.

"Auntie?" I tapped louder. The dog barked. It was the most noise I'd ever heard out of him. Something wasn't right.

I pushed the door open a crack and saw Auntie Momi was still in bed. Hulu jumped down and came to the door. Momi didn't stir, even as the dog jumped back up on the bed and began whining again.

"Come here, Hulu," I hissed. "I'll take you outside."

His eyes darted my way, but he stayed put. He whined louder.

"Oh, for Pete's sake. Come on."

I went in to get him. In the gloom of the shuttered room, I saw Auntie Momi's face. It was the color of plumber's putty.

I tightly clamped my hand over my mouth to prevent myself from screaming. With my other hand I reached out and gently touched her arm. Her cool, rigid arm.

I ran from the room and skidded into the kitchen. Then I grabbed the phone and called Aidan's cell number.

"Please pick up. Please, please," I prayed. I knew he was busy with his sculpture contract and often ignored the ringing phone.

He answered.

"Aidan," I said. My voice sounded breathy, as if I'd just finished a long run. Then—nothing. I couldn't find the words.

"Hi, gorgeous," he said. "What's up?"

"Oh," I choked. "Momi's gone."

"She's probably out walking the dog," he said.

"No. I mean she's here, in bed. But I think she may have died."

"Don't move. I'll be right there."

Aidan burst through the door a few minutes later. We went to Momi's room and found Hulu still tucked up next to her on the bed. His fierce protective stare stopped us in our tracks.

"Oh, Aidan," I said. I gripped the molding around the door frame. "I had no idea she wasn't feeling well."

"What did she eat last night? Was she upset about anything? "

I felt a stab of defensiveness.

"I, uh, I ..." Try as I might, I couldn't recall what we'd eaten for dinner. And I wasn't ready to talk about asking Momi for a raise, or that I'd told her I'd be heading back to Seattle.

"We need to call 9-1-1," he said in a measured tone, as if making a big effort to mask his irritation. "Look, I wasn't implying anything. I just want to be able to relay information to the paramedics."

"Let me think." I blew out a breath and turned away from gazing at Momi's inert body. "After work yesterday you dropped me off at Al's and we ate chicken stir fry. Then when we got back here she went to bed a little early—around nine, I think. And now that I think about it, she's been complaining that her arm ached. She thought it was from holding onto Hulu's leash too tightly."

I was justifiably proud of my powers of recollection given that my housemate was lying no more than ten feet away—dead. I peeked into the dimly-lit room and wondered about her unwillingness to pay me a decent wage. Had she felt guilty? Had she fretted over what she'd do once I quit? I should have been more persuasive in my negotiations and told her about my plans to add the dine-in business. Maybe I could have put her mind at ease if I'd simply explained how I'd planned to bring in more money every week. Had I given her cause to fret and worry? Had I *killed* her?

When the paramedics arrived, they couldn't find a pulse. They immediately called the police. A Maui county police car arrived a few minutes later.

"There will be an autopsy, since she died at home and she wasn't under medical supervision," said the police officer. I watched the paramedics pull a sheet-covered gurney out of the back of the ambulance. "She'll be taken to the morgue at Maui General. Are you family? They'll need a family member to sign for the autopsy."

Aidan and I exchanged a grim glance. Finding Auntie Momi had been horrible. Telling Al he'd have to sign off on an autopsy to cut open his beloved sister would be ten times worse.

A strange unsettled feeling came over me. Since I'd arrived, all kinds of havoc had befallen the Kanekoa family: Al's heart attack, Pookie's death, and now Auntie Momi. It was ridiculous, not to mention narcissistic, to assume my being there had anything to do with the barrage of bad luck. But I was having a hard time selling that to my conscience.

CHAPTER 22

After the paramedics left it was deathly quiet in Momi's cottage. Hulu huddled at my feet trembling like a rabbit. Every now and then he'd get up and search from room to room, as if he'd already forgotten the morning's events. Momi had trimmed the clump of hair over the dog's eyes and his beseeching stare was heartbreaking. Since Hulu was Momi's stand-in offspring, I directed my condolences his way.

"I'm so sorry. I feel terrible about this. She was a good woman, and she treated me like *ohana*."

I left out telling him about how she expected me to work for prison wages because it seemed inappropriate given the situation. Besides, it's never wise to dish flak at someone else's mother. My own mother could probably have beat out Joan Crawford for the lead in *Mommy Dearest,* but I never allowed my friends to put her down.

The cottage walls closed in tighter with each tick of the clock. I needed to get out of there, but I couldn't go because I knew the phone would start ringing at any moment. Word travels fast on an island, and at least half a dozen neighbors had seen the paramedics pull up.

Around noon, I went to the kitchen to make a cup of tea. The phone on the wall jangled. I jerked as if it was a gunshot. I sucked in a breath and picked up the receiver.

"Mmm, wiss eek tee," said the caller, gargling the words. Then there was a huge clearing of the throat.

"Malia? Is that you?"

"Yes," her voice quavered like a witch cracking open the spooky mansion door to some unsuspecting trick-or-treaters.

"Oh, Malia. This is horrible. I'm so sorry."

"What happened? I need to know *everything*." She said 'everything' with such force, it sounded as if she figured I knew way more than I did.

"Malia, there's not much to tell. Momi was tired last night and went to bed early. She didn't eat much dinner, but I thought maybe she just wasn't in the mood for chicken stir fry."

I waited for her to chime in, but all I heard was snuffling and then a swishing sound. I figured that must have been a Kleenex brushing against the mouthpiece.

"They took her to Wailuku." I balked at saying anything more.

"I know," she said after another throat clearing. "Jim's on a corporate jet on his way over there now. I'll be flying commercial in the morning."

I was dumbstruck. I mentally started Frank's stupid counting routine to give myself time to think, but caught myself, stopping at four-thousand.

"Jim's flying on what?"

"One of the drug companies keeps a corporate jet at Sea-Tac Airport and they offered to fly Jim to Maui. He's going to witness the signing of her death certificate and make sure they treat Auntie with respect."

Wow. Now I understood why mothers wanted their kids to be doctors—or at least marry one.

"That's good. No, that's great. So, now your dad won't have to deal with it."

"Jim said he needed to get on that plane or he was afraid we'd end up going to two funerals." Leave it to Jim to cut to the chase.

"You'll be here tomorrow night?"

"Yeah—" She'd continued talking, but Momi's call-waiting bleated a long beep, cutting out the rest of the sentence.

"Malia? Excuse me, but I just got the call-waiting tone. I need to check and see who it is."

"That's okay. I'm hanging up now. I'll see you tomorrow."

I clicked the hang up button. "Hello?"

I heard a garbled static sound. Finally, a male voice said, "Mom?"

I thought he might have said "Momi," since it wasn't a very good connection.

"She's not here right now." I flinched at my deceit, but I hadn't figured out a good way to disclose the grim news to friends and family.

"Who is this?" the guy said.

"I'm Nola, Momi's..." What was I? Her houseguest? Her employee? The person who found her dead body? "I'm her brother Al's caregiver."

"Well, when my mom comes back would you tell her to call me? This is her son, Tommy, over in California. Tell her I've got some good news."

I felt like a ghoul, but I deepened the deception, still unable to come up with the right words for the truth.

"Would you like to leave a message?"

"Yeah, okay. Tell her it looks like I'm finally coming home. I got an offer from the Maui Sheriff's Department. I'll tell her all about it when she calls."

"Fine," I said. I felt like I'd managed to ramp up a bad situation into the appalling category. "I'm sure she'll be happy to hear that."

I hung up, vowing to not answer Momi's phone for the rest of the day.

About an hour later, my cell phone rang. It was Aidan.

"How're you doing?" he said.

"Not so great."

"Me neither. I got the paramedics to stop by Al's after they dropped off Momi. I wanted them to be there when I broke the news."

"How's he doing?"

"Better than I expected," he said.

"Did you hear that Dr. Jim's on his way over?"

"Yeah, Malia asked him to call me from the jet. Must be nice to be able to just trot out to the airport and grab a ride like that."

I wanted to remind him that with a three hundred thousand dollar contract he could more than afford to fly in a private jet, but I stifled my envy. After all, green wasn't my color.

"Is Al still at the house, or did they take him to the hospital?"

"Are you serious?" Aidan snorted a laugh. "He barely let them put the blood pressure cuff on him. He's lying down in his room. They offered to call his doctor to prescribe a sedative, but he got totally belligerent."

"I'll bet. Does he know Malia's coming tomorrow?"

"Oh, yeah. I think that's what's holding him together. Oh, by the way, Malia doesn't know about the autopsy and Jim doesn't want her to know."

I searched my fuzzy memory to recall if I'd let it slip. I remember her saying something about him making sure they treated Momi with respect, but I was pretty sure the A-word hadn't come up.

"Do you think I should stay here at Momi's tonight?" I said. "Or go over to Al's?"

"He needs you here. I'll come get you in ten minutes if you can get ready that fast."

"I'm already more than ready to get out of here."

I packed my little suitcase as well as Hulu's dog bed, chew toys and food. I looked around the tidy cottage as if I'd never see it again. It was a rental, so no telling when the lease might be up, or even if there was a lease.

When Aidan pulled up, he looked a lot better than the last time I'd seen him. The color had returned to his cheeks and his eyes were no longer dulled by shock. I was also pleased to note he'd regained most of its 'guy in charge' swagger. Hulu and I scrambled into the front seat of the truck. As we bounced along on the way back to

Al's, I finally allowed the reality of Momi's untimely death to sink in.

I swiped away a tear and broke the silence.

"I've got some more bad news," I said. "Well, actually good news. Just bad timing."

He glanced over at me, squinting in the brilliant sunshine that poured through the windshield.

"Momi's son, Tommy, called. He said he's gotten a job with the sheriff's department over here."

"How'd he take it when you told him about his mother?"

I placed my hand over my mouth in a kind of speak-no-evil gesture and shook my head. He rolled his eyes.

"You didn't tell him?" He seemed to be pondering what I'd done, or in this case failed to do. Then he blew out a breath. "It's probably best. The Anakua boys have been gone a long time. They hardly ever came to visit her. I bet the guilt is going to hit them hard." He sounded less than sympathetic.

I was surprised to see Jim climb out of a taxi at a little after five o'clock that afternoon. Apparently what took almost six hours on a commercial jet had taken only four and a half in the sleek Learjet. He said the pharmaceutical company that owned the plane had authorized the pilot to remain on Maui and take him back in a few days, but he'd declined the offer.

"I bet I didn't make any points with that pilot," he laughed. "He was probably planning to hit the beach or maybe the golf course. But I'm already into those guys big-time for hauling me over here. My chief of surgery will not be amused when he hears I accepted a free ride. And if I asked them to take me back, I'd lose my hospital privileges for sure."

"I'm so glad you're here," I said. I gave him a quick hug. "Now Al won't have to know about the autopsy. He's such a worrier. I hate to think what it would have done to him. But I didn't realize you could get in trouble for riding in a drug company's plane."

"Well, here's how it stacked up for me: I could accept a freebie from a vendor, which is considered unprofessional, or I could decline and probably put my wife's father back in the hospital. I'm not stupid. My job is only a small part of my life; my marriage is 'til death do us part. That made it a pretty easy decision."

While Aidan explained to Jim how to get to Maui General, I went back to Al's bedroom to check on him.

He was sleeping peacefully on his back, his hands at his sides, just as Momi had been that morning. I slipped in and lightly placed my fingertips on his chest. I blew out a breath when I felt it rise and fall.

"Don't worry, Noelani," he said, not opening his eyes. "I'm still here."

I fought back the urge to apologize for Momi's death. Why did I feel so responsible?

He slowly rose and propped himself up on one elbow. Then he took my hand.

"I know you feel bad. I do too. But she's never been happy since Koma's passing. She missed him too much. Now she's with him."

I nodded. I couldn't talk because my throat had closed up tight.

"You know," he went on, "I miss my Lokelani too. But I've got Malia and Lani and my granddaughters. I love being a grandpa. Momi didn't have no one. Her boys left and they never came back."

Al probably thought the tears I swiped from my eyes were for Momi. And some of them were. But what really hit hard was the realization that sometimes children leave their mothers who love them and they never come back. Or, sadder still, they come back too late.

CHAPTER 23

On Sunday afternoon, Jim, Al, and I were getting ready to go pick up Malia at the airport when we heard a commotion outside. I peeked through the kitchen window and saw the charge of the not-so-light brigade ambling across Al's lawn.

"We're going with you," Lani said, her arm gesturing in a sweeping motion to include at least a dozen assorted aunties, uncles and cousins. "Malia needs us there for support, and it'll give us a chance to talk about the funeral."

"I think Momi's son, Tommy, is coming in tomorrow," I said. "Shouldn't we wait for him before making plans?"

"Eh," Lani said. "What does he know? He's been gone fifteen years."

Had it been fifteen years since Momi's son had been home? I had at least a dozen questions, but it wasn't the time or the place.

We all piled into the same three decrepit vans that had come to the airport when Malia and I arrived in

December. Lani's husband took the lead, Al's van was in the middle, and cousin Paulo brought up the rear. I pitied any drivers who attempted to pass our little convey. The vans remained bumper-to-bumper as if they were driving in dense fog on an unfamiliar road. A guy in a red Mustang convertible made an attempt to swing out into on-coming traffic, apparently to dodge in front of the rear van, but Paulo nudged up closer, leaving no room for him to slip in. The Mustang dropped back. I was glad we were wedged in the middle so I couldn't see the more-than-likely mid-finger salute that accompanied his retreat.

At the airport, Malia squeezed past other travelers coming down the escalator. Her eyes were puffy and her hair was pulled back in a sloppy ponytail. She looked exhausted.

"Daddy!" She fell into Al's embrace.

"*Ku'uipo*," he said, "My little sweetheart. It's so good to see you again."

"But Auntie Momi." She slipped into full boo-hoo mode.

"I know, I know," he said, "But she's with Koma now. They're back together again."

I marveled at his ability to remain stalwart. The rest of the relatives joined Malia in a chorus of sniffling and sobbing.

Jim turned to me. "I think this may be the dress rehearsal for the funeral."

I waved him over to a spot away from the crowd. "When is the autopsy scheduled?" I said in a hushed voice. I had no idea how he'd manage to attend the gruesome procedure without alerting Malia to the fact it was taking place.

"First thing tomorrow," he said. Then in a booming voice he added, "Oh, did I tell you I'm going to try out that new Gold's Gym in Ka'anapali tomorrow morning?"

I squinted at him in confusion. Then I figured it out.

"Oh, yeah?" I said. "Good idea to get there first thing in the morning. I've heard it gets really crowded later on."

"That's right," he said. "It'll probably take me two or three hours. You know, signing up and then figuring out how all the stuff works. No two gyms are alike, you know."

I shifted back to whisper mode. "You're so great," I said. "I hope Malia knows what a prince you are."

"I remind her all the time."

"Well, don't worry. I'll keep her busy tomorrow. No doubt we'll be feeding this entire crowd."

"By the way." He lightly grasped my bicep and I jumped in surprise. "Speaking of busy: it looks like you've been working out. You look amazing."

I felt my blush spot start to form.

"Oh, thanks. It's not from hitting the gym, though. I've become a regular pack mule since I got here. Up from the farmer's market to Al's, then hauling in all the stuff that comes through the back door at the Shore Store. I can one-arm bench press a thirty pound bag of Maui onions—no sweat."

"I hear the lunch business is going well."

"Yeah, it is. But I don't know what'll happen now."

The autopsy showed Momi died from a massive heart attack. The news hit Al hard, probably because he'd come so close himself. Of course, Jim never told Al or any of the other family members that Momi had been subjected to a full-blown autopsy. He said only that he'd talked to the doctors and they'd determined the cause of death.

Jim left the next day. He had surgeries waiting, and as he put it, "Funerals are tough for me. I need to stay focused on keeping folks alive."

Momi's memorial service was held in her church. Friends and family from all over Maui attended, as well as some from Oahu and the Big Island. The service was similar to a mainland funeral. However, the interment at the cemetery was a whole different matter. It was conducted by a *kahuna*—a local spiritual leader—who spoke in Hawaiian. No subtitles, no interpreters. I'd heard the Hawaiian language sung, or in scattered words sprinkled throughout everyday English conversation, but I'd never heard it spoken sentence after sentence. I was moved by how soothing it sounded. It seemed to be all vowels, with a few soft p's, m's, and clicking k-sounds. Although I couldn't understand the words except Momi's name and the words *mahalo* and *ohana*—the words for 'thank you' and 'family'—it felt right to hear the *kahuna* say farewell to Momi in the language of her ancestors.

I had to leave early, because just as I'd predicted, we were holding the reception at the Shore Store. As soon as the service was over a wave of hungry mourners would stream in looking for Hawaiian-style comfort food.

When the last person finally left around seven, I plopped down in a chair. I was exhausted. Malia, Aidan and I needed to get the store cleaned up and ready for re-opening the next day, but I needed a break.

"I've got a good bottle of wine next door," said Aidan. "How about we take it up on the lanai and watch the sun go down? Then we can attack this mess."

"Sounds great," said Malia.

We clomped up the dark stairs and Aidan opened the smudged French doors to yet another stunning Lahaina sunset.

"We must've had a hundred people," I said.

"At least," said Malia. "And they ate enough for two hundred."

We chatted until almost dark, and then we went back downstairs. The place looked even worse than before the wine break.

"What do you say we call it a night and I'll come back early tomorrow morning?" I said. "I'm beat."

"No. You go," Malia said. "Dad will want a bite to eat before he goes to bed and Aidan and I can get this whipped into shape in no time."

Aidan shot her a look that said, *I don't remember volunteering for KP duty.*

"I can't leave you guys here to deal with this disaster. Look at this." I picked up a half-full glass of guava juice that had been used as a receptacle for shrimp tails and a wadded-up paper napkin. "It's disgusting."

"Don't worry about it," Malia said. She took my elbow and steered me toward the door. "We've got it covered."

Malia gently pushed me onto the front porch. Aidan stepped around her and gave me a quick kiss. I glanced back to see Malia's reaction. She seemed to take it in stride, blowing me a kiss of her own as she waved good-bye.

I walked to Momi's cottage. I hoped I could get Tommy to drive me to Al's in his rental car. On a good day I could walk to Al's in half an hour, but I wasn't up for it after standing around at the gravesite, then cooking, serving, and socializing. Not to mention the soothing glass of wine that had turned my legs to rubber.

I came through the screen door without knocking. "Hey, Tommy. How're you doing?" He jumped at the sound of my voice.

"Oh. I didn't hear you come in," he said. Then he blurted out, "You know, it wasn't my fault I didn't get over here very much."

I had a feeling I was about to get buried in excuses.

"No really," he said. "I've been with the LAPD for the past eighteen years. It's hard work. When I'd get a few days off, the last thing I want to do is shoehorn myself into an airplane seat for six hours."

"Oh yeah, coming to Maui is tough duty," I said. "Did you know your mom kept a guest room all ready for you? She prayed every night that you and your brother would come see her."

He hung his head; then snapped it up as if he'd remembered something.

"So, what were you doing in our room? Did you pay rent for staying here?"

Oh Tommy, bad question.

"I guess I'm more Hawaiian than you are," I said.

He looked puzzled, but let it drop.

"So," I said. "Would you mind giving me a lift over to Al's? I need to make him some dinner. You're welcome to stay, by the way."

"Stay? I don't think I need your permission to stay in my own mother's house."

"No. I mean you're welcome to stay for dinner. At Al's."

"Oh. Thanks, but I'm not hungry."

I looked at his six-foot three, two-hundred-thirty-pound frame. "Look, you've hardly had a chance to sit down all day. Come over and eat something. Besides, it'll give you a chance to *talk story* with your Uncle Al."

"Okay," he said, finally cracking a smile.

As we made our way through the dark Lahaina streets, the low murmur of the car radio was the only thing disturbing the quiet. Tommy spoke as he turned up the hill to Al's.

"I feel horrible about my mom. She's the best person I've ever known. It probably sounds stupid, but I thought she'd live forever."

"Yeah, she had an *aloha* soul. And she loved you and your brother more than you'll ever realize. What baffles me is why you stayed away so long. You know how important family was to your mom."

By then we'd pulled into Al's driveway. Neither of us made an effort to get out.

"I'd been gone a long time," he said. "Then I came back for my dad's funeral. It was horrible. My mom and brother got after each other and tried to drag in the whole family. I left as soon as the funeral was over."

"What did your mom and brother argue about?"

"Everything."

"No, really. There had to be something in particular."

"They mostly fought over what most families fight about," he said. "Money."

"Oh."

I knew how obstinate Momi could be on that subject, so I steered clear. But Tommy wasn't done.

"My brother Sam thought my mom should sell the Shore Store after dad died. She refused, and they wrangled over it tooth and nail."

I opened the car door and the overhead light came on. I didn't want to weigh in on who I thought was right.

"Thanks for the ride," I said.

"No problem."

We went inside Al's. Lani and the cousins stopped talking when they saw Tommy come in behind me.

"I came to fix some dinner. Anyone hungry?"

They laughed as though I was kidding, but then one brave teenager piped up, "What're you gonna make?"

Aidan and Malia came over an hour later. Malia was all smiles. I gave Aidan a long sidelong glance but he shrugged as if he had no idea what was going on.

"Hey, Nola," she said. She draped an arm around my shoulders and steered me toward the sofa. "I've been thinking."

"Should I be worried?"

"No, no. It's a good thing," she said.

"I think you should seriously consider doing a full-blown restaurant. Forget about just fixing up the deli."

"What exactly do you mean by 'full-blown restaurant'?" I said.

"Turn the Shore Store into a fine dining place. With tablecloths. And waiters. And a bar. And the best view in town."

At least I agreed with her about the view.

"I don't know. The Shore Store might not be a good location for a restaurant." I didn't want to let on I knew Momi's sons would sell the property in a heartbeat if given half a chance.

"Well, at least think about it. I know you'd be incredibly successful."

"Yeah," Aidan chimed in. "I've always thought if you put your mind to it you could give ol' Lech a run for his money."

I went to bed thinking about what it would be like to own and operate a restaurant. I thought back about my dream of being a flight attendant, and how I wanted to serve people in the first class cabin. Maybe I could build my own first class restaurant space. But first I'd need to convince the Anakua boys to keep the building.

The next morning I got up and made my usual trek to the farmer's market. When I returned, Al was sitting alone at the table. He had the newspaper stretched out in front of him.

"What's for breakfast?" he said as I hefted the heavy bags onto the counter.

"I think I'll cut up some of this fresh pineapple and then make banana pancakes."

"Oh, good. I love pancakes. Am I allowed to have 'em?" He glanced furtively around the room, as if he thought the cardiac police might swoop in and arrest him for trying to score some cholesterol.

"No problem. I know how to make them 'heart smart'."

"Will they still be good like the ones you used to make?"

"You can be the judge of that, Al. I'm just going to add a little wheat germ and use your special margarine."

"I like real butter."

"I know. But your heart prefers the margarine. When you pour on the syrup, I'll bet they'll taste just as yummy as the old ones."

I had pancakes on the griddle when the kitchen phone began to ring.

"Al, would you mind grabbing that? I've got to flip these over before they burn."

He picked it up. As he listened, a scowl clouded his face.

"She's busy. She's making me breakfast."

"Here," he said. He handed the receiver across the counter. "Aidan doesn't believe me that you're too busy to talk to him."

I tucked the phone in the crook between my shoulder and neck. "What's up? I'm making pancakes here."

"I'm over at Momi's. I found something you've got to see. I'll come and get you. Oh, and tell Malia she needs to come too."

CHAPTER 24

I wasn't a big fan of guessing games. Unlike Frank, who thought it proved his genius if he could spit out, "What is Constantinople?" before the flustered contestant on *Jeopardy!* could hit the button, I found Alex Trebek's nightly trivia contest about as fun as breaking in a stiff pair of shoes.

"What do you think Aidan found?" Malia asked, as we stood elbow to elbow in the tiny guest bathroom. She'd pulled her long black hair into a high ponytail. Looping the tail into a knot, she stuck a chopstick down the center, creating a sleek, exotic look.

"No clue," I said. I tried arranging my own hair in a style that looked a little less like Crack Head Bozo and bit more like Malibu Beach Barbie. "I hope he didn't find something embarrassing like an old rubber douche bag. Can you imagine trying to explain *that* to the island boys?"

"Ugh," she said.

"Why wouldn't he just tell me over the phone?" I wondered aloud.

I ducked into the kitchen to grab a quick cup of coffee and saw Aidan's truck slide into the driveway. He banged through the kitchen door as I rummaged through the refrigerator looking for creamer.

"Hi, gorgeous," he said. He put his arm around my waist and gave me a quick squeeze.

He smelled so good. He was wearing bay rum after shave. It made me want to duck my head under his tee-shirt and take a big sniff.

Al's face was still buried in his newspaper, but I was sure he was tuned in to everything going on.

"Hey, Al," Aidan said to the outstretched paper.

Al lowered it just enough to peer over the top and grunt an acknowledgment. Then he made a big production out of snapping the page and repositioning it in front of his face.

"You two ready to go?" Aidan said to me, ignoring Al's slight.

A plaintive voice piped up from behind the newspaper. "You taking both my girls and leaving me here all alone?" Al had learned to play the frail cardiac patient card when it suited him.

"Just for a little while," said Aidan. "I'll bring them back within the hour."

We went out to the truck. In an unspoken changing of the guard, Malia opened the door to the back seat to allow me to ride shotgun.

It felt odd to pull up in front of Momi's cottage and realize she wouldn't be inside. I dreaded seeing her things and smelling her still-lingering gardenia perfume.

Without a word, Aidan led us down the hall to Momi's bedroom. The shades were tightly drawn, bathing the room in a steel-gray gloom that sucked the color from everything inside. It made the scene look like a grainy black and white photo. A tremble skittered down my arms as I glanced at the bed where I'd found her lifeless body only six days earlier. Aidan crossed the room and opened a tiny drawer in the nightstand. He pulled the drawer all the way out and carried it over to us.

He lifted out a piece of lined paper folded in fourths. The paper had a jagged edge, as if it had been torn from a spiral notebook. Scrawled on the diagonal across one side of the fold I could make out the word "Noelani."

I unfolded the paper, but in the dim light it was impossible to read the small, loopy script.

"We need some light," said Malia. She grasped one side of the paper and bent closer to get a look. "I can't read this."

Aidan ceremoniously flipped the switch for the overhead fixture. It threw about sixty watts at the problem. It wasn't bright, but it was enough to do the trick.

Malia and I huddled over the note. It was dated a month earlier, around the time when I'd first asked Momi to pay me for working for her.

I, Momi Luka Kanekoa Anakua, hereby give my Shore Store and the property it sits on to my friend, Noelani Stevens. She has done a good job for me and she has helped out my brother, Kailealoha Kanekoa. My sons are on the mainland and don't need the store. I love them, and wish them much hau'oli, but they want to sell the store and I don't want that.

This is my will. Good luck and God bless you, Noelani, for helping me out.

P. S. The land is on Kingdom of Hawaii Crown Land, so no taxes!

It was signed by Momi using her full name and then dated once again at the bottom of the page.

"Oh, shit. Wow," said Malia.

"How do you say that in Hawaiian?" I asked.

Aidan smiled. "I think 'oh shit, wow' is pretty universal."

"Well," Malia said. "Looks like you can open your restaurant."

"What?" I said.

"This is a sign from the universe, can't you see? You can turn the store into a full-blown restaurant. It's the perfect location."

"Yeah," said Aidan. "You were already thinking of putting in some seating. Maybe you should go whole hog."

"I don't know."

"So," Malia said. She gave a quick look at the closed guest room door, and then turned to Aidan, "What did Tommy say when you showed this to him?"

"He doesn't know yet. That's why I hauled you two over here. He needs to see it, but I don't think I should be the one to show it to him." His eyes never left hers. It was clear he was counting on a family member to handle the dirty work.

"What? You expect *me* to throw this in his face? That property was pretty much all Momi had. Tommy and Sam are as good as disinherited."

"Well, Nola can't say anything. It looks bad enough as it is. She was living with Momi when this was written."

I took some offense at the implication but kept my mouth shut.

"Yeah, that's true," said Malia. "But as you know, land ownership is a real hot topic around here. This is going to have repercussions far beyond what the Anakua boys think about it."

I felt a little woozy and expected the black splotches at any moment. I considered plopping down on the edge of Momi's bed but then thought better of it. Instead, I groped my way to a low trunk and sat down, my head resting in my hands.

"Nola, don't sweat this," Aidan said. "It's not like you've done anything wrong. Maybe I should take this note to my attorney and have her tell us if it's even legal. If it's not, then I say we keep it to ourselves and don't say anything."

"I agree. That's smart." Malia looked relieved at Aidan's stay of execution in making her rile up the Kanekoa-Anakua clan. Telling her cousins their mother had bequeathed a multi-million dollar Lahaina property to a *haole* woman was probably right up there with peering over the edge of a volcano about to erupt. Not a safe place to be.

We puttered around the house for about half an hour, boxing up Momi's personal items and sorting things to take to the Salvation Army on Shaw Street. Tommy said he'd send a box of mementos and photos to his brother Sam in Los Angeles and he'd put the rest in storage until he found a place to live on Maui. He'd decided against living in Momi's cottage because he'd be working at the sheriff's office in Kahului and rents were cheaper on that side of the island.

"We need to get back to Al," I said, checking my watch. "I worry about how he's handling Momi's death. He acts like he's fine, saying 'she's with Koma,' and all that. But I'm afraid it hasn't sunk in yet that his little sister is really gone."

"That's just the way my dad is," said Malia. "I remember when my mom died. I kept waiting for him to fall apart but he never did. He was quiet for a couple of weeks and then he seemed to make peace with it and he got on with his life."

Aidan drove us back to Al's. We chit-chatted on the trip over, but thankfully no one mentioned Momi's startling bequest. I knew the simple solution was to pretend I'd never seen the note. Most of my life I'd simply ignored things I didn't want to deal with, so I was already pretty skilled at self-deception.

The next morning I wasn't surprised when Malia announced she'd booked a flight to Seattle and she'd be leaving at ten o'clock that night. Her reaction to Aidan asking her to be the one to tell Tommy about Momi's handwritten will made it clear she'd have snagged a canoe and paddled her way home rather than have to face that task.

"Seems I'm always taking you to the airport," I said that night as I gunned the van to pass a dawdling rental car.

"Yeah. I wish I could stay," she said. She turned her head to gaze at the moon reflected in the placid ocean. I gave her credit for at least not looking at me while she lied.

"You know your nose will grow," I said, "or anyway, that's what my mom always said. I guess if that were true, Frank should have a snout the size of a hothouse cucumber by now."

"I really don't want to leave. Losing Auntie makes me realize time is passing. And I miss being home."

"But isn't 'home' with Jim back in Seattle?"

"With Jim, yes. But I've been trying to talk him into moving his practice over here."

"Here? Do you think Jim would actually agree to live here?"

"Don't jinx it by saying anything. But I've got a plan." She cleared her throat a little, signaling she was changing the subject. "So, tell me what's going on with you and Aidan. He said you guys are 'kind of a couple.' What the heck does that mean?"

"Did you know that Mr. Aidan Lawson already has a *Mrs.* Aidan Lawson?"

"No! Get outta here. No way."

"Way."

"Who is it? Someone I know? Did he just get married? Have you met her?"

I attempted to take the questions one at a time. "Her name is Claire. No, I don't think you know her. They've been separated for more than twenty years. She lives with a woman friend in Vermont."

"Vermont? A *woman* friend?" she said. It was followed by a long 'hmm' like she was solving a riddle. "You mean she's gay?"

I laughed. Leave it to Malia to trump me on figuring it out with only a few sketchy clues.

"Hey, you beat me to the punch line. How'd you know?"

"It's not exactly rocket science, Nola. I was thinking if they've been separated that long maybe they just didn't bother to get divorced. And, Vermont has a pretty liberal attitude toward same-sex couples and you said she lives with a woman. It all kind of adds up."

"Yeah, Aidan told me he stayed married to her to keep her parents from suspecting anything. I guess they're kind of old school about the girl-on-girl thing."

"Ah. See, I told you the guy was a sweetheart. I'm not surprised he offered to marry a friend to be her alibi."

By then we'd pulled in front of the airport. We said our good-byes and made promises to keep in touch. I'd managed to dodge explaining my perplexing relationship with Aidan. I did give some thought to her comment about coming home, though. And I concluded that for me, there was no place that I considered *home* anymore.

I spent the next week cleaning out the store in anticipation of adding my tables and chairs. It helped keep my anxiety in check while I waited for news from Aidan's attorney. I managed to avoid Tommy for the rest of the week, but on Saturday, Al invited him over for dinner. Since I was Al's cook, server, and clean-up crew there was no getting out of it.

Tommy banged through the kitchen door and hefted a twelve-pack of Budweiser onto the kitchen counter. "Hey, Nola," he said. "Thanks for letting me come to dinner. I'm getting kinda sick of eating at Maui Taco, you know?"

I nodded. I felt like such a sleaze. Maybe it would've been better to just blurt out about finding Momi's will and get it over with. But since we hadn't heard anything from Aidan's lawyer, I kept my mouth shut and plastered on my happy face.

"I made lettuce chicken wraps tonight. They've got garlic, roasted peppers, chilis, and lots of fresh ginger. They're one of Al's favorites."

"Sounds good. My mom said you were a great cook."

"When'd you talk to your mom?"

"Oh, I called her nearly every week. I'd phone her from the station when my shift was over. Usually on weekends."

Momi never mentioned talking to her son, and I didn't remember overhearing any phone calls when I was at her house.

"How about Sam? Did he call her, too?"

"Nah. Mom and Sam had one of those weird relationships that parents and kids sometimes have. They loved each other, but whenever they'd get on the phone—or even worse in person—they'd end up fighting. Like I told you before, they bickered about *everything*."

"I know what you mean," I said. I gave the chicken a final stir. "My mom and I pretty much stick to talking about the weather."

He smiled and shook his head. "With those two, if my mom said the weather was nice, Sam would argue it was too hot."

I scooped the chicken mixture into a bowl and put out a plate of crisp lettuce leaves.

"Don't we get tortillas?" Al surveyed the table as if I'd forgotten the turkey at Thanksgiving.

I shot him some stink eye.

"What?" he said, feigning innocence.

"They're *lettuce* wraps, Al. Tortillas have a lot of calories and fat."

"That's why they taste *ono*." He turned to Tommy with a scowl on his face that said, *See what I have to put up with?*

Tommy picked up a lettuce leaf and filled it with the fragrant chicken mixture. He rolled it up and stuffed about half of it into his mouth. Nodding his head in approval, he made "mmm-mmm" sounds while he chewed, just like Momi had done. It made me think of Frank Jr. and wonder if he ever instinctively echoed my quirks.

"Wow, that's some great stuff," said Tommy.

"Yeah," said Al. "See? Momi was right."

I marveled at how easily Al mentioned his sister. She'd been dead less than a week, yet Al talked about her as comfortably as if she'd been gone for decades.

On Tuesday morning when Aidan came to take me down to the store, his eyes gleamed like a guy eager to share some news.

"What'd you find out?" I asked as I slid onto the passenger seat.

"What makes you think I know anything?"

"Aidan, give me a break. You look like you're about to explode."

"Okay, you're right. My attorney, Elizabeth, thinks it's a go."

"Which means what, exactly?"

"She says it's called a 'holographic will.' It's a little dicey because it wasn't witnessed, but if everyone agrees it's Momi's handwriting, then it's probably going to hold up in court as a legal will. Elizabeth checked with most of the other attorneys in town, and so far no one else claims they made out a will for Momi."

"But what about her sons? They can contest it, can't they?"

"Oh, sure. And they probably will." He braked for a red light. "I would."

I would, too.

"Tommy already knows the bad news," he said, popping the clutch and pulling away from the light.

"Oh?" I felt my chest tighten. I clenched my hands.

"Yeah. Elizabeth said she called Tommy to ask if his mother ever mentioned a local attorney's name. He asked her point blank if she knew how he could find out if his mom had a will. She felt an ethical responsibility to advise him that a handwritten will had been found and she was checking into it."

"Did she tell him his mother left her entire estate to *me*?"

"No, of course not. She simply told him Momi left it to someone or something other than her sons. She said he seemed to take it pretty well."

"Oh, sure. No biggie." I said. "His mom literally gave away the store, and he's cool with it. C'mon, Aidan, the guy's mellow, but he's not stupid."

"Okay," he said. "Let's just say she thought he seemed pretty calm for a guy who'd just lost out on a multi-million dollar inheritance."

The only things I ever saw Momi get agitated over were money and land. If Tommy was as much like his mother as he appeared to be, his calm reaction was merely testimony to the professional demeanor he'd learned working the mean streets of LA. Just because a cop smiles at you when he asks for your license and registration doesn't change the fact that he's packing a loaded gun.

CHAPTER 25

Aidan's attorney, Elizabeth Campbell, agreed to represent me in handling Momi's estate. She advised me the first step was to file the holographic will with the court in Wailuku.

"The worst that can happen is they reject it," she said. "And, if they do, there's really no downside. You wouldn't be any worse off than you are right now."

"Except I'll owe you for attorney fees. To be honest, I'm pretty much broke."

"Don't worry about it. I won't bill you until it's all over." She stood and extended her hand, signaling the end to my free consultation. "I don't think this will be too costly. You'll have some filing fees; then some fees for my time at the court appearance; and maybe a few correspondence charges if the sons contest it. That'll be about all. But I think it will be worth it. I think you've got an excellent chance of winning."

She sounded a lot more confident than I felt.

I kept going to work at the Shore Store, hoping the ownership issue would be decided within a month or two. That left the matter of what I should do with the money I brought in every day.

"I don't know what to do with all the money in the cash drawer," I said to Aidan one afternoon while he was helping me clean up. "I used to give it to Momi every night, but now it's just piling up in there."

"Why not just take it? It's yours; you earned it."

"But Auntie Momi paid me fifty dollars a week."

"So? Give yourself a raise." He laughed as if I was an idiot not to have thought of it myself.

"I can't do that. When I go to court I need to be completely above-board. Elizabeth advised me to 'avoid the appearance of impropriety'."

"I don't think she expects you to become a bag lady while this thing gets sorted out. When she said 'impropriety' she was talking about trying to take out a loan against the store, or getting uppity and changing the name to 'Nola's Shore Store.' Stuff like that."

"I'd never do that," I said. "But I'm in a pretty tight bind money-wise. In fact, I was hoping I could ask you for a small loan." I puckered my face into a beseeching look.

He glared at me, silent.

"I'm serious," I went on. "I persuaded the guy at the furniture store to invoice me at the end of the month for the new bistro tables and chairs, but now I don't know how I'm going to pay for them."

"Take it out of the till, Nola," he said in a measured voice. "You're being ridiculous."

"Well, whether you help me out or not, I still can't take Momi's money." I reached under the counter and pulled out a blue zippered deposit bag from the Bank of

Hawaii. It bulged with more than a week's profits from the Shore Store. "You have a safe where you lock up your jewelry pieces, right?"

He nodded. His eyes glowed with annoyance.

"Would you mind putting this in there until the court decides who it belongs to?" I handed him the bag.

He weighed the heft of the bag and then tucked it under his arm. "You can play the martyr," he said. "But trust me, it won't change anything. Tommy and Sam's lawyers are going to come after you no matter what. You've got to be prepared for that." He wiped his hands on a towel and kissed me on the forehead. Then he headed for the door.

"So, I guess that's a 'no' on the loan?" I said, but he'd already closed the door.

I spent the next week rearranging the store to accommodate the four bistro tables and dozen chairs I'd ordered. Just to cover myself, I called Tommy and left a message about the proposed changes, but I didn't expect to hear back from him. Every night, I put the money from the day's receipts into Aidan's safe. I avoided commenting on his look of irritation as I locked it back up.

Most days Aidan didn't come over for lunch. He used the excuse he was behind schedule in finishing his hotel contract. But he still came every afternoon to help me clean up.

"It's been three weeks," I said. "And still no word from Elizabeth about a court date."

"You know what they say about Maui time. It took me almost a year to get my vendor's permit to open my studio."

"A *year?*"

The next day I called Elizabeth's office. Her assistant advised me they hadn't gotten a court date yet, but she'd check on it.

"It's kind of soon, though," she said.

"It'll be a month next week," I reminded her.

"That's what I mean," she said. "Not nearly enough time."

Rather than sit around fretting, I opted to move forward. I borrowed Al's van to drive to Wailuku to apply for my food establishment permit. I'd learned I'd need a permit to offer any type of sit-down dining, no matter how meager the ambiance.

I left at eight in the morning expecting to be back by ten-thirty to prep for lunch.

The address of the state administrative offices turned out to be an ancient gray stone building. It looked like it'd once been a high school or maybe a courthouse. A sign on the lawn indicated the county permits department was located in the basement. Trudging down an outside stairwell, I imagined a dusty hallway leading to a grizzled little man with a dried-up Bic pen and a rubber stamp. I'd smile, hand him my paperwork and a check for fifty dollars, and he'd wish me *aloha* and hand me my permit.

At the bottom of the steps, the entry door was locked. I should have taken the hint right then.

I trudged back up and went in the double doors on the main level. The place was jammed with people who looked as if they'd camped in the hallway all night. I moved through the crowd, glad I wasn't there to get whatever they were handing out on the first floor. Everyone looked pretty testy, both employees and citizens alike.

I stepped into a shabby elevator to go down to the basement. It smelled like stale cigarette smoke, even though I'd seen at least three 'no smoking' signs. The elevator took a half-minute to drop down one floor, and then another half-minute to settle itself before opening the doors. I nervously waited, imagining myself entombed in the airless fingerprint-smudged stainless box. I vowed to locate the stairwell for the trip back up.

Finally the doors opened. The downstairs hallway was as crowded as the one above. Some people tried to fill out forms as they stood against the wall. A fortunate few had snagged the eight or nine battered one-armed school desks that were riddled with the initials of students that had probably attended school before Hawaii became a state.

"Is this where they give out the restaurant permits?" I asked a big local-looking guy. He was standing in the entrance to the only open door in the hallway. He filled the entire doorway, as if daring anyone to try and slip past him.

"I guess," he said. "Not sure, though. I'm here for my contractor's license."

Maybe I was in the wrong place. I squeezed down the hall, searching for the end of the line.

"Are you here for a restaurant permit?" I asked a woman about half-way down. She wore a tattered brown gauze skirt with a tank top and no bra. In her arms she held a tiny infant. In the chilly air-conditioned basement, I wasn't just assuming she was bra-less—it was a visible certainty.

"Nope," she said, shifting the baby from one hip to the other. The baby's eyes were focused on the thin cotton knit separating him from mom's pointy nipples. I looked up and down the line, but no one appeared inclined to talk. I couldn't even establish eye contact.

I finally made it to the end of the line. Then I waited. And waited. After an hour only five or six people had moved through the doorway at the other end. There were still at least two dozen people ahead of me.

"What's the deal?" I finally asked a guy who'd joined the line right behind me. "Is this the line to beg the Wizard of Oz for a heart or a brain or something? What's taking so long?"

He grunted and turned away, as if disrespecting the minions who worked for the State of Hawaii might get him tossed out of the building.

At ten-forty-five, eight people stood between me and victory. My early customers usually arrived by eleven-thirty and it was a forty-minute drive back to Lahaina. I considered my inventory and tried to come up with a daily special I could make on the fly—maybe a cold cheese sandwich, or a spicy egg salad.

At eleven o'clock, I gave up and slipped my completed application form into the mail slot outside the office. I was pretty sure it was one of those 'must be present to win' kind of things, but maybe they'd call me and I could make an appointment to come back. I jostled my way toward the elevator—I was in no mood to search for the stairwell—and dodged vicious looks from people who probably thought I was trying to cut in line.

As I walked back to my car I began to contemplate whether four little bistro tables really constituted a 'food establishment.' By the time I arrived back in Lahaina, I'd determined the whole permit process was merely a formality. The 'better to beg forgiveness than ask permission' rule definitely applied.

Every day when the mail came I'd flip through the stack hoping to see an envelope from my lawyer. Nothing. But I did get an eight hundred dollar invoice for the bistro tables and chairs. Since I didn't have any money to pay it, I tucked the bill in a drawer. I'd never been a deadbeat before, so I wasn't clear on the best technique for dodging a creditor. After a couple of weeks, I got a call from the bookkeeper at the furniture store.

"That bill was due on receipt," she said. Her tone implied she considered me a shady character that she, personally, would never have extended credit to, but her boss was a soft touch. She sounded like she was pressed for time and she wasn't at all pleased to be spending it cleaning up his messes.

"I know. I'll get to it right away," I said. I cringed at the lie. For my entire adult life, I'd been maniacal about paying my bills promptly. The two or three times I'd forgotten and a finance charge had been tacked on, I'd sent an apology note along with the payment. I even drew a happy face next to my signature to show I was really a good person.

Monday morning, three weeks after my futile attempt to score a restaurant permit, I got an early-morning phone call on my cell.

"This is the Maui Health Department calling. We need to meet you at the food service premises," the man said. He had a Joe Friday voice that brought to mind black and white reruns of *Dragnet* on middle-of-the-night TV.

"Sure. I can be there within half an hour. But how'd you get this phone number?"

"Did you, or did you not," he said, as if I was handcuffed to a battered table in a windowless room; a single high-wattage light bulb swaying overhead, "complete an application for a food establishment permit?"

"Well, yes, but—"

"We have your inspection scheduled for Wednesday."

"Okay. What time?"

"We'll be there at nine a.m., prompt."

I stifled a chuckle. Everyone who's lived in Hawaii for more than a month knows the word "prompt" has no local translation.

"I'll be there."

On Wednesday, two gentlemen dressed in beige and gray print aloha shirts and khaki slacks showed up at the store. It was almost ten-thirty, but one look and I lost any urge to chide them for being late.

"*Aloha*, welcome. I'm Nola Stevens," I extended my hand, and then mentally kicked myself for not referring to myself as "Noelani."

"Yes, well..." said the first man, ignoring my offer of a handshake. Instead, he pulled a business card from his shirt pocket.

I read the card. It introduced him as Benjamin Yamasato. His title was "Commercial Business Inspector" from the Maui County Health Department.

"Welcome, Mr. Yamasato. And Mr...?" I waited for the second man to give his name, but Ben must have considered such formalities a waste of his time because he brusquely intervened.

"We are here to inspect your premises."

"Yes, I figured as much. However, I haven't gotten my restaurant permit yet. Shouldn't you come back once I'm fully operational?"

"You get the permit *if* you pass the inspection. Not before."

"Oh." I led them past the few remaining grocery shelves and back into the spotless deli which now sported the brand-new tables and chairs. Gesturing like a car show model at a shiny red convertible, I said, "This is where the magic happens."

They glared at me, seemingly not amused by my attempt at banter.

Ben whipped out a clipboard with a blank inspection list attached, and he and Mr. Nameless began whispering and pointing. After a few moments, Ben scribbled something on the list.

"I'll show you around, if you like." I said, chirping like a cooperative inspectee with nothing to hide.

"Excuse us, but we need a few minutes alone— please," said Mr. Nameless. His attempt at civility earned him a scalding glare from his partner.

I went next door to Aidan's to allow them their space. My hand shook as I tapped on his door.

He peered through the window before opening the door. He was working bare-chested, as usual, and I marveled at how his tanned, chiseled body never failed to distract my attention from the problem at hand.

"Can I hang out here for a few minutes? I've got the health inspectors next door and they've got a go-get-'em look in their eye that rivals Tom Hanks in *The DaVinci Code.*"

"Oh, no," he said. "Those guys can be brutal."

"I'm not worried. I keep that place squeaky clean. And I only put in four little tables. Tables I can't pay for, I might add." I threw in the last part hoping he'd take pity and finally offer to lend me the money.

"Let's go upstairs and have a soda," he said, slipping on a dusty gray-green tee-shirt. He grabbed my hand. "I could use a break, and you need to come up with a strategy."

"I don't know if I have time. They said it would just be a few minutes."

"Trust me," he said, turning his head to glance at the wall adjoining the store. "You've got time."

The health inspection report totaled eight pages. A long string of check marks in the 'Fail' column marched down the right side of each page. Looking at the report you'd think I was cooking up strychnine in a toxic waste dump.

Later that evening I showed Aidan the report. "What's this?" I said. "'Mite and dust particles present'?

Are they nuts? It's a century-old building with a wooden floor. What do they expect?"

We were in Al's backyard watching the light fade from the sky. Aidan had made a pitcher of "lemon-Aidan," which consisted of frozen lemonade with a few shots of vodka and some other secret ingredients thrown in. It was one of Aidan's less ambitious concoctions but it still had the ability to make a crummy day seem a whole lot better.

"Some of this stuff is impossible to fix," I went on. "Look at this. It says, 'Scrapings taken from floorboards on porch indicate possible soil contamination beneath building.' Are they saying I've got to clean the *dirt*?"

He silently refilled my glass.

"I should have left things the way they were and not even applied for that stupid permit. Now, I don't even know how long the store can stay open."

He held a fist to his mouth as if considering a response, but remained quiet.

"Why are they doing this to me?" I continued. "What did I ever do to Mr. Yamasato and Mr..." I peered at the bottom of the inspection report for Mr. Nameless' name. I found it. It was Tanaka.

Aidan finally spoke. "You ever hear people say, 'You ain't on the mainland, brudda'?"

"Yeah."

"Well, believe it. This isn't the mainland. You're not a local, so you need to play the game. Trust me, I've been there."

So, for the next few days, I cleaned every morning before the store opened. I cornered the market on Pine-Sol, along with wire scrub brushes and even sandpaper. I went back to Al's every night with lobster-red hands and an aching back in the hopes that I'd be deemed worthy of the coveted 'food consumed on premises' permit. Until I had it in hand, I'd been warned I needed to put away my new tables and chairs. Actually, the threat didn't hold much of a sting. I'd stashed my unpaid-for furniture back in the original cartons figuring the repossession would be easier for all concerned if everything was already boxed up.

On Thursday night, I received my first response to Momi's handwritten will. A registered letter was delivered to Al's address from a Mr. Sanborn Lawrence, Esq. informing me that his clients, Samuel and Thomas Anakua, had retained him to contest the proposed disposition of the estate of their mother, Momi Kanekoa Anakua. That was the bad news.

The good news was that the next day I got word we had a hearing date for probate court. It was scheduled for the following Friday. One way or another it would be over soon. But just thinking about facing down Tommy and his brother, Sam, in a Maui courtroom made me yearn for a double shot of lemon-Aidan.

CHAPTER 26

The third horse in my trifecta of 'guys out to get me' showed up on Monday. First, I'd had the health inspectors, then the Anakua brothers contesting Momi's will, and, rounding the turn to finish by a nose—the county fire inspector.

"Where are your exit signs?" he said as he stared at the crossbeams above the front door. He looked the part of the handsome fire department officer: broad-shouldered and tall, with striking, angular features and close-cropped dark hair. He wore a crisp white shirt with big official-looking patches on the sleeves and a shiny gold badge above the breast pocket. His name badge said. 'Watson.'

"I suppose since people come in through that door," I said. "It seems reasonable they'd know it's also the way out." I didn't mean to sound disrespectful, but puh-leeze.

"Fire code says you must have lighted exit signs above every public doorway." He scribbled on a tablet with carbon copies like a policeman's ticket book. "You've got a bunch of other code problems here, too.

But this one's a shut-down violation, so no sense going any further until you get this fixed."

"What's that mean, a 'shut-down violation'?"

"It means," he said in a voice you'd expect from a cop slapping the cuffs on a DUI driver who'd just mowed down a family of five, "You're *shut down* until you get this fixed."

"Today?"

"This minute. You need to lock the door and get those exit signs up. No further business until we can come back and clear you."

Eli, a regular customer who usually comes in early to make sure he gets a chicken wrap, popped through the door.

"Sorry, sir," said Inspector Watson. "This establishment is closed due to fire safety violations. Unsafe environment."

Eli's eyes bugged out as if he'd been told I'd spiked the salt shakers with anthrax.

"What are you doing?" I said turning back to the fire inspector. "You're going to kill my business."

"Better to kill some business than a bunch of civilians."

I turned off the lights, hung up the closed sign, and stumbled over to Aidan's.

"How do you cry 'uncle' in Hawaiian?" I said, dropping into his rattan rocker.

"That bad, huh?"

"The store's closed until further notice."

"Let me guess. The health inspectors found a dead insect in the parking lot."

"Nope. They're probably going to cry foul 'cuz they got beat out by the fire inspector in shutting me down first."

"Ah. The fire department—America's heroes. What's your crime? Multiple outlet strip?"

"Nah, they haven't even seen those yet. They're up in arms because I don't have lighted exit signs over the doors."

I looked up at Aidan's studio door. There was no trace of an exit sign, lighted or unlighted.

"How do you stay open?" I pointed out the infraction.

"I didn't get this place until I had insurance."

"Insurance?"

"Yeah. I waited until I'd sucked up to the right people in Wailuku before I even applied for a business permit."

I thought the probate hearing would clear up the question of whether I owned the Shore Store or not—but no such luck. The judge put on tiny reading glasses and shuffled through a stack of papers. While we waited in the hard pews of the courtroom, I read the bronze nameplate on his desk, "The Hon. Judge Lewis Stanton." It wasn't a very Hawaiian-sounding name, maybe I had a fighting chance. The judge called me to approach the bench. Elizabeth scrambled up next to me as if I couldn't be trusted to answer without first consulting legal counsel.

"Were you well acquainted with Mrs. Anakua?" he asked.

I glanced at Elizabeth. She nodded.

"Yes, Your Honor."

"In what capacity did you know her?"

Again, I got the nod to wing it. But how should I answer? What was my relationship with Momi? Houseguest, employee, friend?

"I lived in her home, Your Honor. I also helped out at her store, and I was a caregiver for her older brother."

Elizabeth beamed as if I'd aced a killer word in a spelling bee.

The judge didn't appear to be as delighted as my lawyer. "Did she offer to give you the property on Luakini Street in exchange for those duties?"

"No, Your Honor. I had no idea she planned to give me the property. Her death was totally unexpected, and sad. Distressing—really."

He made a *hurrumph* noise that sounded like a polite way of saying, *Gimme a break.*

Tommy sat at the table with his lawyer. He wore an expression that smacked of time spent in front of a mirror practicing his 'grieving son' face. As phony as it appeared to me, it looked as if the judge was buying it.

"You found no other wills, Counselors?" he said, peering over the top of his glasses. He glowered at Tommy's lawyer; then turned his glare on Elizabeth.

"None, Your Honor," they said in unison.

"Well, we're talking about a valuable piece of property being bequeathed to an unrelated person while there are living heirs present. I'll need to take this under advisement." He gathered the papers together and tapped them into a tidy stack. Then he handed the stack to the court clerk. She stamped the top page and then called the next case.

"Now what?" I asked Elizabeth as we stepped out into the hallway.

"We wait."

Tommy came out of the courtroom and turned down the hall. He pointedly avoided looking my way. A part of me wanted to run after him and tell him to forget it. Momi was his mother and he and Sam should get the property. In fact, a year ago I would've done just that. To heck with what Momi wanted, I just wanted to be liked. Even more, I wanted to avoid conflict at all cost. But that was then and this was now. Even though I was probably going to lose, it felt good to not wimp out.

Elizabeth looked over at me. "I'm afraid it didn't go as I expected. Are you okay?"

"I've never been better."

I told Al I'd probably be leaving for Seattle soon. He said he understood, that he'd be fine on his own, but his eyes betrayed him.

"You've been a good girl to me," he said. "No better cook than you. Not even my Lokelani, and she made *ono* stuff for me every night."

"I've had a wonderful time here with you, Al. But I've run out of money, and now with you feeling better and the Shore Store closed, it's probably best for me to go back to the mainland."

"But what if you get the store? Momi wanted you to have it."

"I know. But the judge didn't seem too thrilled with the idea of Tommy and Sam getting nothing from their mother's inheritance. And I'll bet if Tommy had come back a month earlier, Momi probably wouldn't have written that will at all."

"Could be." He looked conflicted. After all, Tommy and Sam were his nephews, members of his bloodline *ohana*.

A few hours later, I steeled myself for one last act of groveling; one final phone call to Frank.

"Hi, it's me," I said when he picked up.

"Nola! I was just going to call you. Say, I've been thinking about you. What's going on, babe?" His voice sounded oddly enthusiastic, as if he was trying to impress someone within earshot of what a swell soon-to-be-ex-husband he was.

"I hate to ask again, but I really need a little money." I waited for the hostility to creep into his voice.

"How much?" He sounded neutral. Maybe he was playing me. Wouldn't be the first time.

"I need airfare home. Probably about five hundred dollars."

"One way?" Leave it to Frank to make my begging more painful than it already was.

"Yes. I said I'm coming home." I prepared myself for the gloating that was sure to follow. The funny thing was I'd winced even more at using the word 'home' than asking for the money. Seattle wasn't home anymore, but that wasn't something I cared to discuss with Frank.

"Are you okay?" he said. "I've been worried about you since our last phone call. I would've called you, but I've experienced a few setbacks."

Setbacks? I was shocked to hear Frank, a firm believer in positive mental attitude, use such a word.

"What's happened? Have you heard something about Frankie?"

"No, no. He's fine. Last I heard he was still in Mexico, selling timeshares or something."

"That's what I heard too." I wanted him to know I had access to the same information he did.

For reasons that will forever remain a mystery, I started to cry.

"I'm sorry," I burbled into the receiver. "I'm broke, I'm tired, and I need to come home. Would you please help me?" Then I blurted out the whole story—minus any reference to Aidan, of course. I told him about being accused of running over Momi's dog, and about working so hard at the Shore Store and getting paid slave wages. Then I told him about Momi dying, and the holographic will, and my failed attempts to get the restaurant permits I needed. By the time I got around to describing my run-ins with the health inspectors and the fire inspector, I'm pretty sure I was incoherent.

"Give me a couple of days," he said. His voice had a caring tone I hadn't heard in ten years. "By the way, I'm sorry about what happened."

Perhaps a stronger woman would have replied, *You damn well ought to be.* But, God help me, I said, "Thanks, Frank. It's okay."

Later, I mentally rehashed my response over and over. What was I—nuts? It's *okay* to cheat on me with a young man only a few years older than your own son? It's *okay* to bring a complete stranger into my bed while I'm staying over at a friend's house? It's *okay* to try to starve me out by not giving me the settlement we'd agreed on?

But I was too beat down to say anything. I felt like a caterpillar who'd begun to sprout wings but in the struggle to leave the cocoon just gave up. Yeah, it'd be nice to fly, but the effort was too exhausting.

I spent the next couple of days cleaning Al's house and readying myself for my return to reality. I went to the farmer's market and said my farewells. I drove the van up to Kapalua and watched the waves crashing at Fleming Beach. No more sherbet-colored sunsets, no more lemon-Aidan, or stunning views from the Shore Store lanai.

On Saturday afternoon, my cell phone rang. Frank's cell number flashed across the caller ID screen.

"Hi," I said. "I hope you're calling to say you have the ticket money for me."

"I've got it all handled," he said. "Do you know where the Hawaiian Airlines ticket counter is at the Maui airport?"

"Yes, Frank," I forced myself to refrain from chiding him about never coming to Hawaii. If he'd ever been here before, he'd have known that Kahului Airport is tiny, and the Hawaiian Airlines ticket counters are pretty much front and center.

"Well, what you need is waiting for you there. They're expecting you within the hour."

"What's the rush?" Perhaps he'd bought me a same day ticket. "Should I bring my luggage?"

"No, you won't be leaving today. But the ticket agent said there's a shift change in an hour. I'll feel better once I know you've picked it up."

I asked Al if I could borrow the van.

"You want to come?" I said. "It'll just be a quick trip over and back."

"No, thanks," he said. "I gotta fertilize the orchids this afternoon. And then Kilia's coming over to play cribbage."

"Okay," I said. "Maybe I'll stop off at Costco and pick up some things." I didn't want to be around when that busybody showed up. She was still telling people I'd run over Momi's dog. "And I'll gas up the van while I'm at it."

I'd already climbed into the driver's seat before I remembered I didn't have any money for shopping or gas.

CHAPTER 27

A sense of loss rolled over me like a rogue wave when I pulled into the Kahului Airport parking lot. The next time I came out there, I'd be leaving Maui for good. I parked the van and walked toward the terminal. The view of cloud-shrouded Mt. Haleakala that had greeted me when I first arrived still took my breath away.

I waited for the crosswalk light to change and then hurried across the street, squinting into the shadowed interior of the open-air ticketing area. I'd forgotten to ask Frank which agent I should ask for. There was a milling throng of mainland-bound vacationers swirling around the baggage check area. They looked tanned, but cranky about leaving.

I got in the line that read 'Buy Tickets.' While I waited, my cell phone started chirping. I took the call.

"Nola?" It was Frank. "Where are you?"

"I'm at the airport. I'm in line at the ticket counter."

"Oh, I see you now," he said.

Huh?

I turned and there he was, striding across the ticket lobby. He was towing a large black soft-sided suitcase. Not good. Not good at all.

He pushed his way through the people behind me. I couldn't make myself move to meet him halfway. I doggedly maintained my position, trying to come up with a good reason why he'd shown up. I still held out hope there might be a ticket for me at the counter.

"Surprised?" he said when he'd finally pushed his way to where I was standing. Behind him, waiting passengers glared in indignation, but Frank didn't seem to notice.

"Yes," I sputtered. "I'd say that's an understatement."

"You look absolutely wonderful," he said, grabbing my arms to pull me in for a hug. I turned aside at the last moment and my shoulder dug into his chest—his bony chest, compared to Aidan's. The side of my head clomped him on the chin.

I couldn't think of anything to say. I was literally dumbstruck with shock. Was I happy to see him? Or still furious? The truth lay somewhere in-between.

"Did you buy me a ticket?"

"Yes and no."

I waited, unwilling to beg for more information.

"Look, Nola, I've just gotten off a grueling flight with screaming babies and some kind of sports team throwing Nerf balls around the cabin. Can we just get out of here?"

I led Frank back to the *ohana*-mobile. I could only imagine what he'd think of the pitiful vehicle, but I'd already decided I wasn't going to be his chauffeur.

"What's this?" He grinned as I opened the driver door. "Going native?"

"It's your ride to the rental car desk." I opened the back doors and waited for him to throw in his suitcase. "Where are you staying, Frank?"

His mouth tightened into a straight line and his eyes darted from me to the van.

"I didn't mean to offend you," he said. "I'm just surprised at your choice of ride. You were always so fond of your comfy Taurus back home."

"It's borrowed, okay? And just for the record, I hated that stupid Taurus. I drove it because it matched everything else in my life—beige and dull."

Frank ignored my attempt to start an argument. "I was hoping I could stay with you."

"That's not possible. Malia's dad's house isn't big enough, and besides, he's recovering from a heart attack, remember?"

What I didn't say was I was through playing unpaid cook and maidservant. I'd willingly helped Al, but Frank's ticket had been punched months ago.

"Where's your boyfriend?" I said. There was no way I'd allow him to pretend his extramarital affair hadn't happened. "I'd think a little hottie like him would love a trip to Hawaii."

"Nola, is there somewhere we can talk? I didn't come all this way just to bring you home. I have some things I need to say."

"You already said you were sorry and I accepted your apology. What more is there?"

"Please?" He turned on his super-salesman smile. "I know you'll be glad you said 'yes' if you'll just hear me out. Let me take you to dinner."

I called Al and told him I'd run into a friend at the airport and we were going to grab a bite. I reminded him about the leftover fried rice and barbecued pork tenderloin in the fridge.

"I'll be okay," he said. "You'll be back before dark?"

I assured him I would. When I hung up, I felt like laughing out loud. There I was, sneaking off to dinner with my gay, almost-ex-husband and furtively calling my girlfriend's father to beg off from my unpaid caretaking job for a few hours. If I weren't living it, I wouldn't have believed it.

We went to Buzz's Wharf in Ma'alaea. When the waiter asked if we wanted a drink, I ordered a mai tai. Frank shot me a withering look and ordered a club soda and lime.

After the drinks were served, he reached for my hand. I started to pull it away, but decided it was a small price to pay for a ticket home.

"I think you may still feel some anger toward me," he said.

Good thing I didn't have a mouthful of mai tai, or I may have spit it all over the table. I gave a small nod, staring into the intricate folds of the napkin in front of me.

"I went a little nuts there for a while, but it's over, Nola. I don't know what happened, but I felt so trapped, so bored. I mean it when I tell you I'm truly sorry.

I looked into his hang-dog face. His eyes drooped at the outer corners. Funny, I'd never noticed that before. And his pale flaccid skin was as rumpled and creased as a wadded-up dollar bill.

"My relationship with Jason is over. It wasn't much to begin with, believe me. He was looking for a meal ticket and I fit the bill."

"And what, exactly, were *you* looking for, Frank?"

"I guess I wanted to see another side of life."

"Did you?"

"It's not what you think." He blew out a quick breath. "It was mostly platonic, believe me."

"But some of it wasn't, right?"

"I was very careful. I got an HIV test and everything."

As if that should make me want to hop into his lap in gratitude?

"Well, I appreciate you owning up to your mistake," I said.

"There's more." He pulled out a business-size envelope from the inside pocket of his sport coat. I flinched and choked back a gasp when I noticed the All Seattle Realty logo. Had I really worked there? It seemed like a dream.

He handed me the unsealed envelope. I flipped the flap open and saw a business check. It was made out to me for the sum of ten thousand dollars.

This time I did gasp. I felt a hot tingling in my sinuses and knew I'd be sniffing back tears in a few seconds. I almost said, *I can't take your money*, but luckily I managed to keep my mouth shut.

"I haven't put the house up for sale, but I wanted you to have something," he said. "It's got to be hard for you to have no money."

It took all the strength I had to avoid pointing out that I'd worked for him for more than ten years without a paycheck. But I didn't want him to snatch away my ticket home—and my down payment on a place to live once I got there—so I just flashed him a smile and slipped the check into my purse.

Our food came. I had the char-grilled mahi-mahi accented with a yummy mango salsa. It smelled wonderful, but when I tried to eat, I found my throat had pinched closed and I could hardly swallow.

"Aren't you hungry?" he said, after ten minutes passed and I hadn't taken another bite.

"No, not really. You have to realize seeing you is quite a shock."

"I know. I've upset you a lot in the past few months. But if you'll allow me to make it up to you, I will. I mean it, Nola. I messed up pretty bad, with both you and Frank Jr., but I swear I'm a changed man."

I'd already come to accept Frank as a so-called 'changed man.' The question was, could I dare to believe he'd changed back?

After dinner he followed me in his rental car as I led the way down the Honoapi'ilani Highway to the Ka'anapali Villas Resort. He checked in and asked if I wanted to come by his room, but I declined.

It was inky dark when I pulled into Al's carport. He'd turned the porch light on for me, probably more a subtle statement about me missing curfew than a nod to security.

All was asleep on the sofa. I went into his room and got him a pillow and blanket. I felt a twinge of guilt he'd waited up for me, but I didn't want to wake him. He'd be comfortable enough on the sofa to sleep through the night.

As for me, I didn't expect to sleep at all.

CHAPTER 28

The next evening I finally confessed to Al that my cheating, former gay, soon-to-be ex had come to town. He shrugged it off, his level stare not signaling much of an opinion. His biggest concern seemed to be how it would impact his meal schedule.

"I'll make you breakfast and fix you a cold lunch for the fridge. I'll be going back to the mainland soon anyway, so you need to get used to doing things on your own."

He dropped his head like a scolded dog. I felt guilty, but held my ground.

"What about dinner?" he said after a moment of silence. "You gonna make me dinner until you have to leave?"

"I'll make it most nights. But Frank will only be here for a little while. He and I may go out to dinner a time or two."

I would've invited Al to join us, or asked if I could bring Frank to the house sometime, but I didn't want Al relaying too much information to Malia. I still wasn't convinced of Frank's professed change of heart, so I didn't want to be forced to defend it.

But keeping the two men apart didn't diminish Al's pique over my spotty attention to him. I knew it was just a matter of time before he'd start complaining to Malia.

My cell phone rang. Frank had offered to get us tickets to Warren & Annabelle's, a chic Lahaina nightclub with an amazing magic show. I'd asked him to call if he'd managed to get tickets for that night.

"Hi," I said, chirping like a chickadee. "Are we all set?"

"I don't know," said Malia in her *you're in deep doo-doo* voice. "Are *we*?"

"Oh hi, Malia," I forced myself to sound pleased to hear from her, but my heart raced in anticipation of the dressing-down I knew was coming.

"Don't 'oh hi' me," she said. "What the *hell* is going on?"

It pretty much went downhill from there.

I explained Frank had come to take me back home, and he'd helped me out financially. I added that he seemed genuinely contrite about his infidelity.

"I suppose this means you're dumping Aidan?"

No fair. I hadn't allowed myself the luxury of thinking about Aidan. But instead of admitting my uncertainty, I played major dodge ball.

"He's busy working on his hotel contract." I moved the phone to my other hand so I could wipe my sweaty palm on my shorts. "We haven't seen each other in almost a week." That part was pretty much true. Ever since the fire inspector closed the store I'd avoided going down to Lahaina. But Aidan still called every day, and he'd been over for dinner the weekend before Frank arrived.

"Don't duck me, Nola. I talk to Aidan every week. He has no idea you've thrown in the towel on him. And he sure as hell doesn't have any clue about you getting all kissie-face with Cowboy Frank."

"Don't call him that," I said.

"What? Too close for comfort? Nola, get a grip. How much cash did ol' Frank throw your way? A thousand, five thousand? What's your price for turning a blind eye to adultery and trashing your wedding vows?"

"I can't talk anymore. I've got to go." I started to hang up, but then I added, "You know, I made my bed more than twenty years ago. It's a little late for me to go mattress shopping."

"Oh, please. Don't head down the victim road. It leads nowhere. All I'm saying is you deserve better. And you know it."

"Thanks," I said. "But I've got to see this through."

"I think you're making a huge mistake. Especially since Aidan worships you. Don't kid yourself; this is going to hit him hard. But if this is what you need to do, then I wish you well."

"Thanks for understanding," I said. "You're the best."

"No, you are. I just wish you could see yourself like everyone else does."

We hung up. My armpits were damp, but my mood lifted now that my furtive reunion was no longer a secret.

For the next week, Frank and I focused on tourist activities. We went snorkeling at the Olavine Pools in Kapalua. We took a helicopter ride around the island. We even joined the throng at the Old Lahaina Luau. Every evening Frank made dinner reservations at a nice restaurant, but I always made a point of fixing a hot meal for Al before I left.

On Thursday, we drove the road to Hana and stayed two nights at an unbelievably romantic—and ridiculously expensive—beach hideaway. The place had no TV, no telephones, and no alarm clocks. It didn't even have cell service. It was as if we'd stepped back to the early years, before a cloud of tedium had settled over our marriage.

"I love you, Nola," Frank said on our second morning in Hana. We were sitting on the lanai enjoying fresh croissants and Kona coffee while gazing at the surf pounding hypnotically against the black sand beach below. "I always have and always will. I think we ought to get remarried. You know, wipe the slate clean and start over."

For a millisecond, my mind flashed on the sound of the young man's voice answering the phone in my bedroom the day after I found the "nooner" card. I took a deep breath and it stuck in my lungs.

"What's that?" he said. "You're thinking about something bad; I can tell."

"I was thinking about how much it hurt, Frank."

"It hurt me, too. I was like a drug addict. I knew I shouldn't be doing what I was doing, but I couldn't stop. I'm over it, though. You know I stopped drinking. I'm a guy in recovery. But in order for this to work I need you, just like I needed you for the drinking."

I bit my lower lip. My eyes darted from his pleading eyes to his creased brow. They finally settled on the white knuckles of his fisted hands.

"This has got to be a 'pinkie-swear, hope to die' pledge, Frank."

"I'd rather be dead than live without you."

We went back into the room and made love. At first I felt awkward stripping off my clothes at ten o'clock in the morning, but when I stood naked before him, Frank's jaw dropped. He gave a low whistle that made me tingle.

"You look better than you did when we got married," he said. "Look at you—all tanned and buffed out."

The term "buffed out" didn't sit well with me, but I pushed down my unease and accepted the compliment.

Everything about Frank was so familiar—his scent, his body, his moves. It felt like crawling back in your own bed at home after spending time in the hospital. .

"I love you, too," I said afterward. "What happened to us? We got in a rut and couldn't get out."

"Yeah, babe, that's what I was trying to say. I'm sorry it took me going nuts to realize we were meant to be together. But now that it's over, I'm kind of glad it happened."

Well, that made one of us. I would've given anything to have not found that card, or heard that voice on the phone, or had Frankie vanish to Mexico. But an opportunity to take the high road had been laid out before me, so I gave a half-hearted nod.

On the long ride back from Hana, Frank offered me yet another high road opportunity.

"I've been thinking, Nola. There's not much waiting for us back in Seattle. Maybe we should consider a complete change of scene."

"What do you mean, nothing waiting for us in Seattle? We have our house and the business."

"The house has built up a ton of equity. We could sell it in a week." He smiled as if he was about to pull a quarter out of his ear. "And, you're going to love this: The price of the business went up with the second valuation. They're now saying is worth closer to two million."

My bullshit radar started pinging, but I muted the bell.

"What are you saying?"

"I'm saying, why not here? You love it here, right?" He looked over, eyebrows raised as if he expected me to scoot across the seat and throw my arms around his neck.

Instead, I shot him a one-bob nod.

"Well then, why not start over in Hawaii? I could get my real estate license here and sell multi-million-dollar properties. Think of the commissions. And with the payout from the Seattle house and the business, I wouldn't have to do more than a couple of deals a year."

I gave my forehead a quick fingertip massage to release the tension between my knotted brows.

"And, we could open a little restaurant, you know, like you were saying. Hell, we could open a *big* restaurant. With the money we've got and your flair for cooking, the sky's the limit."

Frank obviously hadn't researched Maui commercial real estate prices, but I didn't want to dampen his enthusiasm with a cold blast of reality.

"You want to stay here?" I said. "And you'll help me open a restaurant while you study for your real estate license?"

"Yep, that's the plan. What do you say?"

"Sounds good. But I'm wondering if you really know what you're getting yourself into. It's not the same here, Frank. Believe me, this place is a hundred eighty degree turn from Seattle."

"I'm aware there'll be some differences. But look at you. This place is like the fountain of youth or something. If we start over here I know it will be *fabulous* for both of us."

The emphasis with which he'd gushed the word 'fabulous' caused my radar to *ping-ping-ping* in double-time alarm. I couldn't remember ever hearing Frank use the word with such gusto, except perhaps when describing an over-priced condo to a well-heeled buyer.

He reached for my hand, but then he quickly pulled it back and grabbed the steering wheel as we met another car coming straight at us on a narrow hairpin turn. When we'd safely negotiated a series of switchbacks and were within a mile of the town of Pa'ia, I finally spoke.

"Why don't we stop at the Shore Store on the way home?" I said. "If we decide to open a restaurant, that's where I'd want it to be. It's a *fabulous* location." My turn to volley the word back at him. I watched for a flicker—a hint—of annoyance at my mockery, but if he felt it, he didn't let on.

"Great," said Frank, releasing a whoosh of breath it seemed he'd been holding since we left Hana. "I can hardly wait to see it."

Ping-ping-ping. I wanted to trust him; to be a willing partner in his starting-over plan. Everyone makes mistakes, and I believed Frank's apology was sincere.

Question was: why did my mental radar keep going off like that?

CHAPTER 29

I don't know what I imagined would happen when Aidan met Frank, but a schoolyard scuffle never crossed my mind. We parked in front of the Shore Store on our way back from Hana. Aidan had been watching the store for me since it'd been closed, and I knew that within a few minutes he'd come out to eyeball the unfamiliar car parked in front. Sure enough, he showed up as I was jiggling the key in the front door lock.

"Hey, Nola, long time, no see." He smiled at Frank as if angling for an introduction. He'd probably pegged him as some type of county inspector and wanted to make sure the guy knew I had a *kama'aina* neighbor willing to go to bat for me.

"Hello, Aidan," I said.

"Everything okay?" Aidan glanced from me to Frank and then back again.

"Just fine. We'll only be a minute."

At that, Aidan shot me some stink eye to let me know he wasn't pleased with my lack of manners. By then he'd figured out my companion was no inspector.

Fortunately, he left it at that and walked back over to his side of the building. He pulled his door shut with a bang.

"Who's your little buddy?" Frank said. His eyes stayed riveted on Aidan's studio door.

"My neighbor. He's a sculptor."

"Somethin' going on between you two?"

I did my best to act annoyed, as if his assumption was way off base, but I felt the hot spot sprouting at the base of my neck.

"Hey, no problem-o," Frank said. "We've both had our little indiscretions, and now it's time to put all that behind us, right?"

Frank reached for me, but I stepped around him, pretending I didn't notice.

"Here's the store part," I said, gesturing to the few remaining shelves of groceries lining the walls. "And back here is the deli counter. It's called a *bento* over here. The other word for it is *okazuya*, but that's kind of a mouthful, so I just say deli or *bento*."

Frank glanced around the room as if calculating the square footage.

"This is the place you might inherit?"

"Well, it's a long shot. Remember I told you about the handwritten will? Her two sons are contesting it and the judge took it under advisement, so I don't think it looks good. Funny thing is, the sons don't want the store; they just want to sell it."

"That's okay. If they get it, we'll buy it from them."

"It would take everything we've got."

"Are you kidding? This dump should go for, what, three hundred thou, maybe half a mil?"

"The tax assessment is more than two million dollars."

"Who told you that? That's total bullshit. In Seattle, even close to the waterfront like this, an old commercial building in this condition would go for two-fifty, maybe three hundred thousand. I'm being generous with the half-mil."

"We're not in Seattle, Frank. That's the tax assessment—believe it."

"Right. When pigs fly."

He poked around and soon found the stairs leading to the upper level.

"It's got an attic?"

"It's a complete upper floor. It's only used for storage right now, but it's got a balcony with a killer view. I'd put the bar up there."

"Really? Let's see it."

As we made our way up the rickety stairs I warned him the upstairs was still pretty grungy. At the top, I turned and caught a glimpse of Frank's face scrunched in disgust.

"Everything okay?" I asked.

"Sure, sweetie," he said, pushing down the scowl. "It's fine."

We crossed the room and with a tah-dah gesture, I opened the French doors to the lanai. The view never failed to astonish me.

"That's it?" He nodded indifferently toward the uninterrupted expanse of ocean with the dusky brown of the island of Lana'i to the south and a glimpse of cloud-shrouded Molokai to the north. His eyes squinted in the harsh sunlight, and he'd pulled his mouth down into a tight frown.

"Isn't it amazing?"

"It's all right, I suppose. But looking over those rooftops makes it a second-tier ocean view."

I felt a pinch of irritation he didn't consider my killer view so killer. I imagined sitting out here, mai tai in hand, while the kitchen below hummed with activity turning out state-of-the-art Pacific fusion cuisine. But none of that would fire up Frank. He couldn't drink alcohol, and his preferred dinner fare was overcooked pot roast next to a mountain of mashed potatoes and gravy.

We'd turned to go back inside when the upper doors to Aidan's side burst open and he stepped out onto the lanai.

"Oh, sorry. I didn't know you guys were out here." He looked uncomfortable with the lie. He and I both knew the thin clapboard walls kept no secrets.

This time I couldn't avoid an introduction.

"Aidan, this is my, uh, this is Frank Stevens. From Seattle."

If I were a sadist, I would have gotten a big kick out of the look on Aidan's face. But since I'd never been comfortable watching other people thrash around in distress, I squirmed instead.

"Frank?" He spit it out like a watermelon seed. "You mean, *that* Frank?"

"I see my celebrity precedes me," Frank said. He smiled and extended his hand.

Aidan hesitated, then stepped forward and grabbed Frank by the collar of his polo shirt. He pulled him in close. With Frank's face hovering about four inches from his, Aidan gave him a little shake like a Rottweiler checking out a new chew toy.

"I don't know what the hell you're doing here," he said in a low voice. "But I want you to know if you do anything, and I mean *anything*, to cause this woman one more second of pain, I will personally take you out. Got it?"

I take back my comment about being a sadist. I must've had a tiny streak, because I took some pleasure in Aidan's threat. I'd agreed to forgive Frank, but the wound was still tender.

"Let me go, you smelly hippie," said Frank. Aidan released his grip. Frank reached up and fiddled with his collar as if it'd been ruffled by the wind. "I have no intention of causing her harm. And, although it's absolutely none of your business, you can be sure I've already apologized for our previous personal problems. Nola has forgiven me, and we are planning to renew our marriage vows. So, now I'm telling *you*—get the hell out of her life."

Aidan turned to me. "I guess I won't be helping you wire those exit lights, after all," he said. His piercing eyes locked on mine while a muscle in his jaw twitched like an external heartbeat.

"Oh, okay," I said. I tried to come up with something more—an apology, an explanation—but I drew a blank.

Aidan stalked back to his side of the lanai and banged the doors closed with a pane-rattling crash.

"It seems your neighbor has a penchant for slamming doors," said Frank. He tucked his rumpled shirt into the waistband of his shorts. "Also it seems you two are well-acquainted." He leaned in close. "Intimately, I presume?"

"Don't go there, Frank. I'm not going to apologize for getting on with my life these past few months. If that's going to be a problem for you then we better just go forward with the divorce."

Frank reached out and enveloped me in his arms.

"I'm sorry. I didn't mean to pry. I love you, Nola. We've been together for almost twenty-five years—laughing, crying, just *being* there for each other. It's just hard for me to imagine you with someone else."

The high road was getting steeper. I bit back half-a-dozen zingers.

He must have seen the cloud skitter across my expression, because he went in for the knock-out punch, "Can you imagine how happy Frank Jr. will be to hear we've patched things up?"

I pulled in a lung-filling breath of ocean air. No doubt my life had been a thousand times easier when I was married. I had a gorgeous home, a no-stress job working with my successful husband, and a delightful son. Now I had no money, no place to live, and I was smack in the middle of an inheritance squabble with someone else's family. Everyone makes mistakes, especially mid-life men. It was so common it was a cliché.

"I love you, too," I said. "And I'm sorry about Aidan roughing you up."

"He didn't even come close," Frank said in a huffy tone. "I could have pounded his sorry butt into the pavement if I'd felt like it. But I've got nothing to prove."

I stifled an eye roll. I'd seen both men naked. End of story.

"Sure," I said. "Let's get back downstairs and go out and get some lunch. I'm starving."

Right after lunch, I dropped Frank at his hotel and drove to Lahaina to cash the ten thousand dollar check. I ended up opening an account at Bank of Hawaii. I'd never had any financial accounts in my own name, and I hesitated when the teller asked me if I wanted to add a co-signer.

"No, just me."

I went back to the Shore Store and called an electrician about wiring the lighted exit signs. I wasn't kidding myself; I expected more violations to be pointed out once I'd fixed the signs. But I couldn't get the fire inspector to return until I'd dealt with the exits.

West Maui Electric gave me a three o'clock arrival time, but I knew that could run into four or five o'clock; maybe even the next day.

The electrician showed up at two-thirty. Aidan showed up at two-thirty-five.

"I said I'd do that for you," he said, steering me into the back by the empty deli counter.

"You said this morning you weren't going to."

"I know. But I didn't mean it."

"I'm sorry," I said. I took his hand. "Frank showing up was a real shock. But I feel like I've got to give him a chance. I think he's sincerely sorry. And, if we can get the Anakua brothers to sell us this place, he said he wants to stay here and help me open a restaurant. Maybe even an upstairs bar."

"You think the Maui powers-that-be are going to give you an occupancy permit, let alone a liquor license?"

"Money talks, Aidan. I think with enough cash to the right people we can make it happen."

"Good luck with that," he said. He started for the door, then stopped short when he saw the electrician's ladder was in the way. "Mind if I use the upstairs doors?"

"Sure."

"Oh. I almost forgot," he said. "I got a call from a guy over on Kauai. He owns a pretty good-size gallery in the Poipu area. He's offered me a studio and part ownership in the gallery if I'll move my operation over there. I'm going over for about a week starting Saturday. I'd appreciate you keeping an eye on my place while I go check it out."

"You're thinking of leaving?"

"Why not? Looks like we're both moving on. Or, in your case, moving backward." His eyes were as flat as pewter buttons.

I nodded. I didn't trust myself to say anything without crying.

The electrician finished installing the lighted signs in half an hour.

I puttered around, wiping down the already spotless deli area. I chastised myself for not calling Frank as soon as the electrician finished, but after a week of being with him almost every waking moment, I wasn't ready to give up my alone time.

At about five o'clock, Frank called my cell and asked if I'd mind not going out to dinner that night.

"I laid out in the sun all afternoon and I've gotten a little burned," he said. "I think I'll turn in early."

"That's okay. I'd like to spend some time with Al. He's getting cranky about me being gone every night."

"Good," he said. "So, what's next?"

"Next?"

"Yeah. Now that you have your exit lights can you open the store back up?"

"I guess so. I'll call the fire inspector's office tomorrow and tell them I got the signs. I'll open up tomorrow and see what they do about it."

What was the worst they could do? Shut me down again? I'd remedied the violation, so if they want to come back and cite me for something else, they could. The ball was in their court.

By the following Tuesday, they'd returned with a vengeance. I was cited for combustibles creating an unsafe fuel load. I hadn't provided wheelchair accessibility—although almost all of the older buildings in Lahaina hadn't done so either. I was guilty of an ignition source too close to a fuel source. I didn't have fire extinguishers rated for wood, grease, and electrical fires. The list went on and on. My work wasn't just cut out for me; it was piled to the rafters.

I stomped over to Aidan's to whine and wail about the unfairness of it all, but then I stopped short when I saw the "Closed" sign on his door. I'd been so busy getting the store back up and running I hadn't noticed he'd already left on his fact-finding trip to Kauai. A fist tightened in my chest as it dawned on me I had no reason to seek sympathy from Aidan: Frank was my business partner now.

But where was Frank? That morning at around ten, he'd offered to run to the hardware store for a box of heavy-duty garbage bags. It was almost two-thirty. In the four-plus hours he'd been gone, I'd hauled two dozen huge boxes of paper plates and napkins down the stairs; met with the contractor about installing a ramp to the front porch; washed all the upstairs windows; and fixed lunch for sixty-two hungry customers.

"Where the hell have you been?" I said when he finally walked through the door.

"Excuse me," he said. "Maybe I should go out and come in again." He spun around.

"No, Frank," I said. "I'm sorry. It's just that I expected you hours ago."

"Why? You got a million little chores up your sleeve for me?" He came around the counter and began kissing my neck. I smelled beer on his breath.

"Frank, have you been drinking?"

"What? No." He dragged out the 'no' a little longer than an innocent—or a stone sober—man would have. "I went back to my place and dozed a bit by the pool. A clumsy barmaid came by, bumped the edge of my chair and spilled a glass of beer on me."

I sniffed his shirt.

"I changed clothes, Nola. But I needed to get back here, so I didn't take time for a shower. It's probably still in my hair and on my skin."

Ping-ping-ping. Quite a story. I wanted to believe him, though, so once again I mentally threw a pillow over the annoying little warning bell.

Too bad I'd been born in the twentieth century. I bet I could've given Cleopatra a run for her money as the "Queen of De Nile."

CHAPTER 30

Aidan came back the following Friday. He told me he'd accepted the position on Kauai and would be leaving by the end of the month.

"I'm happy for you," I said. "But I'll miss you."

I wanted to say a lot more.

"Yeah, well, Frank's helping you out now so you'll be fine." He glanced around the store taking in the improvements.

What I didn't tell him was Frank's idea of helping out meant coming by after the work was finished and passing judgment. I felt like the Little Red Hen—where the animals have a million excuses why they can't help, but they show up at the end to eat the bread. I shrugged it off. I actually preferred working alone. Frank didn't know squat about cooking or the restaurant business, so it was easier for me if he stayed away.

"You guys have done some good things. How's the permit process going?"

"It's not. I know I have to pay my dues, but it's starting to feel like a French farce. As soon as I fix one thing, they come back and find fault with something else."

"Patience. That's the best advice I can offer."

Frank was taking an online prep course to get ready for the Hawaii real estate license exam. Every day he'd report on how the laws in Hawaii were "weird" or "wrong."

"This Kingdom of Hawaii crap is a joke," he said one night when we were eating a late dinner at Al's. Kilia had invited Al over for ice cream so we were alone.

"Don't say that in front of Al or any of the other Kanekoas. They feel very strongly about their country being stolen from them."

"Oh, for crying out loud. This place was a string of desert islands inhabited by naked savages. The best thing that ever happened to them was when the U.S. Navy showed up."

I waited for the ghost of Momi to strike him dead— or at least make him choke on his *haupia* pudding.

"This is good stuff," he said. "What's it made of?"

"It's *haupia*—coconut. I thought you'd like it because it's beige."

"Hmm." Frank wrinkled up his nose. "But coconuts are round, aren't they?"

"Frank, the coconut *meat* isn't round. It comes out in hunks, like beef jerky." That was stretching it, but Frank loved his jerky.

"True. And, it is pretty tasty." He scraped the last of the pudding from the bowl. "Guess what? I talked to a friend back home who's going down to Cabo next week. I told him to keep an eye out for Frank Jr."

"What?" I pushed back my chair. "Do you know where Frankie's living?" I ran out of air by the end of the sentence.

"Don't get your panties in a wad," he said. "I'm not exactly sure where he is. But I figure Cabo's a small town. A light-haired American kid like Frank Jr. working at a timeshare resort shouldn't be that hard to find."

My heart pounded at the thought of Frankie hearing his parents had gotten back together. I hoped it might put an end his self-imposed exile.

Frank ran his fingertips up my arm. "You know, I was thinking we ought to go out tomorrow and buy you something nice. You've been spending all your money fixing up that restaurant. I think you deserve a present."

I tried to read his face. He looked like he already had something in mind.

"How about it?" he went on. "Can you pull yourself away from the salt mine long enough to go with me to a jewelry store?"

Frank rarely bought me luxury gifts. The one time he did—it was a fox fur coat for our tenth anniversary—I never wore it because I swore I could hear the screams of little ghost foxes whenever I slipped it on.

We went to an upscale jewelry shop in Kahana. The clerks were dressed as if they were working in Beverly Hills rather than a shopping mall anchored by an Outback Steak House and a McDonald's. I felt a bit dowdy in my jersey knit shorts and tee-shirt, but they warmly welcomed us in. I'd seen photos of big-name celebrities in Lahaina restaurants and shops and they were always wearing tee-shirts, ball caps, and no makeup.

Store clerks were smart to not judge their customers by their appearance.

"*Aloha*," said a young male clerk. "Are you enjoying your stay?"

"It's very nice here." Frank gave him his *I've got money to spend* smile.

If it'd been up to me, I'd have gone the *kama'aina* route and pushed for the locals' discount, but Frank seemed to prefer to play tourist.

"What can I show you today?"

We made a quick sweep around the glass cases. I stopped in front of a display of exquisite gold necklaces.

"These are beautiful," I said.

"Oh, you picked wisely," said the clerk. "These are made on Maui, by a very talented local artist. A sculptor, actually. "

I stifled a gasp and mentally kicked myself for not recognizing them sooner.

"You want to try one on?" said Frank.

"No," I said, turning away from the case. "I'd prefer something else."

Frank drifted over to the engagement rings. "Remember when I told you I'd upgrade your diamond?"

How could I forget all those years of disappointment?

"You did? When was that?" I said. Too bad the Oscar committee wasn't in earshot.

He bought me a one-and-a-quarter carat solitaire in a platinum setting. It cost as much as a compact car, but Frank insisted. On the trip back to Frank's hotel room I kept flipping my hand up to gaze at how it caught the light.

"You love it, don't you?" he said.

"It's incredible. Thank you so much. This is really such a surprise."

"Well, you deserve it. You've been such a good sport about all of this."

A good sport? *Ping-ping-ping.*

"I've got some really big news to tell you," he said. "And I wanted you to be in a good mood to hear it."

"O-kay," I said, drawing out the word.

"I've decided to buy a brokerage over here."

"Wow. That's a pretty big step. What does something like that cost?"

"The down payment would take most of our money, and we'd have to negotiate a commission split for a few years. But I met a guy who wants to go back to the states, and he's anxious to sell."

Frank had yet to comprehend that Hawaii is already in the "states." The locals refer to the continental U.S. as "the mainland." But I shrugged off the urge to play smarty-pants.

"What about the restaurant, Frank? We'll need money to get that going."

"I know. That may need to get postponed. But with me back in the brokerage business, you won't have to do the restaurant. You can work with me."

I caught the not-so-subtle change in his attitude. In the past two weeks, he'd gone from '*I'll do anything to make it up to you*' to '*Here's what I plan to do.*' But realistically, my goal of turning the Shore Store into a restaurant had shifted from a dream into something more like a delusion. The ownership of the property was still in question, the inspectors seemed unwilling to ever hand me a food service permit, and now Frank had plans to spend all our money on a real estate brokerage.

The months I'd spent with the Kanekoas had been fun, but real life beckoned. I was proud of myself for my decision to forgive Frank and move on. At least by reconciling I was assured of a comfortable future. Most importantly, I felt certain it was only a matter of time before Frank Jr. would be back in my life.

I knew I was doing the right thing. Oddly, I kept having a weird dream where I was some kind of little burrowing animal—like a prairie dog. Every time I'd pop out of my hole, there'd be some kind of disaster: a fire, a flood, a huge tree crashing down. I'd be forced to scurry back down the hole. I'd awaken with my heart pounding, wondering what it meant.

CHAPTER 31

It's funny how childhood cruelty stays with you. Whenever I got emotionally trashed, not only would I usually see the black splotches, I'd often hear the jeering voice of the kid who lived next door when I was a little. He'd say things like, *fatty, fatty two-by-four, can't get through the kitchen door...*, or *I'm rubber, you're glue, anything you say bounces off me and sticks to you.*

On Wednesday morning, I went over to Aidan's studio to see if I could borrow a roll of paper towels. As I opened the door, I heard the low rumble of his voice followed by a woman's giggle. I stepped back, hoping to quietly close the door before being seen. No such luck.

"Nola?" said Aidan. "Is that you? C'mon in."

His tanned face glowed with satisfaction as he fastened a gold necklace around the neck of a stunning young woman with tawny skin and waist-length glossy black hair. "You remember Emme, don't you? From the jewelry show?"

Oh, if only I could forget. Emme and I had vied for Aidan's attention all night. Me in Momi's gorgeous kimono, and twenty-something Emme in a tiny, midriff-baring white halter top and a Bali print wrap skirt that dipped below her belly button showing off perfectly sculpted abs and a navel ring.

"Nice to see you again," I said. "Aidan, I just came over to see if you had towels...a roll. No, I mean, a roll of paper towels." I took a breath. "Sheesh, I've been breathing too many cleaning fumes over there." I laughed, but my stammering gave me away.

"Sure. Back behind the counter there. Help yourself."

He finished fastening the clasp and bent to give her a peck on the shoulder. She turned and reached her perfectly manicured hand up to his chin and gave him a quick kiss on the cheek. My knees buckled as my breath stalled in my lungs.

She languidly crossed the room in a model's sashay and stood before an oval mirror on the wall. Turning from side to side, she admired the jewelry.

"This is the best one, Aidan. For sure." Gliding back to where he stood, she put an arm around his waist. "How can I ever thank you enough?"

I grabbed the roll of towels, knocking over a can of cleanser in the process. I didn't stop to sweep up the grit. Instead I headed straight for the exit. A cool breeze hit my face as I opened the door and I resumed breathing.

"Bye, Nola." Aidan's voice sounded mocking through the almost-closed door. "Come again anytime."

I shakily made my way across the long porch and back into the store.

You only want it, 'cause you can't have it, said the taunting eight-year-old voice in my mind.

I scrubbed like I was determined to get down to the molecular level. I vowed not to stop until every shelf shined, every window sparkled, and the burnished floorboards gleamed like the deck of a yacht.

At ten-thirty, I knocked off the cleaning and started prepping for lunch. My list of regular lunch customers had grown to more than sixty people, so it took more than a full hour to prep the meats, salad fixings, and breads needed to feed them and get them on their way. I'd paid for the bistro tables with the Frank money, but without the food establishment permit I still couldn't put them out. My eat-in customers were forced to lean against windowsills or sit cross-legged on the porch.

At around four I was nearly finished. I missed Aidan's help with the dishes almost as much as I missed his affection. Frank called at four-thirty to ask if I wanted to go out to dinner.

"If it's okay with you, I think I'll pass," I said. "I'm beat."

"That's fine," he said. "I'm right in the middle of this online class on titles and deeds. You can't imagine how screwy things are over here. They've got government land, fee simple private land, leased land, and then some stupid thing they call 'crown' land. It's a freakin' mess."

"Uh-huh," I said. I didn't feel like going into the whole story about how I knew about the different kinds of title holdings due to Momi's property tax situation. "It's complicated because Hawaii was a conquered country with a legitimate government."

"What country? What government? It was an outcropping in the Pacific with sugar cane fields worked by slave labor."

"Yeah, Frank. Whatever."

"Anyway," he said, "You want me to call you later?"

"Sure. I'm going to be going to bed early, though. Call before nine, okay?"

We acted as if we were dating. Since he'd arrived, I'd only slept with him that one weekend in Hana. We'd planned to resume "marital relations" when we did our re-commitment ceremony and bought a house together. Until then, I was fine sleeping in Al's guest room. Frank seemed content with his little bachelor pad at the villas.

Driving back to Al's, I passed the *okazuya* in Honokowai. I drooled over the memory of their fabulous lemon caper mahi-mahi. It was beige and certainly not round, so I figured Frank might like it. He had to eat dinner anyway, and staring at a computer all day is brutal when the ocean is beckoning and a warm breeze is wafting through the sliding glass door.

I stopped at the deli and had to wait almost twenty minutes for my order to be ready. The expert staff seemed to work at warp speed, but there were a dozen orders ahead of me. It was okay, the food always more than made up for the waiting time.

I pulled into the parking lot at Frank's hotel. Sure enough, his rental car was parked in its assigned stall. It was a perfect night to eat on the little glass table on his ground-floor lanai, so instead of going to the front door I went across the lawn to his first floor patio and set the food on the table.

I peered into the darkened room through a six-inch space between the almost-closed drapes. Frank needed to keep them closed to cut the glare on his computer screen.

The room was dark. Not a single light on or window shade open. I would've gotten eyestrain working in such total gloom.

I didn't see him at the desk.

I rapped lightly on the door, but there was no response. I nudged the handle. The door was unlocked.

Sliding it open, I heard a low moaning coming from the bed at the far side of the room. As my eyes adjusted to the dim light, I saw Frank's head appear from under the covers.

"Are you okay?" I said. "I brought over some dinner."

I saw a second head pop up. It was the young male clerk from the jewelry store where we'd bought my diamond ring.

Look up, look down. Look at my thumb. Gee, you're dumb.

CHAPTER 32

Finding Frank cheating flashed me back to that scene in the *Titanic* movie where the ship's starting to tilt and the people know they're going into the water. Some people spent their last moments performing acts of sacrifice and dignity; others just slid mutely into the black abyss like lobsters at a clambake.

With that in mind, I pushed aside any idea of quietly skulking off. Once was enough.

According to my best recollection it went something like this: I picked up the food I'd brought and stomped into the room. By then they were both hiding under the covers like little kids afraid of the dark. I pulled back the sheet, exposing Frank—naked and cowering. His hands were hiding his face. I pushed his shoulder down to allow for a straight trajectory of the steaming fish onto his privates. As he howled in distress, I launched the Styrofoam containers, Frisbee-style, against the opposite wall. Then I left, slamming the slider shut with such force I'm pretty sure I heard the glass crack. I'm not certain about that, though, because I didn't bother to look back.

Firing up the old van seemed to take minutes instead of seconds. My black stress blotches were back—big-time. I careened out of the parking lot, my vision so obscured I was barely able to make out the road ahead. But I'd driven that route so many times I could've made it back blindfolded.

Pulling into Al's driveway, the van's headlights slashed across the front of the house. Momi's dog, Hulu, was in the front window draped across the back of the sofa. His limp body had the forlorn look of an ancient afghan knitted by a beginner who'd dropped way too many stitches. As a "pet parent" I'd been lousy—I'd forget to change his drinking water until the bowl was dry and, more often than not, I was a no-show for our daily walks.

I went inside and pulled the dog leash out of the junk drawer without so much as a "hello" to Al. He pretended to watch TV, but his eyes skittered my way.

"You mad at me or somethin'?"

"No, Al, not you."

"You mad at Aidan?"

Obviously, Al hadn't been privy to the major twists and turns my life had taken lately.

"No, not Aidan, either," I said. But upon further deliberation, I silently realized his status with me had slipped a few notches since I'd caught him making goo-goo eyes with Emme.

"So, what's up?"

"It's complicated."

"Your ex-husband cheating on you again?"

"Vanna," I said, in an over-the-top impersonation of Pat Sajak on *Wheel of Fortune*, "We have a winner. Hand the man the keys to the brand-new Toyota Four Runner!"

I sucked air deep into my lungs to keep from crying. Then in as normal a voice as I could muster, I said, "Yeah, Al, that's pretty much it."

"Oh, my poor girl. I didn't say nothin' when you brought him over, but that man look like a *mo'o*. He got a bad *kapu* feeling all around him."

"Watch your mouth, Al. On behalf of lizards everywhere, I think you owe 'em an apology. I don't know the Hawaiian word for 'snake,' but even that's too flattering."

"No snakes allowed in Hawaii," he said. "We kill 'em if we find 'em."

"Damn straight."

I gave Al a quick peck on the cheek and told him I'd be back in an hour. I snapped the leash on Hulu, who'd been darting his eyes my way every few seconds as he waited patiently by the door.

We walked and I cried. Big, hot tears pooled in my eyes and coursed down my cheeks. I made no attempt to swipe them away. My nose ran like an upcountry stream after a heavy rain. Every once in a while I'd snuff it back up so I could get some air through my nostrils, but I didn't care what I looked like or how I sounded.

When we turned onto an unfamiliar street far from home, Hulu stopped. He turned his head and shot me a quizzical look.

"I know. We've never gone this far before. It's okay, I know the way back."

But did I? Did I honestly know the way back? And back to what? I'd pathetically returned to Frank's sheltering arms, only to discover he'd been palming a knife to stab me in the back one more time.

I rounded the next corner and found myself squinting to read the street sign in the dark. Time to turn around. I'd promised Al I'd be back in an hour. He was a worrier with a bad ticker so fretting him into another trip to the hospital would just add one more brick of wretched on to an already ghastly wall of shame.

Coming into the house, I flipped on the light and was greeted by three tall stems of kiwi-green orchids. Each bloom was the size of a teacup. The stalks were arranged in a slim, elegant vase. In all the time I'd been at Al's I'd never seen his orchids outside the shed. And I'd certainly never seen any of them cut.

A scrap of paper was wedged underneath the vase. It said, *A little aloha from your makua kane. If I see the snake, I'll kill it. —Al.* He'd drawn a little heart under his name.

Reading the note started up my boo-hoo machine all over again. I carried the vase to my room. My quaking hands nearly knocked it over as I placed it on the dresser top.

"You okay in there?" Al said through the door.

"I'll be all right, Al. *Mahalo* for the beautiful orchids."

"I wish I could make you feel better." His voice was heavy with concern.

"You already have. I'll be fine in the morning, I promise."

"Okay, then. Good night."

I heard him shuffle back to his room.

I had conflicting desires: part of me wanted to call everyone I knew and tell them what a bastard Frank had proven to be. The other part prayed no one would ever hear about this latest betrayal.

At eight o'clock the next morning I called Frank's room at the villas. I'd practiced my little speech all night and I wanted to get it over with.

The call got picked up on the third ring. "Room 132," said a strange woman's voice, barely above a whisper.

Oh, my Lord, I thought. *Now he's got a woman in there? He must be some kind of sex addict.*

"Hello," I managed to spit out. "I'd like to speak to Frank Stevens."

"The guest in this room checked out last evening," she said. I picked up a lilting Southeast Asian accent in the way she said *evening.* "Would you like me to transfer you to front desk?"

"No, thank you." I hung up. The loser. Sneaking out under cover of darkness.

I made breakfast for Al before going down to the Shore Store. I had eight thousand dollars left. And I was willing to spend every nickel of it to convince the nit-picking locals that this *malihini* wasn't about to throw in the towel without a fight. I dredged up Scarlett O'Hara in the radish field, chanting, '*I'll never be hungry again. I'll never be hungry again.*'

At ten-thirty, I heard a rap at the front door of the store. I was just about to shout we didn't open for another hour, when I saw Aidan peering through the window. He had a big smile on his face.

"Hang on," I said, running a hand through my hair and forcing a smile. I unlocked the door.

"Hey. Whatcha up to?" he said. He carried a small backpack in one hand. "I'm on my way to the airport, but I couldn't leave without bringing you something. It's an old Hawaiian custom to bring parting gifts."

He reached into his backpack and pulled out a battered copy of Betty Crocker's *Learn to Cook*.

"Very funny," I said, although I inwardly grinned at the memory of my gaff at Al's birthday party. My stomach churned as I stood close to him, smelling his aftershave, noting the fine hairs below the first knuckle of his fingers. I wanted to recount the whole sordid Frank story, but the sting of humiliation and my sadness over Aidan's imminent departure pressed me to silence.

"No, really," he said, dropping his voice to a whisper. He reached inside his windbreaker and fished around. "These are for you—and Frank. I wish you both well."

He pulled out a white letter-sized envelope. As he handed it to me, I noticed the return address: County of Maui.

"What's this?" I said, ripping it open.

Inside I found three sheets of heavy paper, each one bearing enough elaborate seals and official stamps to pass for third world visas. The first sheet read, "Food Establishment Permit." The second, "Fire Safety Inspection, Passed." The third—and this one really floored me—read, "State of Hawaii Department of Liquor Control, License to Vend Alcoholic Beverages."

I couldn't speak. The tears I'd been holding back from the Frank debacle flowed under the guise of delight at Aidan's extraordinary gifts.

"If that's a 'thank you,' then you're welcome," he said. He dug a neatly folded cotton handkerchief from a back pocket in his pants. "It's clean. You can keep it."

I wrapped my arms around him and hung on tight.

"Whoa," he said. "We wouldn't want Cowboy Frank to see this, now would we?"

He'd obviously told Malia about his unfortunate introduction to Frank and she'd shared her witty nickname for him.

"Thank you. *Mahalo*," I said. "You can't imagine how much this means to me."

"Oh, yes I can. I was a *malihini* once, too, you know."

"How'd you get these?"

"Just like I told you. You pay your dues and become *kama'aina*. In your case, you'd be wise to comp these guys lunch or dinner every now and then. Then you cater their daughter's weddings, and buy 'em a drink when they get promoted. You do that and you'll never have another problem."

He paused and smiled; his eyes shined as if evoking a fond memory. "You know that big bronze piece with the seven dolphins at the entrance to the county courthouse building?"

"Sure, I've seen it." Hard to miss. The sculpture stood at least twelve feet high.

"Never took a dime for it."

"Wow. That has to be worth a small fortune."

"It's worth more than money to me. Like the Mastercard ad says—'priceless.' But it's how we do business. You help me, I help you. I hate to rub it in, but it took me less than an hour to get all these permits. Of course, I had to fudge a bit on the liquor license. Since only an owner can sign the application, I told them I was a partner in the restaurant.

"I know you paid dearly for this liquor permit. How much do I owe you?"

"Nothing. Remember, I work on the investment model. When I come back to visit, I expect free food and drinks."

"You got it. I hope you do come back." I knew how it went, though. The *see ya later; we'll do lunch sometime* that people say is just an excuse to avoid the final farewell.

"Hey. I'll be back now and then," he said. "I've got lots of folks on this rock that owe me and I intend to collect." He leaned in and kissed my forehead. Then he walked to the door. As he put his hand on the doorknob, he turned. "Oh, yeah. And one more thing: Tommy Anakua's going to be calling you. I suggest you take the call."

I nodded.

"I'll get in touch when I'm settled in over there. Is that okay?"

"I'd like that."

"I don't want to get you in trouble with Mr. Brokeback."

"No," I said, trying to sound peeved at the reference. "It'll be fine, I promise."

My throat ached to say, *Don't go. Frank's long gone. I caught him in bed with a guy. Besides, I love you.* But instead, I just forced a bogus grin and blew him a kiss.

That night Tommy Anakua called me at Al's.

"Hi," I said, "Aidan told me you might call." I tried to recapture the positive attitude I'd had toward Tommy before we'd started tussling over the will.

"Yeah," he said. "Well, me and Sam want to talk about maybe working out a deal with you."

"A deal? I thought we were all waiting to see what the judge said."

"We are. But who knows how long that's gonna take?" He took a breath. "You're still working at my mom's store, right?"

"Yes. I've been putting the money in Aidan's safe. I wasn't sure what to do with it."

"Yeah, Aidan told me. Here's the deal: How about you and us split the profits fifty-fifty until the judge decides on who gets the property? I could use a little cash, and that way, with you working there we all come out ahead."

"But what if the judge awards you the property? I've put in a bunch of improvements, and I got the permits—"

"Hey," he laughed, interrupting my snow job. "I know it was Aidan who got those permits for you. And don't worry. If we get the place, we'll work out an arrangement for rent or something. We'll be fair. I know my mom wanted you to be able to stay there if you wanted."

"Thanks, Tommy. I'm actually kind of glad the judge has to make the final decision. It's a tough one."

"Yeah," he said. His voice was barely audible. "I sure wish my mom was still here."

"Me, too," I said. "She only paid me fifty bucks a week, but she was really good to me in other ways."

"Fifty bucks a week? Man, she was a real piker."

"We're talking about your *mother*, Tommy."

"I know. But don't go fibbin' me you didn't know how cheap she was. We used to say she'd squeeze a nickel until the buffalo took a dump."

Hard not to like such a straight-up guy; even if we were in a tug-of-war over a couple million bucks.

CHAPTER 33

I should have been thrilled that I finally had my food service permits and could move forward with opening the restaurant. I'd gone as far as naming it—*Momi's*. It seemed only right to keep Momi's name as a tribute to her generosity. Besides, that's what everyone would call it no matter what I put on the sign.

But hard as I tried to rouse my enthusiasm, it just wasn't there. Every day I'd go in, wander around until it was time to fix lunch, handle the lunch crowd and then clean up. No forward motion at all.

I spent a lot of time sitting on the upper lanai staring at the ocean. In fact, I was up there one late afternoon when I heard the bell tinkle on the downstairs door. The mail carrier shouted he had a certified letter for me to sign.

"I'll be right down," I said. I got up from my chair and scanned the ocean for one more moment to gather strength. I was pretty sure the letter would have a Seattle return address. My final divorce papers at last.

"Is it from the court?" I said as I hit the bottom stair.

He glanced at the return address. "Looks like it."

"Thanks." I scribbled my name on the little green card attached to the back of the letter. "I feel like I ought to tip you or something."

"We don't take money, but you could save me one of those chicken wraps sometime," he said. "I've heard they're pretty *ono*."

"You got it, buddy," I said. I remembered Aidan's advice. "Come by anytime between eleven-thirty and two. It's on the house."

He left, whistling.

I turned the envelope over. It was from a court, all right, but not the court I'd expected. I used a paring knife to slice open the flap.

"The District Court of the County of Maui, State of Hawaii..." it began. I read on, and through the legal jargon and run-on sentences it appeared the court hadn't accepted the holographic will as binding. My heart clutched, and I plopped down on the bottom step to avoid falling over.

I read the rest of it. It declared that the property—the legal description of the Shore Store's address went on and on for at least a paragraph—would be transferred forthwith to Thomas Anakua and Samuel Anakua, heirs of the estate of their mother, Momi Kanekoa Anakua of Lahaina, Hawaii.

What did I expect? This was Hawaii, after all. The word for a local person, *kama'aina*, is translated "child of the land." Land ownership and family ties are the cultural heavyweights. Everything else is just politics. The Shore Store property had been in the Kanekoa-Anakua family for generations. I felt foolish I'd ever held out hope.

I ached that Aidan wasn't next door. I could really use another hankerchief. Now what would I do? Regardless of Tommy's assurances that I could rent the building, I couldn't continue to pour money into a property he might put up for sale at any time.

The final sheet in the thick sheaf of papers was titled, "Life Estate in Real Property." I glanced through the verbiage and wondered if I was reading it correctly. It seemed to imply I might actually have a claim on the store after all.

I pulled out my cell phone and called Elizabeth.

"I don't get this."

"I got my copy today, too," she said. "It's brilliant. The best possible outcome. I'd say Judge Stayton has proved his mettle with this ruling. What it says is you have unlimited tenant rights to use the property, free of charge, until you die. During your lifetime you can't sell it or transfer it for any reason, and when you die, it will automatically go to the two Anakua sons or their heirs. Also, there's a provision that if you abandon the property for more than ninety days it will nullify the life estate."

"Who pays the taxes?"

"You do. Essentially it's yours until you die or you don't want it anymore. Then it reverts to them. Ingenious, wouldn't you say?"

"It's wonderful. So, they don't have to sell the store right away, and I don't have to feel like a creep for stealing it from them?"

"Yes. Everybody wins. I think once you get your restaurant up and running you'll owe that judge a dinner on the house."

"I've never heard of a 'life estate' before."

"It's usually used in situations where you have two unmarried people living together and one of them dies. The other one gets to stay on the property until they die. Then the property reverts to the heirs of the original owner."

"So I can do anything I want and not ask their permission?"

"Well, you can't sell it, or give it away. But other than that, it's pretty much yours. And, of course, any improvements you make will go to them in the end."

I was fine with that. I figured when I'm dead, I wouldn't want to be buried in my four-thousand dollar Viking range anyway.

For a second I imagined running next door to share the good news with Aidan. But it'd been more than three weeks since he'd left for Kauai. A pang of distress shot through me as I realized he hadn't called. But I was pretty sure he'd taken Emme with him. And since he believed dear ol' Frank was still onboard, our mutual attraction had probably already fallen into the realm of ancient history.

That night I told Al about the judge's decision. He listened carefully, but still seemed confused.

"So, now you own it, but later it will be Tommy and Sam's?"

"Yeah. Isn't that great?"

"What if you change your mind?"

"Change my mind? About what?"

"What if you want to leave it to your own boy instead of Tommy and Sam?"

At the reference to Frankie, my chest tightened. But I sucked it up, refusing to let the ongoing hurt override the good news.

"That's the point, Al. I *can't* give it or sell it to anyone else. It goes to Tommy and Sam without question. The property stays in the Kanekoa-Anakua family."

"I think that's good."

"Me too." I gave him a hug. "I think the judge was very fair. Everyone should be happy with this decision."

I called Tommy to make sure he understood what it all meant.

"This is good, don't you think?" I said.

"My lawyer said he thought it was reasonable. He asked me how old you were, and I said mid-thirties or so."

"Why'd he want to know?" I said. I was pleased he'd shaved a few years off my age, but I didn't let on.

"I think he was trying to figure out if you'd outlive me." He chuckled, but I could hear his uneasiness. He may have lived in LA for decades but he still balked at bantering about death.

"Well, I'm not planning to run a restaurant until I die. I imagine you and Sam will probably get it in ten, or at the very most fifteen, years. Think how much it will be worth then."

"A ton."

"Probably a couple of tons," I said. "And for all those years I'll be the one paying the taxes."

"My mom would love that."

"I hope we're still friends, Tommy."

"We're totally friends," he said, his pitch dropping a few notches. "Any friend of my mom's will always be a friend of mine. I'm proud to have you in our *ohana*."

I was once again struck by the power of that word.

With the property ownership decided, all my excuses for not starting renovations for my restaurant rang hollow. I had the building, the permits, and even a decent cash flow from the lunch business. I had enough money in my bank account to buy a basic restaurant package for cooking, seating and barware. So, why was I so sapped of energy every day I couldn't pick up the phone and call in a contractor or get bids from suppliers? Why was I finding it nearly impossible to get the lunch prep ready by eleven-thirty?

At the end of the month, I finally heard from Frank's lawyer. He sent me a registered package bulging with real estate listing forms, final marriage dissolution documents, and a copy of the two valuations on the brokerage.

When I'd sifted through all the paperwork, it appeared the past twenty-three years of my life were worth just a hair over one and a half million dollars. That's sixty-five thousand dollars per year—not bad for a high school graduate who'd barely passed algebra.

Sadly, every bit of good news pushed me deeper into my cave. My financial circumstances had transformed me from a homeless, food-stamp-eligible bag lady to a seven-figure lottery winner. But instead of being elated, I felt miserable. I should have been working to turn the Shore Store into a kick-ass restaurant with a bar sporting a magnificent view. Instead, I spent my afternoons listlessly gazing at the ocean and then going home to fix dinner for Al. When suppliers called on me I ordered my usual: paper bags and take-out trays. And on my trips to the wholesale food market I picked up the same old things, week after week.

One morning I went in to work and felt a shiver run down my arm as I closed the front door. I took a few steps to the right and detected a noticeable chilliness in the front corner. The space was empty now, but it had previously been the area where Momi stocked the baby items—graying jars of strained peas, disposable diapers, and bubble-packed pacifiers.

I ducked in and out of the spot, and sure enough, there was a definite change in temperature. It felt like stepping into an invisible refrigerator.

As a mother, I was pretty sure what was going on. A few times each day, I'd think of Frankie and go stand in that spot. The chill made him real to me, and for some unknown reason, it quieted my gnawing dread.

Five weeks into my funk, Aidan finally called. I was chopping lettuce and nearly took off a fingertip when my cell phone chirped in my pocket.

"Hi," he said. "How's the restaurant coming?"

I considered lying, but didn't have the energy.

"It's not," I said. It came out sounding like "it's snot," but I didn't care.

"What's the deal? Has Frank decided he's too good to wash dishes?"

Aside from my dealings with Frank, I can usually pick up when someone's jerking my chain. I knew that Aidan knew.

"You know what happened with me and Frank, don't you?"

"Yeah," he confessed. "Malia spilled the gory details. I didn't want to tell you because she swore me to secrecy."

"Well, other than that, everything's okay."

"Really? Then why'd you'd call your restaurant 'snot'?"

"I didn't mean to say 'snot.' I meant 'it isn't happening.' I'm moving a lot slower than I'd hoped. How about you? How's Kauai?"

"It's good. Rains a lot."

I waited for more but he fell silent.

"It's raining here, too," I said. "It's nearly lunchtime, and I—"

"I know. I'm sorry to call when you're busy. I told you I'd check in, so I'm just checking in. Take care, Nola. Bye."

"Bye," I said. "Call anytime." But he'd already disconnected.

I slipped the phone back into my pocket. I wanted to hit the redial—to tell him I couldn't even bring myself to flip through the stack of restaurant supply catalogs that begun pouring in after my permits were approved. I wanted to tell him about the chilly Frankie corner that seemed to get colder and colder every week. I wished I could ask him if he thought I was going nuts.

I wanted to cry on his shoulder and ask him why my husband kept cheating on me. Was I ugly? A total dead fish in bed? Maybe I had an annoying trait I should work on. But most of all, I wanted to ask if his relationship with Emme was everything he'd hoped it would be.

I went back to chopping heads of iceberg lettuce into perfect pale green shreds. Chopping and cleaning were the only tasks I found satisfying anymore. Oh, and walking Hulu. That little dog had taken over a whole chunk of my heart. Every night when I went back to Al's, he'd be sitting on the back of the sofa staring out the window. I'd pull into the driveway and he'd disappear. When I went inside, there he'd be; standing vigil by the door, wagging his tail. He never barked, never whined, always ate whatever I put in his dish.

"Do you know who's living in Momi's cottage now?" I asked Al one morning.

"Kilia told me the name the other day, but I can't remember." He scratched his chin, and turned his eyes on me. "Are you thinking of moving back down there?"

"No. I was thinking about Pookie. I'd like to move him up here."

"Why? He's dead."

"I know, but I'd like to keep up his grave, and I don't know if the new person even knows he's buried there."

"I think you should ask before you go digging stuff up."

The trip to Momi's cottage left me shaking at the curb. I looked at her sweet yard; it was still blooming and tidy. The front porch where she and Pookie had greeted me with a boisterous ruckus every night appeared to have been repainted. I broke down, sobbing. I leaned my elbows against the steering wheel and covered my face in my hands.

A tap on the driver's window startled me. I swiped the back of my hand under my nose and looked out.

"You okay?" said the man standing there. He was so short the crown of his head was even with the top of my window. He had a nut-brown face and black hair cut like Moe from The Three Stooges.

I nodded and rolled down the window.

"You look upset," he said. "I'm Ray. I live here now." He cocked his head in the direction of the cottage. He seemed to sense I'd known the former occupant.

"Oh. That's nice," I said, in a faraway voice. "I used to live here, with Auntie Momi."

"I figured as much. People come by all the time to check on the place. You the one who killed her dog?"

I gasped. I didn't know whether to laugh or keep crying.

"I'm the one who *found* him." It dawned on me I could've added *and her*, but I wasn't in the mood to explain.

"You come to see if I'm keeping up the grave?"

The guy was psychic.

"Yeah," I admitted. "I was thinking maybe I should move him over to her brother's place."

"Well, you can if you want," he said. "But I'm a gardener. I keep it pretty nice. Come see for yourself."

He walked me through the house, which was as clean as when Momi'd lived there. Out in the garden, he'd planted a large gardenia bush at the upper end of Pookie's grave. Its waxy white blooms infused the air with a sweet fragrance. Inside the circle of stones, he'd scattered fresh pink and white plumeria blossoms.

"Looks pretty good, eh?" His face flushed with pride.

"It's beautiful. I know both Momi and Pookie would be very pleased."

"Thanks. I know how much that dog meant to her. Too bad it got killed."

"She got another dog, you know," I said. I sounded way more defensive than I'd intended.

"Yeah, but it's not the same."

No, I thought, *sometimes it's better.*

On Saturday, I'd just put in a load of laundry when Al's kitchen phone began to ring .

"You want me to get that?" I said. No reply. I looked out the back window. The door to the orchid shed was open.

I picked up the phone. For a split second I feared it might be Frank.

"Hello?"

"Hi," said Aidan. "I was expecting Al to answer."

"Do you want me to go get him?" My heart rate ratcheted up to near stroke level. "He's out back with the orchids."

"No, it's fine," he said. "I'm just calling to say 'hi.' So, how's everyone doing?"

Truth or dare? Throw him a load of BS and say it's all hunky-dory, or whine about my constant malaise?

"Everyone's doing okay." I figured that more or less split the middle.

"How come I hear something less than 'okay' in your voice?"

"It's probably a bad connection. Kauai's a long way away."

"Maybe," he said. "But I'm not. Check the driveway."

I pulled aside the kitchen curtain. His big black truck was ten feet from the house.

I let out a whoop and dropped the phone. It clattered onto the countertop. I reached the truck as he was slamming the driver door shut.

"Why are you so intent on bustin' my eardrum with that phone?" he said. He wrapped his arms around me and nearly lifted me off my feet.

I nuzzled his neck. Then I remembered.

"Where's Emme?" I said, pulling back and trying to peek over his shoulder to the passenger seat.

"Who?"

"Emme. You know, your girlfriend."

"Whatever gave you the idea she's my girlfriend?" He sounded amused, but after a few seconds he looked more annoyed than pleased. "She models for me now and then, but that's it. Besides, you ought to see the young buck she's marrying. Don't let him hear you calling her my girlfriend or I'll be needing some major dental work."

"Really? She's engaged?"

"That's the plan. I finished their wedding rings last week."

"That's wonderful," I said.

"No wonder you've been so crabby."

I could feel my blush spot forming so I turned and walked to the house. I called out to Al we had a visitor.

He swiped dirt from his hands onto his khaki shorts as he came through the screen door. "Aidan," he said. "Good to see you."

The two men did an intricate surfer-shake—a series of grasps, slaps, and knuckle-pounds—followed by a quick shoulder hug.

"What're you doing back on Maui?" Al pulled out a kitchen chair and sat down. Then he gestured for us to join him.

"I came back to help my girl here get her damn restaurant put together."

"That's good." Al looked at me. "She's been acting all *pupule* ever since you left."

I didn't need a Hawaiian dictionary to figure out that one.

CHAPTER 34

The next few months passed in a frantic blur of activity. Getting a bar and restaurant open is like building a house, planning a wedding and having a baby—all at the same time. So much shopping. So much money flying out the door. And, so much fun. Table cloths or placemats? Which chairs—the comfortable clunky ones, or the butt-breaker gorgeous ones? How many sets of tableware; how many wine glasses?

I brought in contractors to renovate the stairwell and turn the upper floor into an ocean view bar. On the lanai I decided on cozy two-top tables and bolted them in place so every seat would always have a spectacular sunset view.

"I don't want this bar to turn into a wet tee-shirt kind of place," I told Aidan.

"Then charge ten bucks for a mai tai, and only serve micro-brews. No cheap beer and no TVs." For an artist, the guy was pretty savvy about the hospitality business.

I left decorating the bar up to Aidan while I concentrated on the food service area downstairs. My small commercial kitchen was slowly coming together. Piece-by-piece, appliances and furniture trickled in from Honolulu or the mainland.

"*Sixteen weeks* for the cabinets to arrive?" Had I heard right?

"That's if we're lucky and there's room on the ship when they get to LA from North Carolina," the contractor said. "I've seen it go to twenty, but let's hope for the best."

We worked around it. I decided to open Momi's in stages. First, we'd get the bar set up and open. The downstairs restaurant would serve lunch and then only *pupus*—appetizers—after four. As the kitchen fixtures arrived, we'd slowly expand to a full dinner menu.

Not only did I have to equip the restaurant, I had to hire and train staff. Maui enjoys almost full employment, which means everyone who wants a job already has one. The only people available are either new to the island or unhappy employees hoping to change jobs. I considered walking around the airport handing out applications at baggage claim, but Aidan nixed that idea.

"Those kids will swear they're here for the long haul, but as soon as you train them they'll realize how much it costs to live here and—bam! They're heading home to free rent at mom and dad's."

"Seems we're going to have to steal some people." I said.

"It's not stealing, it's 'offering an opportunity'."

"How about 'offering an opportunity' to a few of Lech's waiters?"

"Now, *that* would be stealing."

We named the bar "The Lana'i Lanai," after the serene island floating on the distant horizon. After a few days, it got nicknamed the "Double L," and like a pedigreed dog, it was never called its real name again.

Aidan painted the walls upstairs in gradient shades of blue starting with deep navy at the bottom and growing lighter and lighter to a pale topaz near the ceiling. The effect made it feel as if you were underwater. On one wall he hung a giant canvas with life-size images of fish, dolphins, and turtles. He invited other local artists to submit work to hang on the remaining wall space. Discrete white cards at the bottom of each piece indicated they were for sale, showing the artist's name and the price.

"It's a win-win," he said, scanning the two dozen paintings filling the walls. "We get first-class artwork and the artists get exposure—maybe even a sale."

Every last one of the artists represented on the walls of the Double L came to the grand opening, and they brought along friends and family members.

After closing on our first night, we sat on the lanai sipping mai tais. I'd propped my weary feet up on the rail.

"So, what do you think?" Aidan said.

"It's great," I said. "You've got as much artistic flair with pineapple juice and rum as you do with bronze and paint."

"No, I mean, what do you think of the restaurant? Are you glad you did it?"

"I guess. I don't know."

"You thinking about Frank?"

"Nah. I figure he's got his own demons. I used to wish him all kinds of hideous payback, but now I pretty much don't think about him at all. You know what they say: 'the opposite of love isn't hate, it's indifference.'"

"Then why are you second-guessing yourself about the restaurant?" He drained his glass.

"I've been thinking about Frankie. Now that I've made this investment," I said, "I feel I can't leave. I wonder if I should have gone to Mexico to look for him."

"He's a big boy."

I looked over at him. "Okay, I get it," I said. "Having your mom track you down like Dog the Bounty Hunter is only slightly less humiliating than having your dad come out of the closet with a guy you know from the gym."

"Bingo."

I set my glass down and stood up.

Aidan took me in his arms and kissed me in a way that made it seem almost reasonable to enjoy making love on the scratchy sisal carpet.

One Friday night, after the Double L had been open a couple of months, the place was rocking. Two guys showed up, but every table upstairs was taken. The two didn't appear to be a gay couple. One had a peeling bald head. He wore a garish aloha print shirt and baggy plaid shorts, which made him look like Elmer Fudd goes Hawaiian. The other guy, who could've been Rob Lowe's younger brother, hid behind Von Zipper sunglasses. He wore a butter yellow polo shirt with matching shorts. The shirt sported a discreet designer logo.

The sunglasses guy carried a Halliburton aluminum attaché case that he clutched to his side as if it held ransom money. The bald guy had a black webbed strap running diagonally from shoulder to waist, like a Miss America banner. When he turned, I saw the strap was attached to a messenger bag.

"We're at capacity on the lanai," I said. "But I can seat you here on the first floor until something opens up." I got the uneasy feeling these two might be mystery food critics or even inspectors. I hoped being stuck downstairs might encourage them to come back another time.

"Great. No hurry." Elmer Fudd ordered a Bikini Blond beer. Mr. Sunglasses opted for the Double L special mai tai.

While they waited for their drinks, I became even more alarmed when I noticed them whispering, nodding, and pointing toward the still unfinished kitchen. Elmer slipped the webbed strap over his head and took out a laptop. He set it up on the table and started typing. The restaurant didn't have wi-fi, so I knew he wasn't checking emails.

Meanwhile, Mr. Sunglasses ceremoniously snapped open the lid on the Halliburton case. Inside was an eye-popping array of expensive camera equipment.

When he started screwing a filter onto a camera lens, I'd had enough. It's one thing to show up without a reservation; it's another thing altogether to do a restaurant review when we were still working on the kitchen.

"Can I help you?"

"Are you the owner?" Elmer said, pulling out a business card.

Uh-oh. They were beginning to seem more like inspectors.

"Yes," I nodded. Luckily, Aidan was right upstairs. If push came to shove I might need him to run interference or maybe even throw a block.

"We're from *USA Today*." Elmer said. He held out the card, arching his eyebrows as if checking to see if I was illiterate.

"Yes, of course. The national daily newspaper," I said. I looked at the familiar logo on the card. "Believe it or not, it's available here in the fiftieth state."

"I'm Bob Thorton," he said, ignoring my sarcastic tone. "And this is my photographer, Brad Dial. We're here on assignment for a travel piece."

"*Ho'okipa*. Welcome to Maui. I'm sure you must've pulled the long straw to score this gig." I said. I chuckled, but he maintained his hard news face so I quashed my grin.

"Right," he said. "So, how long have you been open?"

"Would you believe just two months?"

"And what made you decide to open a restaurant in such a competitive market?"

"Long story." I gave him a two-minute summary of my life on Maui, starting with my arrival in December. I left out the part about Frank's open-zipper policy being the reason I hadn't returned to Seattle.

"That's great. Do you mind if we take some photos?" Bob said. He must have decided humor was finally allowed, because he smiled and followed up with, "We need tangible evidence to document our expense reports for the accounting department."

"No problem. But, I'd like you to see the upstairs. It's pretty amazing."

We went up the newly widened stairway and they offered the predictable ooh's and aah's as they took in the stunning undersea décor.

"This place is beautiful."

"Yeah," said photographer Brad. "I hope I can get these colors to come through."

I introduced them to Aidan. Then Bob asked us to stand against the sea creature wall. We beamed like a couple of kids at Disneyland while Brad took our picture.

"I've got to get back to tending the bar," Aidan said. We all shook hands one more time. "Thanks for dropping by."

Six days later, Lech Gorelczenko jogged over to me as I unlocked the front door to Momi's. He wore a sly smile and had a rolled newspaper under his arm.

"Did you see this?" he said, unfolding the paper. His beady eyes reminded me of a praying mantis.

The front page of the travel section of *USA Today* contained a centered six-inch photo of Aidan and me with cheery grins on our faces. A stingray sailed above us on the wall. The headline read, "#1 Island, Maui, Never Ceases to Amaze." Under Bob Thornton's byline the article described new tourist spots, restaurants, and services, ending with a flattering portrayal of the Double L as "an idyllic bar, in an idyllic town, on the most idyllic island in the Pacific." Needless to say, Mr. Bob Thorton would never need to pull out his wallet in my place again.

We were swamped, crushed, hammered every night for the next month. My kitchen was finally starting to take shape, allowing us to offer a menu of eight different *pupus,* including coconut shrimp and tasty crab wontons. When the walk-in cooler was finally installed, we were able to serve a limited menu of chilled desserts after eight o'clock.

Strangely, the nippy corner by the front door remained cold. Even Aidan remarked about it. We placed a few chairs there for guests waiting for a table, but often people would sit for a few minutes and then move, claiming the A/C was blasting them. But there were no A/C vents within fifteen feet of that corner.

One Saturday just before noon, I was in the kitchen prepping additional shrimp for the seafood and caper salad lunch special.

"Nola?" said Misty, a waitress we'd snagged from an upscale restaurant in Wailea. "There's a guy out here who wants to apply for a bartending job."

"Great. Give him an application and tell him to come back after three."

A minute later, she was back.

"He says he'll wait until he can talk to you."

"Well, clue him in that it's lunchtime and I don't talk to applicants until after three." I shook my head in dismay. Although I desperately needed another bartender, I had to draw the line at hiring a prima donna.

"He made it pretty clear he isn't going to leave." She squinted as if preparing to deal with my tirade.

"This is ridiculous. I don't care how short-handed we are, I'm not hiring an ass with an attitude."

I rinsed the shrimp slime off my hands and wiped them on my apron. Misty waited by the swinging door, ready to escort me to the waiting victim.

Charging toward the front of the restaurant, I felt a chill wind, as if an arctic breeze had rushed into the room.

A young man sat in the corner, his head down. In addition to his pushy demeanor, I saw he wore his wavy brown hair much longer than I allowed.

He looked up, and our eyes met. My hand flew to my mouth as I strangled out a single word. "Frankie?"

"Hi, Mom."

I couldn't speak. I could barely breathe.

"I was so blown away when he said he was your son," Misty said. "I didn't know you had any kids."

Frankie's face swam in front of me as I blinked back a wave of tears.

"How did you know where to find me?" I said.

"I saw you in *USA Today*."

"They get *USA Today* in Mexico?"

"I don't know about that. I saw it at the student union at the U of Dub."

"When did you go back to Seattle?"

"A few months ago. I came back to finish. I got a bunch of credits for testing out of Spanish, so I'm nearly done now. When I saw your picture in the paper I couldn't believe it. I had to come tell you I'm sorry."

"I'd be happy to finish up the shrimp," Misty said.

I gave her a smile. "Thanks, I'd appreciate it."

She started to walk away, and then turned around. "Nice to meet you, Frankie."

"Actually, I go by Scott now," he said. "My middle name."

"Okay. Well, Scott, I hope you get the job."

Frankie Scott and I stared; each taking in the changes in the other. Finally, I reached out and squeezed his hands. They seemed too big for his rail-thin body.

He flashed me his lop-sided grin. "So? Are you going to interview me for a job, or am I going to have to look for work elsewhere? I make a mean margarita."

"Well, my dear Scott, you're going to have to expand your repertoire. You're in mai tai territory now."

He stood and extended his arms to hug me. As we embraced, the air in the chilly corner warmed. And it never returned.

I'd been homeless, jobless, and childless. Two down, only one to go.

CHAPTER 35

"Let's take Monday off," Aidan said. It was after closing. I dried wine glasses while he swept the floor. "We haven't taken a day off for more than a month. Misty and Scott can manage for one night."

"What would we do?"

"We could go out to eat."

"Ha! I spend all my time in a restaurant. Last thing I want to see is someone else's better looking menu or sharper wait staff."

"How about I cook for you in the *ohana*?"

I sucked my lips into a grimace of pain.

"Okay, okay. Bad idea. So how about you come over to my place and I'll get some takeout?"

"Sushi?"

"You got it. I'll pick some up at Awe'awe."

I loved going to Aidan's *ohana* cottage. It sat behind a larger main house, and it had a peekaboo view of the beach. If the owners of the big house weren't there—which was most of the time—we'd sit on their open beachfront and watch the sunset.

"Hey," Aidan said when I arrived Monday night. "I've got a few surprises for you." He walked me toward the main house. I looked up at the two-story residence. It was lovely except for the ugly front door. The owners had painted it a shade of bile green that smacked of color-blindness.

"The Jacobsen's aren't here?"

"That's surprise number one." Aidan wore a body hugging steel-gray polo shirt that turned his eyes sea-green. His khaki shorts showed off tanned legs and sinewy calves, making him look a decade younger. "They've gone back to the mainland for good this time. Julie didn't like being so far away from her grandkids. The house is for sale."

"Does that mean you're going to have to move?"

"I hope not. But you never know."

He pulled out a key.

"The Jacobsons asked me to watch the place until it sells."

We went inside. He'd nestled a bottle of Moët and Chandon champagne in an ice bucket on the kitchen counter. I flashed on our aborted New Year's foray into champagne-induced bliss.

"Ever the optimist, huh, Aidan?"

"This time we'll enjoy every bubble." He picked up a thin stack of legal-size papers from off the counter. "Check it out."

On the top page it read, IN THE FAMILY COURT OF THE STATE OF VERMONT.

"Is this what I think it is?"

"Yeah, that's surprise number two."

"Well, congratulations." I looked around the spacious kitchen. "Why don't you buy this place, Aidan? You can afford it."

"I'm not the big house type. Besides, I think there's already someone else interested in it."

"Who?" I felt peeved imagining strangers lolling on our favorite beachfront.

"You."

"Me?" I laughed. Then I stopped. "You think I could?"

"Why not? As you like to say—*you* can afford it. You're a millionaire, remember?"

And that's how I became the owner of a Front Street beach house. The following Christmas, Scott graduated and moved in with me for a while. He offered to pay rent but I explained about showing gratitude in other ways. For the time he lived with me, my car was always filled with gas and he kept it spotlessly clean.

Al often came to visit and mooch a free meal; and Malia and Jim came over from the mainland whenever he could get time off from the hospital. Jim passed on moving his practice to Maui, but he promised Malia they'd retire there after eight more years.

And Aidan and me? Well, that's a story I never get tired of telling.

The night before I was scheduled to sign the final papers on the house, we went in to see it one more time. I asked Aidan if he'd consider going in with me to buy it. To make it *our* house, instead of just mine.

"It's your call. But if I were you, I'd finally want to have a home of my own. Even if only for a little while." He winked.

I hugged him. "I feel like I'm graduating or something."

"Well, then allow let me give you your first graduation present." He walked to the front door and opened it. "As soon as you sign those papers, I'm painting this door. You can choose anything other than this ugly green."

"I like red," I said. "Hibiscus red."

"Then red it is."

He gathered me in his arms. "You know, I think it's great you're finally getting your own place. You deserve it. But it's not gonna be long before I grow tired of just being your bartender at work and your handyman at home."

"You angling for a promotion?" I said.

"Yeah. You think you could see clear to letting me try out for the job of 'husband'? After all, I did get you that liquor license."

"You said it was a gift."

"It was," he said. He grasped my hands and bent down on one knee on the cold marble tile. "And now it's your turn to give me a gift. Tell me you'll marry me."

And that's how *living aloha* became my *happily ever after*.

Glossary of Hawaiian Words and Expressions

Aloha—Love, greetings. Also used for good-bye. Compassion and grace.

Haole—Caucasian, or can be used for any non-Hawaiians of any race.

Hauoli—Happiness, joy.

Haupia—Coconut pudding.

Ho'okipa—To welcome or entertain as a guest.

Huluhulu—Hairy or furry.

Imu—Underground oven or cooking pit.

Ipo—Sweetheart or lover.

Kahuna—Expert in any craft or field; a priest.

Kalua pig—Pork cooked in an underground oven or pit.

Kama'aina—Native born or local person.

Kapu—Taboo, prohibited.

Kupuna kane—Grandfather.

Keiki—Child.

Keiki mo'opuna—Grandchild.

Ku'uipo—My beloved sweetheart.

Kumu—Teacher; from the term for origin or source.

Kumu hula—Hula teacher.

Ma'i—Sick; ill.

Mahalo—Thank you.

Makua kane—Father.

Malihini—Stranger, newcomer, foreigner.

Mo'o—Lizard.

Mu'u mu'u—Loose gown or dress.

Ohana—Family, relatives. Also used to refer to small guest house next to larger family house.

Okazuya—Delicatessen.

Ono—Delicious, tasty. Good flavor.

Pau—Finished, ended.

Poke—Cubed raw fish mixed with seaweed, onions and other condiments.

Pono—Goodness, duty, true nature.

Pupus—Appetizers.

Pupule—Crazy, wild.

"Rubba slippas"—Local term for cheap rubber thong sandals everyone wears.

"Talk story"—To chat, to "shoot the breeze."

Tutu—Term of endearment for grandmother. (Note: Not a Hawaiian word, there is no "t" in Hawaiian).

Wahine—Woman.

Look for other titles by JoAnn Bassett:

The Islands of Aloha Mystery Series--

Maui Widow Waltz

Livin' Lahaina Loca

Lana'i of the Tiger

Kaua'i Me a River

All are available at Amazon.com

Visit JoAnn's webpage at http:www.joannbassett.com

and

her FaceBook page at JoAnn Bassett's Author Page

Made in the USA
San Bernardino, CA
06 May 2019